11-10-16

trans·fer·ence

Montgomey
#1

a novel

AVA HARRISON

trans·fer·ence: a novel
Copyright © 2016 by Ava Harrison
Published by AH Publishing

ISBN-10: 0-9963585-5-2
ISBN-13: 978-0-9963585-5-2

trans·fer·ence: a novel
Cover Design: By Hang Le
Photographer: Leonardo Corredor
Cover Model: Rob Rea
Interior Design: Champagne Formats

Line Editor: Brenda Letendre, Write Girl Editing Services
Editor: Jennifer Roberts-Hall, Indie After Hours
Creative: Argie Sokoli
Proofreader: Virginia Tesi Carey

To those who are looking to find the strength to conquer their fears.

trans·fer·ence: n. in psychotherapy and psychoanalysis, a client's feelings for the therapist. May be used to understand the origins of the client's emotional and psychological problems.

prologue

I'M HOLLOW.

My pain is an open festering wound.

Unbearable.

I hear the words that are spoken but they have no meaning.

They're only words. They will never bring him back.

Grief.

Loss.

Death.

The pain inside me roars out in a silent scream.

Like ice spreading through my veins and numbing me to the outside world.

Sucking me under, until all is gone.

My hands swipe away my stained tears.

My breath becomes short gasps of air escaping.

Cold sweat. Hammering heart.

A distant hum.

The beat of a bird's wings.

I need to leave.

I can't be here.

chapter one

B*EEP*
Beep

Beep

Through heavy eyelids, flashes of white light gleam in. It's like living in a world of solitude. All alone, no connections, no expectations, no pain, no memories, and then suddenly everything rushes back.

Sounds overwhelm me.

Swish

Swish

Swish

Hummmmmmmm

With careful precision I pry my eyes open, but I'm unnerved as the world around me comes alive. The sounds, once muffled, attack me like a passing freight train. They infiltrate every pore in my body, relentlessly. They are an unwelcome attack on my senses.

A voice breaks through. "I think she's waking up."

Beep

Beep

"That's right, sweetie, open your eyes," coos a soft, comforting voice.

My blurry vision focuses and I'm facing two women dressed in purple scrubs. *Where am I?* A plain room that's void of all emotion and warmth. Sterile. The walls are a dirty white, not quite cream, and the smell of disinfectant permeates the air. My mouth opens to speak, to ask them for some explanations but it's too dry. I try to swallow however the thickness of the saliva pooling makes the action feel impossible. With wary movements, I press my fingers toward my lips, but even this small gesture is too much as pain radiates throughout my body.

"You need something to drink. Let me grab you some water."

"Where . . ." It sounds as though I'm talking with a mouth full of marbles, so I try again but my words are jumbled and make no sense. The sound of the faucet running causes even more liquid to collect. I watch in parched desperation as she slowly fills a pitcher and then grabs a cup and straw.

"Where are you? You're at Sinai-Grace Hospital. You were in an accident." My heart rattles heavily at the new information. No wonder everything hurts. *Even my skin burns.*

Finally, the nurse steps over to the bed, carefully fills a cup with water and then offers me the precious liquid. *Thank you, God.* The water feels like heaven against my tongue.

"What . . . What happened?"

"A car accident. You hit your head and were unresponsive. You've got quite a nasty gash on your left temple and on your cheek."

"An accident?" My eyes widen and the sharp bite of the bandage pulls against my skin. I wince in pain and then she gives me a small smile. "Can I see? Do you have a mirror?" I motion to my face and the shorter woman proceeds to leave the room. I turn my attention back to the remaining nurse, who is speaking.

"Yes, you were brought in a little bit ago. I can't tell you much more than that, but from what I hear, there's nothing to fear. You'll be okay." The other nurse walks back in and approaches the bed, placing a mirror in my hand. Just as she had said, a bandage covers my forehead. My eyes are dull today. You can barely see the blue as my pupils are dilated. My once blonde hair is now matted and caked to my skin. I look skeletal and pale. "I notified the attendee that you're awake, so he'll come speak to you once he gets in," she says before stepping out of the room.

My gaze locks on the window, and I watch as the snow softly falls, drifting down the pane and leaving streaks of murky water. The familiar cage closes in all around me, robbing me of air.

I'm afraid . . .

And I'm not ready to face the truth.

I'm not ready to face what's happening to me.

Hearing footsteps, I turn my attention back to the door and am met with a pair of soft brown eyes that I know so well.

"Oh, my God," Sydney cries as she steps into the room. Her face is blanched and her straight brown locks are now back to their curly form thanks to the snow. "You're awake. Thank God. I was so scared." She grabs my hand and it feels so warm wrapped around mine. I welcome the comfort, leaning closer to her to bask in the feeling of home she evokes.

"What are you doing here? How did you know I was here?"

Her brow lifts up in confusion. "How could I not be here? I got the phone call and I came at once."

Of course she's here. She's the type of friend who would always be there for me. That's one of the things I love most about her: how fiercely loyal she is. We've only been friends for a short time, but with Sydney, time doesn't matter. The moment we met at the office, I felt as if I had known her a lifetime.

When my father passed, his best friend Richard had stepped in, assuming a father figure role. After I told him I was uncertain what major I should declare, he volunteered to discuss my options. Richard also happened to own one of the leading marketing firms in the city. Together we decided a degree in marketing would be a great fit, and once I was done, he had a spot ready for me.

I had been at my new job for all of one minute and I already loved it. The energy, sounds and excited voices booming through the hallways were everything I hoped for. As I stepped further into the space, Richard lifted his head. His lips turned up in a giant smile and he strode over to me. Greeting me with a fatherly hug, he walked me over to a set of desks positioned in front of a giant window overlooking Park Avenue.

"This will be your desk." Richard pointed to the desk adjacent to where a pretty brunette worked. "And this is Sydney White. She's on your team." Her eyes were locked on Richard as he spoke and as if on cue her mouth split into a large smile, showcasing a mouth full of perfectly white teeth. "Get settled and then come to my office so I can go over some information with you." He laid his hand on my shoulder and gave me a reassuring squeeze. "It's good to have you here." He gave me one last smile, then turned his back and walked down the hall.

Sydney sighed. "Damn, that was a close call." Her brow furrowed.

"Are you okay? You look a little pale." I asked her as she glanced over her shoulder to see if anyone is behind her. "Is it

Richard? Do you not like him?"

"Oh, no, nothing like that. It's really no biggie. I've just been spending a lot of time lately looking for a roommate instead of leads and I thought I was busted."

"Roommate?"

"Yeah, my current one totally ditched me. She met some guy and skipped out. Didn't even pay this month's rent. Trying to find a roommate sucks." She huffed as she threw her hands up in the air.

"I wouldn't know. I live with my mom,"

"Shut up!" she exclaimed, making me laugh. This girl definitely had a flair for the dramatic. "How old are you?"

"Twenty-two."

"You're twenty-two and you've never had a roommate? Not even in college?"

I shook my head and her eyes grew wide. "My college was close to home. I didn't need to dorm. It's pretty pathetic, actually." I responded in a timid voice.

"Move in with me."

My mouth flew open.

"I'm not even joking. You have no idea what types of freaks I'm finding on this site. I mean, you seem like a cool girl . . . please. Unless you're a serial killer or something, then I revoke the invitation."

"I . . . I . . ."

"Come on . . . You can't live with your mom forever. Time to fly the nest."

She did have a point. "Um . . ."

"Say you'll think about it. Please," she whined and I couldn't help but nod in agreement as I stifled my laugh. I knew, right then and there, that not only would I move in with this crazy girl, but

5

also it would be the best decision of my life.

One week later we were roommates.

Shaking my head to pull myself out of the memory from two years ago, I focus on Sydney and try to remember why I'm here.

"What happened?" My brain feels cloudy. It's as if the information is hovering above me but I just can't reach it.

"We were at the funeral. You remember being at the funeral, right?" Her eyes close, then reopen with unshed tears.

The muscles in my chest tighten, gripping my heart to the point of pain. How could I forget? Richard is dead. My mentor, my boss, my father figure. The only father I know—*knew*. Closing my eyes, I think back to him. He was the one who was there for me through everything for years.

My small, fourteen-year-old body wracked with sobs as I pressed my head to my pillow. Tears poured from my eyes, wetting my long, tangled hair. In the faint distance the door creaked open, followed by footsteps padding on the wood floors.

"Where's your mom?" Richard asked as he walked into my room. Often he stopped by our apartment to check on me and my mom, always making sure we were okay. I peeked up at him, pushing my hair out of my eyes.

"She's sick." My voice cracked as my chin trembled with my sobs.

"Why are you crying, sweetheart?"

"She's always sick. She doesn't do anything but lay around in her bed," I stuttered and he nodded with understanding. This was what my mom did. She said she was unwell and never left her room. Just cried all day and all night. But no doctor could ever

find anything wrong, and that made her cry even more.

"What happened? What did she miss?"

"She didn't miss anything, but you know how she is. There's always something. What if she's sick again? What if she won't leave her room again for days?" Richard sat on the edge of the bed. I scooted closer until his arm draped against my shoulder and I let out a muffled cry.

"I know I'm not your father but I think of you as my daughter. Tell me where you need me to be, and I'll never let you down. I promise."

Life was never easy with my mom, but Richard made it bearable. He never forgot his promise. He was always there.

I open my eyes and meet Sydney's stare.

"When they pulled you out of the car, you wouldn't wake up, so someone called for an ambulance and they brought you here." She bites her lip. Sydney only does that when she's nervous.

"What? What aren't you telling me?" My eyes narrow.

"They tried to call your mom as your next of kin, but she refused to come in to the hospital, so they got in touch with me. Good thing we added each other as emergency contacts when you walked into that wall and had to have stitches." She laughs, but it does nothing to soothe the pain growing inside me.

No matter how much I tell myself not to expect much from my mom, that she's "sick" and can't help herself, it doesn't lessen the ache in my heart. At the end of the day there isn't anything wrong with her other than the fact that she's a hypochondriac. One who, for the last eighteen years since my father's death, has been too scared to live. She wouldn't even go to Richard's funeral and that felt like a slap in the face considering all he's done for us.

Shaking my head, I turn my attention back to Sydney. "Do they know what caused the accident?"

Sydney's nose crinkles and she puckers her lips as she peers around the room. The nurse is in the corner, but she's rummaging through the cabinets looking for something and it appears she's not paying attention to us. Satisfied with this, Sydney leans in closer.

"They're not really sure," she whispers. "But . . . but they said you didn't hit your brakes."

"I don't understand?" My hand rises to my mouth, smothering a gasp. "Oh, my God, they think I did it on purpose?"

"I know, sweetie, I know. But do you remember what happened? What made you crash?"

"I honestly have no clue."

Her hand strokes my arm as I continue to sob. "I'm sure it will come back to you. You were really distraught when you fled the funeral."

I shake my head. "I can't remember anything from the funeral. Is that normal?"

"I don't know, but they did say you had a concussion."

The nurse chooses that moment to make her way to the side of my bed with a blood pressure kit.

"Excuse me, I was wondering if it's normal for Eve to not remember anything from right before the car accident?" Sydney asks her.

"It's actually quite normal, dear. After a concussion, sometimes your memory will be a little spotty. It should come back as the swelling recedes." She smiles down at me as she places the strap around my arm.

"Oh, thank God."

I hear the relief in Sydney's voice and smile weakly at her. "Syd, did I say anything before I ran out?"

"No, not really—"

A man walks into the room before Sydney can continue. "Hello . . ." he looks at my chart, "Ms. Hamilton. I'm Dr. Levin. I'm glad to see you're awake. I'm going to ask you a few questions, if that's okay?"

"Yes," Reluctantly I agree as my stomach clenches tightly against the idea of talking about myself.

"And your friend?" He motions to Sydney, who is now perched on the foot of my bed.

"She's fine. You can speak in front of her." Sydney and I have no secrets. We accept each other, faults and all.

He looks back down at the tablet in his hand. "Have you ever had a concussion before?"

"No."

His fingers tap lightly on the glass. "And how are you feeling right now? Dizzy? Lightheaded?" I shake my head no. "What were you feeling right before you crashed?" He lays the tablet down and pulls the stethoscope from around his neck.

"I don't really remember, but my heart has been racing quite a bit recently and I guess I've been feeling kind of dizzy, like I can't breathe."

"How long have you had these symptoms?" Leaning forward, he places the cold metal against my skin. I start to breathe in deeply, then exhale my breath.

"I guess maybe they started when Richard died."

"And you never experienced any of these symptoms before his death?" He pulls away from me and straightens my gown.

"Not that I recall." My memories are blurry, like a fading dream. I search through them, grasping at anything that will make sense of what happened. A strange clarity forms as I begin to remember feeling a cold sweat, the knots that formed in my muscles and so much more. "I actually kind of remember—"

"What do you remember?" Sydney cuts in, her voice rising in surprise.

A rush of images from the accident starts to play out in my mind. I recall every pain as the memories resurface.

I needed distance.

I needed to escape this reality hovering all around me.

My muscles constrict, alerting me to run. My heart would explode if I stayed.

"Where are you going?" Sydney whispered as she reached out to stop me. I didn't allow her to halt my progress.

I needed out of here.

With shaky arms, I pushed open the door and a sharp gust of wind battered my frail body. Small pellets of water hit me as I stepped out into the cold winter air. The distance to the car stretched out in front of me. Chilled droplets of water clung to every inch of my sweat soaked skin. Rain and tears melded together.

I tilted my head back and looked to the sky. If only the rain could wash away this moment. Transport me back to a time when everything was still right.

But it wouldn't.

It couldn't.

Nothing could wash this pain away. Today was a day of sadness.

Unsteady steps carried me to the zip car I rented to go to the cemetery. I flung the door open and slid into the driver's seat. My body was chilled to the bone from the rain that coated my skin during my walk, but I did nothing to lessen the bite. I welcomed the pain. It reminded me of what I lost.

Pulling out of the parking lot, I made my way back to the city. The farther away I got, the more air entered my lungs. My body was barely able to function in that room. Seeing the body . . .

It was crippling.

My vision blurred as new tears threatened to spill. In the distance, the glare from the opposing traffic shone and stung my eyes. Lights swirled in the distance as rain hit the windshield.

I should have said good-bye.

I owed it to him.

No . . .

I had to go.

I couldn't stay there.

I couldn't see that.

A flash of light descended.

The hiss of tires echoed in my ears.

Then all sound faded away.

"I remember my arm going numb. I remember the flash of lights. I remember thinking I was having a heart attack. Oh, my God, do you think I had a heart attack?"

The machine next to me beeps faster as panic kicks in and my heart rate accelerates considerably. The faces around me start to sway . . .

"What's happening? What's wrong with me?"

"Ms. Hamilton, I need you to take a deep breath. Please, take a deep breath."

My brain feels as if it's stuck in a vice being squeezed tight. My chest constricts. It's too much. Black spots dance in my vision.

Crushing . . .

Suffocating . . .

Thud, thud

Thud, thud

I gasp for air as the world shrinks around me. White noise drifts in. I'm being blanketed by it. Immersed in a storm.

It envelops me . . .

———•———

"Open your eyes. It's okay."

A voice hums in the background.

"You can do it," the voice commands again.

My eyes flutter open. "Wh-what?" I mumble, trying to get my bearings. "I'm . . . What's happening to me?"

"You're okay. Inhale . . . now exhale." Sharp lines etch away at the handsome stranger's face as he studies me.

He has the most mesmerizing pale blue eyes I've ever seen. Hypnotic eyes. They remind me of a cloudless sky on a summer day. I continue to survey him, trailing down to his lips then across his chiseled jaw. It's dusted with the perfect five o'clock shadow.

Lifting my chin to get a better look, his blue eyes pierce the distance between us and I realize I'm openly gawking at this stranger. Heat spreads through my body until it coils deep inside my belly.

"Who . . . who are you?"

"I'm Dr. Preston Montgomery. I'm one of the hospital psychologists."

"Therapist?"

"Yes. Before the hospital is able to discharge you, they wanted me to talk to you. Are you okay to talk now?" *No . . .*

I bow my head in agreement.

"Okay, have you ever seen a therapist before?"

"No." I whisper, wishing we didn't have to talk about this.

"Do you often suffer from panic attacks, or is this something new?" His watchful stare sears me, and I feel restless under his scrutiny. His beautiful piercing blue eyes track my movements. They make my heart beat frantically in my chest.

"New."

We sit in silence. The only sound comes from a cart being pushed in the hallway. My eyes wander around the room until I'm forced to meet his inspection again.

"To the best of your knowledge, have you ever suffered from anxiety or any of the other symptoms that presented themselves to you?"

"I don't know. I mean, I've always been a bit anxious, but I've never felt anything like that before. I honestly thought I was dying. What's going on with me?" My mouth drops open as I feel a sharp pressure in my heart. It hammers violently against my chest. This time I'm *for sure* going to die.

"*Shh*. Breathe . . . Breathe. One. Two. Three. In through the nose, out through the mouth."

Squeezing my eyes shut, I take in his words. Try to follow his prompts. Inhale . . . One. Two. Three.

Exhale.

"Wh-why is this hap-happening to me?" Tears pour down my face. I make no move to wipe them. My arm is lead, weighing me down. *Breathe.*

I finally register the doctor's voice as he answers me.

"You've suffered a traumatic loss, and sometimes it's too much for our minds and bodies to handle."

I don't know what to say. I feel so stupid for freaking out. I want this to all to be over.

"How do you feel right now?" His blue eyes are studying me closely.

"My head hurts."

He chews his bottom lip. "Do you have any current medical problems?" he asks, continuing to scrutinize my answers.

"Not that I know of." I lower my head, needing a moment of silence, but it snaps back up when he continues to fire off more questions.

"Are you currently receiving medical care for anything that I should be aware of, or are you taking any medications?"

"Shouldn't you have this in my file? The other doctor already asked me a bunch of questions." There is more bite to my comment than I intend, but I don't want to answer any more questions.

"Unfortunately, the hospital computer filing system is experiencing some hiccups, so you'll need to bear with me as I figure this out. I know that Dr. Levin is set to run a few tests." He pulls out his phone. "He should be back in a moment to talk with you again."

I close my eyes and wish for all of this to end. I just want to put the whole accident behind me.

"Okay."

"Do you remember what was going through your mind right before the accident?"

My eyelids shut and I will myself to recall more details. Memories flash in my brain. "I was thinking about my . . . my . . . I don't even know what to call him." My chin trembles. "I was crying and I got distracted. Then I looked up and saw the lights . . . But . . . but then it was too late. My foot got stuck in the mat. I tried to stop—" My voice breaks into a sob.

Across the bed, Dr. Montgomery types on his iPad. I

wonder what he's writing. *Does he think I did this on purpose?*
That it wasn't an accident. That there's something wrong with
me? Does he believe me? Why would they send a psychologist in
to speak with me? *Can I ask?*

Dr. Levin enters the room, ripping me away from my
thoughts. "Hello, Eve. Dr. Montgomery," he says as the device
is handed to him. His eyes narrow when he reads the notes
on what must be my chart, and nods to Dr. Montgomery in
agreement.

Dr. Montgomery stands and reaches into his back suit
pocket, then pulls out his wallet and removes a business card.
"Eve, I want to give you my card. If you need me, please don't
hesitate to call and make an appointment. Anxiety and panic
attacks can be serious and, if left untreated, can get worse. I
think therapy can help you discover your triggers and help you
find an appropriate way to manage and treat them." His fingers
brush against mine, and the soft pads cause my skin to pebble.
"I really do hope you will call and make an appointment."

I'm not sure I'm ready for that. To actually face what's haunt-
ing me.

Hours pass, I lie in bed tossing and turning, waiting for the
doctor to return. When he finally does, I'm filled with relief and
foreboding at the same time. Everything is fine. Only a mild
concussion, and a request to follow up with a therapist. *A ther-*
apist. Can I do that? Can I speak to someone?

My hands grow clammy, and a tingling begins in my chest.
With each moment that passes, the fear grows stronger and
stronger. *I don't know if I can.*

I'm waiting for my discharge papers when Sydney walks

into the room and peers over at me. "So now what?" she asks as she rubs the back of her neck.

"We wait for me to be discharged." I try to smile, but I doubt it reaches my eyes.

"Are you going to talk to that therapist? Will you make an appointment with him?" Her left brow quirks up when I shake my head.

"What? Why the hell not?"

"Are you kidding me right now, Sydney? Did you see him? I would have to be all types of desperate to let a man that gorgeous see my crazy."

"Well, you better find someone else, then, and fast. You didn't see yourself, Eve. You were basically catatonic. I have never been so scared in my life. You have to talk to someone. If not him, then someone else."

"Fine, I choose option two . . . someone else."

"Are you sure? I wouldn't mind talking to him, seeing him, being over him, being *under him*." She winks "He was pretty freaking gorgeous."

I can't help but laugh. Sydney makes things feel better, *even if it's short lived.*

Much later in the day, I'm finally discharged from the hospital. Sydney stayed with me the whole time, holding my hand and reassuring me that everything would be okay.

As we exit the hospital, she steps forward and hails a cab. Thank God for that, because I'm too physically and emotionally drained to lift my arms. I swear I could sleep for days. My entire body is weak and fragile. Our cab speeds off into the flow of traffic. It only takes a few minutes to arrive at our apartment building. Sydney pays the driver and we both step out.

The sidewalk is crowded and I find myself having to avoid bumping into bystanders. My steps are slow and unsteady, and crossing the short distance to the lobby door feels like completing a marathon. The wind whips mercilessly against me, causing me to feel chills and tremors.

Finally, we make it into the high-rise and into my apartment. I see a picture of Richard and me at my college graduation on the side table. Suddenly, I can't breathe again. The walls close in as every muscle tightens in my chest, inflicting unbearable pain. Each beat of my heart is a thunderous pounding that threatens to be my last. My oxygen level dwindles to near nothingness as each pull of breath comes faster and faster. *Why won't it stop?* The memories are so vivid, they play out as if it was only yesterday.

The day was finally here.

My eyes scanned the crowd, searching for her, searching for him. It was no small feat, getting my mother to come today. So with excitement, I looked out amongst the mass of smiling faces to find her. I finally did, but it wasn't a look of pride I saw. Her eyes were void of emotion, a blank canvas. She fanned herself and checked her pulse against her neck. There she went again, feigning some imaginary illness. A deep-rooted sadness engulfed me. She couldn't find it in her to pretend to be normal even for a day.

My shoulders slumped forward.

Richard's gaze locked on mine. He squared his shoulders and lifted his chin. I understood what he was conveying to me all the way from across the room.

Stand tall.

Be proud.

And with that, I smiled at him and felt satisfaction swell up within for what I had accomplished.

"Here, drink this," Sydney says while thrusting a glass in front of me. I take a swig, swallowing the water, but the room continues to spin as I breathe frantically.

Sydney's hand rubs circles on my back. "It's okay. You're okay."

My body rocks in place, the movements growing faster and faster as I wait for the impending calm that doesn't come soon enough.

"*Shh*, you're okay. You're okay."

I lean back and close my eyes. I don't know how much time passes, but when I reopen them, I realize I'm back to normal. I'm calm. The fear is once again dormant, but the fuse is now lit. I feel it in every breath. The flame is slowly burning away, and it's only a matter of time before I explode again.

With slow movements, I turn my attention back to Sydney. Seated at the edge of the couch, her face is ashen as she nibbles on her bottom lip while she watches me.

"Are you okay? Do I need to call the doctor?"

"I'm okay. I promise I'm fine. I'm just tired. Really, really tired." I slump back into the couch and sigh.

"That's totally understandable. You've been through so much in the last few days. I swear I've never seen anything like the attacks you've had today. You must be exhausted."

"I am," I mumble as I force myself to answer her inquiry. As the words tumble out, my vision is blurry and it's hard to focus on her.

"Does anything else hurt? You look like you might puke."

"I kind of feel like I might."

"It's probably the concussion. They said throwing up could be a side effect. Why don't you lie down in your room and I'll sit with you while you rest?"

She stands and reaches her arm out to help me up.

"You don't have to do that. I'll be fine." I'm not sure I will be, but I don't have the energy to tell her.

"I don't want to hear it. Between the concussion and your panic attacks, I don't feel comfortable leaving you alone right now." I nod, then walk into my room and lie on my bed. The bed dips with Sydney's weight as I rest my eyes.

———————•———————

My eyes flutter open a few hours later. Sydney's head snaps in my direction. Her eyes are red and swollen from lack of sleep. She rubs at them frantically and I notice moisture collect on her finger. *Was she crying?* Is this because of me? Or is there something else making her sad?

"Are you okay?" I ask her and her back stiffens.

"I will be."

"Is there something you want to talk about?"

"Nah, I'm just tired."

"You do look exhausted. Did you sleep at all, Syd?" I groan out, my voice still laced with sleep.

She gives me a tight smile. "No, not really. How are you feeling? Do you need anything? Some Motrin?"

"I can get it," I say right before I yawn.

"No. It's okay. I'll grab it." She lifts from the bed and heads out to grab me some water. When she returns, I notice how sad she still looks. It makes every muscle inside me tighten, constricting my breathing to the point of pain, and a wave of guilt consumes me. The thought plagues me again. It's an incessant voice in my head playing on repeat. *Is this because of me? Or is it more?*

"I'm sorry, Syd. I hate that I've put you through such an ordeal these past couple of days. Are you okay?"

"I'm fine. Don't worry about me. How are you? Do you want to talk about Richard's death? You don't talk about your family much, but maybe you would feel, I don't know, more comfortable with me?"

My eyes well with tears and I shake my head. "I can't."

"I understand, I do, but don't you think you should? You're still grieving. Maybe it would help to talk about it."

"We'll see."

"Please think about it."

"I promise I will," I lied.

chapter two

PRESTON

EVERY WEEK I VOLUNTEER AT SINAI-GRACE, BUT I DON'T keep regular hours. I'm just here as a free resource for the staff to use when they need a consult.

It never gets easier. Sometimes I'm met with confusion, and sometimes anger, but the hardest is the sadness. Sadness can break a person. It can make a home inside you, slowly building a wall around your soul. At first, my job was part of a reparation I made to myself, then it quickly grew into something I loved. Helping people is what I was meant to do, but everything has changed. What became my passion is now, once again, a constant reminder of what I lost.

Today was different, though. Today *she* was here. *In my hospital.* What were the chances? When our eyes met, it was as if my world fell off its axis. Disbelief, and then worry. *What the fuck happened to her?* Those icy blue eyes were once so dynamic. What happened to cause that much pain?

I remember the first time I saw her. She stole the breath from my lungs.

She was sitting at a table in the far corner of Paradise Diner looking out onto the street. She was beautiful. Serene. But what left me breathless was that she looked just like *her*.

I remember thinking it was her . . .

Sloane.

But that wasn't possible. And as much as I knew that, I still found myself gazing across the space that separated us. The similarities were uncanny.

I stepped forward and her familiar features began to fade. Like an impressionist's stroke on a canvas, up-close formed a new image.

This image was vibrant and alive. This image was not the woman who haunted my waking thoughts, who taunted and tormented me. No. This woman was something else all together. A part of me wanted to cross the space that separated us. Wanted to speak to her. Wanted to discover everything about this girl who reminded me so much of a time before. But I didn't. *How could I? What would I even say?*

I almost fell over in shock today. It took every last piece of my soul to hold myself together as I watched her.

There she was lying in a hospital bed, weak and frail. She reminded me of fresh fallen snow. She had fair skin, pale blonde hair and icy blue eyes. Now I had a name ... Eve Hamilton.

I don't know why I handed her my card. I didn't have to.

I shouldn't have.

A referral would have been enough. But there was something in her eyes. Something I had seen before. A deep-rooted sadness I wanted—no, *needed*—to fix.

chapter three

EVE

THE LAST WEEK AND HALF, I'VE DONE NOTHING AT ALL. I feel as if the world is closing in around me and there's no light at the end of the tunnel. Heaviness sits on my chest. There's a feeling of suffocating with every strangled breath I try to take.

I can't eat.

I can't sleep.

I can't go on like this. Something has to give.

I find myself staring down at Dr. Montgomery's card and wondering what it would be like to sit in front of him and purge my soul. The card is starting to fray and bend from the countless times I've handled it. *Should I call him?* He seemed to know what he was talking about, but at the same time I'm not sure he would be the right fit for me. I'm not sure I want to look into his eyes and let him see my weaknesses.

Since I've been home from the hospital, I've started having nightmares that leave me feeling hopeless and scared. Every night I pray for peace, but as sleep finds me, an array of images and smells and feelings so crisp attack me. They rip me from my bed night after night in sweat and tears. But I know the nightmares will always find me. I have no choice.

This morning, after a dreadful night of tossing and turning, I'm woken from my haze by the sound of glass shattering.

"Shit, shit, shit," I hear as I pad down the hallway and into the kitchen. I find Sydney on the floor picking up pieces of my favorite coffee mug.

I can't help but laugh at the irony. Everything is falling to pieces. Why not my mug, too?

She spins around at the sound of my laugh. "Oh, my God, I'm so sorry. I was trying to make you a cup of coffee and I accidentally knocked it off the counter."

"Don't worry about it." I try to give her a reassuring smile. "Seriously, Syd. It's only a mug."

Nodding she stands, placing the shards of ceramic into the garbage can and then heads over to the cabinet and grabs another coffee cup.

"Want some?"

"Sure, thank you," I say as she pours the coffee.

"So, what do you have planned for today?" She pulls out the chair at the kitchen island and takes a seat.

"I need to call my mom, see if she needs anything. That's pretty much it." Sydney's lips set into a hard line. "I'll be okay," I try to reassure her, but she's smart to worry about me. Talking to my mom is emotionally draining on a good day, and with my current condition, I'm not sure I can handle speaking to her. But I have to.

I take one more sip and stand from the table, grab my phone and start to dial. She picks up on the first ring, as if she's desperate for someone to hear her neurosis.

"Eve," she groans.

"What's wrong, Mom? Are you okay?" I know she's not. She never is. Her hypochondria knows no bounds. It encompasses every breath she takes.

"I'm dizzy and I can't move. It's as if my face is numb. I might be having a—"

"You're not, Mom."

"How do you know? I could be. My heart beat is slow—"

"Did you take anything?"

"Just my insulin." And there it is. My mom doesn't have diabetes. She has "self-diagnosed" diabetes, and with enough money and a crooked doctor, she now has insulin to treat an ailment she's never had.

"I'm coming over right now." I bite my lip and draw blood. The coppery taste coats my tongue as it swipes to wipe it. I'm not strong enough to deal with this now, but it falls on me regardless.

I'm all she has.

An hour later, I find myself on the Upper East Side in my mom's apartment. My whole body is on edge. Richards's apartment is in the same building, and a part of me feels empty knowing I can't pop over to see him.

I walk into my mom's living room, but it's empty, so I continue to the bedroom. It's where I find her, half-dressed and disheveled. There's make-up smudged against her face and her eyes are closed.

"Mom, are you okay?" I rush to her side of the bed, grab her arm and check her pulse.

She groans at the contact. "Cold," she mutters.

"Mom, can you open your eyes?" She does, but I see instantly that they aren't focused and they look hazy. "Did you take anything else, Mom?"

"N-Nothing."

"What did you take, Mom?"

"Nothing," she mumbles. "Just my insulin." And with that I know her blood sugar is dangerously low. I dash out of the room and into the kitchen to grab some orange juice. When I'm back, with my help, she drinks. Within a few minutes, the color returns to her cheeks.

Taking insulin could kill my mom. When she takes it, her sugar level is never high enough for the quantity she takes. I want to scream, but I don't. Instead, I get into bed and rock her to sleep.

Reaching out my hand, I stroke her face, and she mutters unintelligible words. I don't know what set my mom off today. All I know is today is worse than most. Normally, most of her ailments are fictional. They reside inside her brain and feed off the fear that lives there. But this time, she is actually psychically ill. She's harder to deal with like this. On days like today there is no calming my mom. On days like today there is no asking questions or getting truths. On days like today I just have to treat the symptoms and pray it passes quickly.

She lies peacefully in my arms and, for one moment, my heart tugs in my chest.

This is so backwards. She should be holding me, comforting me, not the other way around.

She should be the one doing the mothering.

———————•———————

I'm exhausted when I arrive back at my apartment. Every muscle in my body hurts. Heading into the living room, I submerge myself into the fluffy white couch that sits adjacent to the wall. It was our first purchase when we moved in together two years ago, and to this day it provides the sanctuary I always need after leaving my mom's. Reclining back, I close my tired eyes. They burn from all the fallen tears I've shed in the last week. Like sandpaper scraping against the grain of wood, they remind me of all the defects in me I need to smooth out.

"How did it go with your mom?" Sydney asks as she lazily strolls into the living room.

"Not good." I breathe out a chocked groan as I run my hands through my hair and pull at my roots.

"What's going on?"

"She's sick." My fingers tense in my lap. "This time she was dizzy." Sydney knows what this means. Today it's dizzy, last week it was a stomach ulcer, and the week before that a blood clot. I swallow with difficulty as the familiar anxiety weaves its way through my blood stream.

"She's having a reaction to her insulin. It's making her weak and lethargic." A silence surrounds us as she takes in what I've said. My stomach churns uncomfortably at the void. She has a puzzled look upon her face.

"Insulin? For diabetes? Since when does she have diabetes?"

"You know how it is. She's had it for a few weeks now, but it's not real, obviously. Like everything else, it's in her head."

It's a sad truth, but this is how it's been for as long as I can remember. No doctor ever finds anything wrong. They only humor her with a false diagnosis. It breaks my heart, and I wish I could help her, but there is no helping someone like her. The scary part is that every day since Richard's death, I understand her more and more as my own panic disables me.

"How can that be?"

"With the right amount of money and pressure, a doctor will diagnose you with anything. In this case, her sugars are normal, but for her they're "high," so the doctor gives her insulin. Then she gets "sick" and a horribly vicious cycle starts."

"What can you do?"

My eyes lock with Sydney's. Her forehead is furrowed and I feel a stab of pain for putting that look there. "All I can do is be there for her and take care of her, I guess."

Her cheeks pinch in and little lines of worry appear on her brow. "I'm so sorry."

"Not your fault."

She gives me a tight smile and sits beside me on the couch. "I know it's not my fault, but I care about you, so your pain is my pain."

"You have no idea how much that means to me. I know I'm not the easiest—"

"Eve—"

I hold up my hand. "No, Syd, let me finish. I never really had any friends. In high school, even in college, I always had to be there for my mom, and it didn't lend well to fostering relationships with my peers. Sure, I had *some* friends, but eventually they got sick of me always canceling or leaving early. But you never care if I have to disappear for hours to check on her, or if I'm evasive or closed off, and I thank you for that. I know it can't be easy being my friend, but I thank you for putting up with my endless pile of shit."

Sydney moves closer and pulls me into her arms. Her embrace is warm and comforting. My shoulders drop forward as I let some of the built-up tension be absorbed into this hug.

"This isn't a one-way street, babe. You're there for me, too." I pull back and look into her eyes. She smirks at me. "You help me pick out all my outfits for dates, and you deal with my endless crazy diets." She laughs, lightening the sober mood lingering in the air.

"Yes, totally the same." I giggle back, joining her. Together we laugh until she stills, and every muscle in her face tightens as she grows more serious.

"I love you, girl. No matter what," she says and tears well in my eyes. "And even with everything you are going through, you're still the strongest person I know."

"I don't know about that."

"I don't know many twenty-four years olds who are the sole caregiver to their mother. Even if she doesn't need you all the time, I know her health wears on you. But every day, no matter how bad your own day was, you are still there for her when she needs you."

"Thanks." Her words act like a balm. As if they are a magical elixir that mends my troubled soul.

Even if it's only temporary, I welcome the feeling.

———————•———————

The smell hits me. Unmistakable, yet indescribable at the same time.

Coppery.

Sweet.

Pungent.

It seeped through our house like mist on a hazy day.

Blanketing the world around me. It filled my nostrils.

Suffocated me with fear.

"No!"

My whole body flails as screams leave my mouth. Everything is closing in on me. Fear, stark and vivid, glitter behind my lids. Trying to escape the confines of my mind, my eyes flash open. A half-dressed Sydney rushes in. The door collides with the wall, causing the room to shake.

"Are you okay? I only left you for a minute." *Am I okay? Am*

I okay?

The words echo around the space. Jumping off the walls. Bouncing through my brain.

But they have no meaning. Nothing has meaning. The only thing I understand is the feeling of the blood coating my skin.

Blood.

Wildly, my eyes dash around the room like a crazed animal clawing at myself. "Get it off! Get it off!"

"Get what off?" She eyes me with confusion as I scrub my hands over my body, trying desperately to clean it off.

"It's everywhere! Don't you see it?"

I can feel it. Taste it. It's everywhere. Controlling everything.

"See what? I don't see anything."

"The blood! The blood is everywhere!" My shrill voice echoes through the room as Sydney flips the light switch and the room floods with light, blinding me. "There's no blood." As my eyes adjust, I lift the blanket. There's nothing there. "I saw it. I smelled it. I swear it was there!" I cry.

"It was only a dream. You're okay. *Shh*, you're okay. Here, let me get you some water. I'll be right back."

It was so real, but she's right. There's nothing here. But the tension still lingers in my bones. It still resides in my heart, in my mind.

By the time she comes back, my tears have dried but I can't shake the feeling that I'm missing something. That the dream was a piece of a puzzle, but I don't know where the piece belongs. "Here." She hands me the glass and I take a long gulp of the water. It cools my body, quenches my thirst, but it doesn't stop the wave of apprehension sweeping through my body. "Do you need me to get you anything else?"

"No. I'll be fine. I promise." She raises an eyebrow at me. I steady my breathing to convince her I'll be fine. Plastering on a reassuring smile, my head bobs up and down a few times. "Really, I'm okay. Please, go back to sleep. You don't have to stay up and watch me. I'll just watch some TV or read a book." My voice sounds fake even to my own ears.

She crawls out of my bed. "You sure?"

A part of me wants to beg her to stay to comfort me, but instead, I bow my head.

"Yeah." I exhale.

She eyes me one more time before turning around to leave the room. My life pre-accident seems so far away right now as my body shakes like a leaf falling from a tree. It's as if I don't even know who this person I've become is, but it reminds me of my mom. I need to snap out of it. Return to the version of me that I know. That makes sense. I haven't been back to work since the funeral. Between Richard's death and my head, no one is in a rush to have me return. But being alone all day is starting to wear on my sanity, so I need to go back. The only problem is, my body is psychically exhausted. I only have a few more days before I go back and I'm scared. I don't think I'll be able to function on this little sleep.

I lie in my bed and pull out Pride and Prejudice. I always find comfort in Jane Austen's words. Maybe that will take my mind off having to return to my real life in a few days. Maybe it will bring some semblance of normalcy.

Somewhere between Mr. Darcy insulting Elizabeth and them falling into an all-consuming love only possible in stories, I must have fallen back to sleep. This time, no visions danced behind my eyes. There was no taste of fear so terrifying that

I'm sure it will haunt me for days. Peace finally found me and although brief, I welcomed the reprieve.

I wake with a new resolve this morning, and that is to start preparing for work. It's inevitable that I must return. It's been almost two weeks since I left the hospital, and I can't hide forever. My two-week leave of absence is coming to an end, but the idea of all that I missed at work suddenly makes my head ache. I knead at my temples. No, I will not get a headache right now. I have too much to do. For the first time since Richard died, my appetite has returned. I can't imagine how sickly skeletal I must appear to Sydney. When she's around, I sense her studying me. The concern is evident in her eyes.

Today my stomach rumbles and turns with the need to be satisfied. It needs strength and substance. Heading into the kitchen, I pull out cereal and milk, and sit down when my phone rings . . . *Sydney*. I'm not surprised; she checks in often to make sure I'm okay.

"Hey," I answer but it comes out muffled as I chew the corn flakes in my mouth.

"Hi. What's going on over there? You okay?"

"I'm good, just eating." I lay the spoon down and stand to grab some water. The faucet comes to life and I pour myself a glass from the cold stream. "How's work? Anything I need to know?"

"Nope, you're on break. I'm not going to talk work with you," she says in a stern voice that makes me smile. "Oh shit, the other line is ringing. I'll call you back." I don't even have time to say goodbye before I hear silence. Sitting back down with my now filled cup, I reach for my spoon when my cell phone rings again. My mouth splits into a smile. *That was quick.* When I peer down, I realize it's a number I don't recognize. *Should I answer?* Curiosity wins and my finger swipes the screen.

"Hello?"

"Is Eve Hamilton there?" The voice is unfamiliar and it puts me on edge.

"Yes, this is she. Who's calling?" My shoulders tense, the time going still as I wait.

"Hi, this is Pamela calling from Milton Schwartz's law office. He's the attorney handling Richard Stone's estate. Do you have a moment to speak?"

"Yes. Sure. How can I help you?"

"Mr. Schwartz would like to schedule a time to meet with you to discuss Mr. Stone's estate. Would you be able to come in to our office tomorrow?"

Tomorrow, tomorrow, tomorrow, the word rolls in my mind multiple times. *Will I be able to meet him? Can I handle it?* I'm scared of what he will tell me. But I don't have a choice. I have to say yes.

"Yes, I can meet Mr. Schwartz tomorrow."

"What time would be convenient for you, Miss. Hamilton?"

"I can be there around noon. Would that work?" The sound of fingers tapping a keyboard can be heard through the phone.

"Yes, Mr. Schwartz can see you then."

Pamela proceeds to rattle off the address, and once done, I hang up the phone, already dreading what tomorrow will bring.

With sleep-blurred eyes, I wake. The nightmares last night were the same as all the previous nights. I need to get help, but I'm scared. Sweat coats my upper lip and I find myself chewing on the inside of my cheek. My stomach clenches that I have to meet with Richard's lawyer soon. A strange feeling of dread

AVA HARRISON

gnaws at me, as if ice is crawling through my veins. I try my best to plaster on a fake smile, to pretend I'm okay. Instead, I let the smile fall off my lips.

You can't lie to yourself.

An hour later when I finally walk through the door to his office, I meet with an elderly man. He looks to be about sixty and he's dressed in a crisp navy suit with a matching tie.

"Hello, Ms. Hamilton. Please come in. Can I have my assistant Pamela get you something to drink? A coffee perhaps?" He smiles. It's a fatherly smile and reminds me of Richard.

"Hello, Mr. Schwartz. Please call me Eve, and yes, a cup of coffee would be lovely." I'm exhausted from a rough night and my muscles are so tight that I'd welcome anything right now to keep my mind busy. I'm hoping a warm cup of coffee will do the trick.

"Okay, please take a seat and I'll be right with you." He motions to the chair, and I sit down across the desk from him. After he hangs up the phone with his assistant, he pulls out a file from his desk.

While he sorts through the papers, his assistant enters the room and places a steaming hot mug in front of me. The warm fluid coats my throat and evokes heat to flow through my body. It helps to calm my nerves that are strung so tight I fear I might snap.

"Thank you so much for agreeing to meet with me today. I wanted to discuss Mr. Stone's estate. Normally, I wouldn't discuss this in absence of the rest of the beneficiaries, but when Richard drew up his will years ago, he gave me the authority to discuss all matters of the estate—including the company—with you first, especially since this concerns you."

"I'm not sure why the company would concern me."

"From my understanding, you are aware that The Stone Agency, although primarily owned and run by Mr. Stone, also had a silent investor."

"And this concerns me because?"

"The silent investor is Laura Hamilton." I almost drop my coffee cup as my hand shakes from the news.

"My mother?" I straighten my spine, trying to compose myself in front of this virtual stranger. It doesn't help. Instead, my knee bounces with nerves.

"Yes, when your father passed, your mother invested some of his life insurance money in the business. It's been quite a lucrative investment. You can find comfort that although your mother won't work at the company, she and her medical bills will be taken care of for the rest of her life. There is a stipulation in the will, however, barring your mother's mental condition. The will states that Michael Durand is to be left in charge of the company."

"Okay. That makes sense. Is there anything else I should know about?" Finding out my mom owns the company I work for is a bombshell. I wonder if there are any other big secrets lurking in those papers. The whole thought makes me break into a cold sweat.

"Yes," He pulls out a paper from the pile on his desk and hands it to me. It's a deed. "The real reason I wanted to see you today is that the you inherited Mr. Stone's apartment." My mouth drops open and I brace myself in my chair.

"I got his apartment?"

"Yes, he said that you were like a daughter to him. He talked about you very fondly."

"I can't live there," I blurt out, already feeling my chest muscles tightening at the thought of living in the same building as my mom. "I have to sell it."

"Are you sure?" he asks and I lift my hands to cover my face. "God, I don't know."

"How about you think about it? If you choose to sell, I can find you a real estate firm to list it with."

"Thank you for all your help, Mr. Schwartz. I have a lot to think about and I'll have a talk to my mom regarding the business, too."

"I'll be at the office finalizing some paperwork with Michael in the next few weeks, so we can touch base then. If you need anything in the meantime, here's my card. Please feel free to call me with any questions, or if your mother needs anything."

"Thank you." I stand and make my way to the door. In a daze, I walk the streets back to my apartment. The city passes in a rush of movement, but nothing is in focus.

When would it get easier?

chapter four

EVE

THE EARLY MORNING SUN BEAMS IN THROUGH THE DRAPES. It casts a shimmery light into my eyes, forcing me to wake. Checking the clock, I see it's only seven in the morning. A part of me wants to close my eyes and hide for the whole day, but with going back to work tomorrow, I have a bunch of errands to run. I need to grab some groceries for myself, and some for Mom as well.

The idea of dragging Sydney along is tempting, but in the end as I quietly pad down the hall to freshen up, I decide to let her sleep. I'm sure she'll slumber the day away. She hasn't been herself since the funeral, either. I feel as though it's my fault. She also lost someone. I can't imagine how hard it must be for her to want to grieve but feel she can't because of me. I'll let her sleep. Let her have her space to feel what she needs to feel.

After a long shower to wash away my restless night, I grab a bite to eat and then head out for the day. First I hit the supermarket down the block from my apartment, stopping back home afterward to put my food away. Then, with Mom's groceries in hand, I hop in a cab and head uptown to her place. The architecture and people rush by in a sea of color, and I get lost in my own thoughts of the impending conversation I intend to have with her. Today I need to confront my mom about her investment in The Stone Agency.

I'm a little scared of what I will find today. There is never a certainty of the mood or ailment one will encounter when entering Laura Hamilton's home. Nervously, my hands start to run through my hair, pulling gently at the roots as I enter her home and make my way into the kitchen.

It's a disaster. The pristine marble island has medicine sprawled across it. Pill bottles are open and spilled haphazardly across the surface. It doesn't look like I'll be getting any answers from her today. Throwing the bags of food down, I make haste to find my mom.

The wind is knocked out of me when I find my mom. She's thrown over the toilet dry heaving. Her whole body wracks with sobs as tears stream down her face. Kneeling down, I try to comfort her but it's no use. Through hysterics, she mumbles words I can't understand. It sounds like "my fault," but I can't be sure.

"What happened?" I ask as she finally silences and takes a giant gulp of air.

"Dying," she mutters as my fingers run down her back, comforting and soothing her.

"You're not actually dying, Mom. But if you keep overmedicating, you just might."

"I am. I really am." She's not, but in her state of mind, she will never understand that. She shivers violently as I pull her to standing and lead her to her bed. She rocks back and forth.

———————•———————

By the time six p.m. rolls around, I'm officially and utterly exhausted. Spending the afternoon taking care of my mom has me on edge. I want to go to bed, crawl under my covers and hide from the world. When she's sick, she sucks the life out of me.

As much as my bed beckons to me, the idea of another restless night has me itching for a nightcap. I'm not much of a drinker, but an anxious feeling lurks in my mind. The thoughts tell me my racing heart is having a heart attack, and I'm going crazy with my own impending doom. *I'm becoming my mother.*

With a shaking hand I apply a fresh coat of lipstick and run a brush through my hair. I'm not necessarily feeling up to this, but the knowledge that it will drown out the fear lurking inside is enough to will myself to head out the door to grab a drink.

The Corner Bar is located on the corner of Thirty-Third and Third, hence the name. It also happens to be right underneath our apartment building, which has been extremely convenient when trying to quiet the nightmares.

I enter and take in the mixture of suits and college kids. The surroundings and ambiance are what I love most about this neighborhood. The healthy mix. I have lived here for a little over two years, and it has everything a recent college grad could want. Plus, when I moved here, I was leaving the bad memories behind. I instantly felt lighter being away from my mom's latest ailment hanging above my head.

After taking care of her for so long, I remember the excitement of having my first apartment like it was yesterday.

"You're here." I walked into the apartment—my new apartment—and Sydney squealed. "I'm so excited. Here, let me show you your room. Then we can go grab some food."

"Lead the way." I smiled broadly. I wanted to jump up and

down too, but feared she'd think I was a nutcase. Together we walked a few steps through the living room and she pushed open a door. The room was completely vacant except for a bed sitting adjacent to a large window. "I know it's small and the closet space sucks, but—" I stopped listening.

"It's perfect." It didn't matter how small the room was. This was my place.

"Really?"

"It's more than perfect," I exclaimed, and this time I allowed myself to be excited, too.

"Yeah! Isn't it great?"

"The best."

It's funny how fast things have changed in the last few years. Back then, I welcomed the night and sleeping in my new bed. Now, I fear what that sleep will bring. The irony isn't lost on me. All the things I hate about my mom are starting to plague me as well. With a shake of my head, I follow the path of men in perfect three-piece suits to the bar. This will take the edge off.

Drown the fear.

Allow me peace.

After spying an empty seat at the bar, I sit down. My phone vibrates in my purse, so I pull it out and see that a new text has come through.

Sydney: Where are you?

Me: Having a drink at The Corner Bar

Sydney: I'll be there in five.

A cute bartender in his mid-twenties with shaggy blond hair gives me a wicked smirk. "What can I get for you, sweetheart?" he asks with a southern twang that's just as cute as his appearance.

"Shot of Patron," I shout back over the loud music filling the air. A few seconds later, I'm snapped out of my wandering thoughts as a small glass hits the wood.

"Twenty bucks."

I snap my gaze up to him. *Did he just say twenty bucks?* "For a shot of tequila?" His face splits into a wicked smile. "Yep."

"Better be the best damn tequila I've ever had."

With that he laughs. "Oh, it will be." He smirks as I lift the glass to my mouth. I wink and swallow the fiery liquid. Cutie gives me a smile as he lifts his eyebrow.

"Another?"

"Keep them coming." I smirk and a few seconds later, I'm lifting my second shot to my mouth. This one burns less than the first and makes my stomach feel warm.

"Hey there, killer. Take it easy with the shots. How many have you had?" I peer over my shoulder to see Sydney standing behind me. Her brow is furrowed and her mouth is in a tight line.

"Only two, but who's counting?"

"You should be. Tomorrow you're going back to work, or did you forget that?"

"I wish I could." I wave my hand to get the attention of the bartender. "One more."

"Eve, you need to take it easy." She steps in closer, placing her hand on my arm to try to usher me up.

"I don't want to," I huff.

"What's going on with you?"

Turning my head, I lift an eyebrow at her. "What do you mean? Can't a girl go to a bar and grab a drink?"

"I have known you for two and a half years, lived with you pretty much just as long, and you've never been a big drinker.

Sure, you have a cocktail here and there after work, but to go the bar and throw back shots before bed—on a night when you have to work the next day, too? Well, that's not like you at all. I mean, I get it, but still."

I close my eyes and a strangled moan escapes. "I just want to sleep, Syd. I went to see my mom again, and it was bad. She was really bad. On top of that, the idea of another sleepless night, or worse . . ." I stop myself from telling her I'm trying to drown out the voices and silence the dreams. She wouldn't understand.

She reaches out and takes my hand in hers. Her eyes are soft as if she hears the words I haven't spoken. "Drinking won't make the nightmares go away, babe. I think it's time you reach out to someone."

"Maybe," I whisper. I search out the bartender and lift my hand to signal I want another.

My body feels loose. There's no tension anywhere. With each shot I take, the cute bartender becomes the "hot bartender." Apparently, his name is Austin and his jokes get funnier and funnier until I'm hunched over into a fit of laughter.

"Are you ready to come home?" Sydney asks from beside me.

"Nope." I giggle, eliciting a laugh from Austin.

"I can't just leave you here." Her eyes narrow and I wink at her.

"I'll be fine. Austin will take care of me."

"That's what I'm afraid of."

I laugh and Austin smirks.

Sydney moves closer to me and whispers in my ear, "Are

you sure?"

"Totally. I'll be fine. Go to bed."

———— ————•———— ————

Where the fuck am I?

The aching in my skull feels like a jackhammer is drilling away. My mouth is dry and my lips stick together as I pull them apart. It's as though I'm choking on chalk. A grimy film coats my throat. *Gross.* I try to rub the sleep away, but instead come up with a handful of what's collected on my chin.

Maybe the tequila wasn't such a great idea.

However, it did work. With the booze seeping into my bloodstream, I passed out, *even if it wasn't in my own bed.* It's the first time in weeks I got a full night's sleep.

Sitting up, I survey myself. I'm fully dressed and alone in the bed. *Thank God.* This could have been bad. Not that I wouldn't have enjoyed a night in the sack with Austin, but I'd hate to be so drunk that I didn't remember it.

Stepping out of the room, I take a peek around his apartment. There he is, curled up on the couch, snoring away. I don't even bother to say good-bye. It's awkward enough without me calling attention to the fact I was a drunk lush last night. Shit, I hope I didn't say anything dumb, or worse, make an ass of myself. Sydney and I might need to find another bar.

Still sleeping, he grunts as if he's about to wake. I take that as my cue to make a beeline out the door.

New York is quite peaceful at six a.m., albeit still dark. The only sound is the soft hum of passing taxis. It reminds me of a sound machine you listen to at night. As I walk back to my apartment, my hangover starts to pass. The sounds and architecture distract me. Looking at the intricate nature of each building I pass is fascinating. Like fingerprints, no building is the same. Each is unique and beautiful in its own way.

As I approach my street, I pick up my pace. Work isn't for a few hours, and I don't need to be there until nine, but I still need to shower and get ready.

An hour later, I'm ready to go. Since I've missed so much work, I decide to go in early and get a jump on the day. I've fallen so far behind, I find myself running there to beat the morning rush. With labored breath, I swing the revolving door, and then dash to the elevator. It opens almost instantly.

Everything inside me feels as if it's begun to seize. Muscles twitch, eyes water, shoulders slump forward, I brace my shaking hands on the cold metal surface of the wall. *I have to face my fears.* Going back to a place that reminds me so much of my loss feels as if somebody picked and reopened a scab on my heart. I try to will the emotions away as I plaster a smile on my face and enter the suite. But my smile is an imposter. It lies. It says I'm okay. But I'm not. Every smile is a plea. Every smile is a prayer that they don't see my pain. That they don't see how much I'm hurting since Richard's death.

My heartbeat quickens. *I'm okay. I'll be okay . . .*

It's odd being here. Everything is wrong. The soul of the company is gone, and while the people around me have moved on, I can't ignore his absence. Richard wasn't only a boss, he was for all intents and purposes the life of this company. Now with him gone, this place feels like a shell of what it used to be. It's as if I need a road map to figure it out. Nothing has changed, per se, but everything is different.

I make my way further into the office space. A haze of sadness lingers over the few employees already here for the day. From the corner of my eye I notice them staring, scrutinizing, judging. They whisper and wonder where I've been. I want to crawl in a hole and hide. Instead, I square my shoulders and walk with purpose. I say good morning to them as I make my way to my desk, and hope they don't see through my façade.

For the next few hours, I get caught up on all the emails I've missed these past two weeks while I was on leave. Thankfully, Sydney stepped in and took some of my workload while I was away. Without her, I would never have made it this far after the funeral.

As if my thoughts have conjured her, I see Sydney walking in and straight toward me. "Hey, are you okay? I didn't see you this morning. What time did you come in? Did you . . ." She leans forward, closer to me. "Did you go home with that bartender?"

I groan. "Yes." Her eyes widen, but I shake my head. "No, none of that." I lift my hands to message my temples.

"Are you hungover? Does your head hurt?"

"I'm fine. It really doesn't hurt anymore. Just a bit tender." I set my hands back into my lap to prove that I'm okay. "Sorry if I scared you. I shouldn't have stayed behind. I should have gone home with you." I shiver from the memory of last night and how drunk I was, a small convulsion—*hopefully not noticeable*—but Sydney grimaces and I know she saw it.

"I left there early. I tried not to wake you when I got home, and then came straight here." I open another email and groan loudly. "God, I'm so far behind. Thank you. I'd be lost without you."

"If you need anything, I'm here. How are you, by the way? Are you okay being here?" Her voice is lowered, and I know she's concerned about the inner office gossip that is sure to be circulating from my incident at the funeral.

"I don't know. I guess I'm okay."

Sydney leans in. "It's okay to not be okay." When I don't respond, she reaches out to squeeze my hand. "I think you really need to see someone. You have the card the doctor in the ER gave you. Can you please consider calling him? It's okay to ask for help. It's hard to lose someone so close to you."

The memory of Richard makes my heart lurch in my chest. "I just don't know if I can talk about it, and with Mom always needing me, I'm not sure I'll have time, you know?"

"You have to start putting yourself first. You're the strongest person I know. Taking care of your mother, that's not easy. Maybe now it's time you find someone to help take care of you. It's always been hard for you to let people in, to talk about her, but I think it's time to try. I think this is for the best. No more excuses, Eve."

"It's not that . . ." I shake my head.

"What is it then?"

I open my mouth to speak but no words come out. A sweat breaks out across my brow and my heartbeat picks up. A sharp pain radiates down my arm. I reach across my far shoulder and rub at the knot in my left shoulder blade.

"Can we talk about this back at the apartment?"

"Yeah, of course," she whispers. Her face scrunches as she grimaces. "Oh, I forgot to tell you. Michael called a company meeting after lunch. Everyone is afraid we're getting sacked."

Michael is now the executive vice president of the agency. If he's calling a company meeting, it's a big deal. She shrugs before she heads over to her desk that's directly diagonal from mine.

I pull out the latest project I'm working on and try to distract myself, but the wait is driving me mad. The walls feel as if they are closing in around me. I wish Richard was here.

I stretch my arms above my head and yawn. I've been sitting at this desk for hours. I consider drinking the cup of cold coffee on my desk, but I fear even that won't do the trick. Glancing at the clock, I realize not only have I worked through lunch, but I'm also about to be late for the meeting. My heels click softly on the marble floor as I make my way to the conference room.

Most of the staff, including Sydney, is already there when I enter the brightly lit room. Taking a seat beside her at the long Lucite table that spans the center of the room, I look out the floor-to-ceiling windows overlooking Park Avenue. Snow has started to fall again. Clumps of wet flakes cling to the surface of the nearby buildings, and I lose myself in the white haze.

Muffled sounds reverberate through the room and I turn my attention back toward the center of the table. The atmosphere swiftly changes as Michael Durand walks into the room. Tension swirls in the air.

The fear is palpable.

"Good afternoon, and thank you all for being here. This will be a short meeting. I just want touch upon some rumors that have been floating around. No, we're not closing," he says abruptly. A rush of air is expelled from everyone in the room. "However, things will be changing. Over the next few weeks, the attorney will be going over Richard's will as well as some other pressing business matters that I won't go into today. I know this is vague and I wish I could give you more assurances, but unfortunately, this is all I have for you. In the interim, I will be in charge. As you are aware, Richard had a silent investor in the company, so until they decide who takes over as CEO, any questions can be directed to me."

When he finally stops speaking, his eyes flick over to me. Simultaneously all the eyes in the room follow his gaze. They all seem to narrow in suspicion, as if I know something.

I do, but I won't tell them that.

After Michael leaves, the room erupts in a series of loud whispers. Sydney turns to me and I shrug.

Someone grasps my shoulders from behind. My back stiffens as I turn to find Barry standing there. Where most everyone who works for The Stone Agency is a team player, Barry travels to the beat of his own drum. He's reserved and prefers to work alone. We've never gotten along.

"Hi," Barry says. He doesn't make eye contact with me. He never makes eye contact with anyone. "Do you know who's taking over?"

"Hello to you too, Barry."

His fingers start to tap at his leg. "He told you everything. You have to know something."

"Sorry, can't help you." His brow furrows at my words, but before he tries to press any further, I walk away. Until I speak to my mother, I don't really know anything, but even if I did, I wouldn't share it with this creep.

chapter five

EVE

THIS WEEK SUCKED.

Fear gripped me often, nightmares infiltrated my sleep, and my appetite dwindled.

But today is Saturday.

So today is a good day.

Anything is better than the hell I suffered being back at the office. The rumor mill ran rampant at The Stone Agency, and work was so stressful, it was no feat at all to get Sydney to go out. She didn't judge me on the copious amounts of alcohol I drank to help put me to bed. Work has been stressful for her too, so she happily drinks alongside me.

After waking up at Austin's apartment and doing the walk of shame last week, I tried to convince Sydney to find another bar to go to, but she said I needed to man up and get over it. That once I ripped the Band-Aid off and act normally, it would no longer be weird and that's exactly what I did. Austin was cool about me sneaking off. He even bought us a round of shots to make light of the situation.

After freshening up, my phone starts to ring. It's my mom. *I can't deal with her now.* I send her to voice mail, and then throw on nicer clothes. After I'm dressed, I make my way down the street to my favorite diner. With my concussion and then having to go back to work, I had completely skipped my weekly ritual. I'm hoping this little sense of normalcy will help aid me in allowing my life to return to ordinary.

Paradise Diner is famous for their amazingly delicious chocolate chip waffles with extra yummy homemade whipped cream. Well, maybe not world famous, but in Murray Hill it was the only place to go.

Just as I make it to the familiar door, my phone vibrates in my pocket and an unknown number appears on the screen. I shudder inwardly when I wonder who it could be, especially on a Saturday morning. It's never a good thing when an unknown number calls me.

"Hello."

"This is Sinai-Grace. Is this Eve Hamilton?" My quickening pulse pounds in my ears.

"Yes, it is. What's going on? Is it my mother?" *Please say she's okay. Please.*

"Your mother was brought in today from an adverse re-action to one of her medications." Guilt sweeps through me, filling my veins with despair. That's why she called. She called me and I sent her to voicemail.

"I'll be right there." I hang up the phone. I don't even ask where she is, which room number. Is she even in a room? I just run. I run as fast as I can to help my mom.

Dashing in the entrance of the hospital thirty minutes later, I head straight to the information desk.

"My mother was brought in today," I huff out on labored breath.

"Name?" The attendant doesn't even look up as she

addresses me, her expression one of indifference.

"Laura Hamilton." Her fingers type away at the computer in front of me, and with each tap of the keyboard, the raw and primitive grief I had suppressed overwhelms me and makes it hard to stand.

"She's just now being moved into a room," she answers, and I so desperately want to beg her to hurry and tell me the room number. Every second that goes by is a second I'm losing before I can make sure she's okay.

I'm frantic and desperate by the time the receptionist tells me where I can find her. Turning on my heel, I race down the corridor, then take the elevator up. My footsteps thunder down the hall until I find my mother's room. When I finally step inside, my legs give way.

She's lying frail in the bed. Her skin is hollow, and her once dewy glow now looks dull and grey. I sit beside her bed and hold her tiny hand in mine. It's all bone. Everything inside me freezes for a second. My mind and body are numb. Time stops as I watch her breathe. I silently thank God I didn't lose her too. Lose her the way I lost my father. The way I lost Richard.

She's all I have left. She can't leave me.

Tears well in my eyes. It's too much. This feeling is too much.

My back tightens, my muscles cord and a soft hum sounds in my ear. The impending doom is all around me.

I can see it. It's lurching its ugly head, ready to strike. *Air.* I need air.

The need to turn and run is all-encompassing, it sweeps over me, carrying my feet out the door and into the hallway. In my haste, I collide into something, causing a strangled gasp to escape as I drop to the floor. It feels as though I'm floating underwater, trying to break through the surface.

White knuckles, uneven breathing, suffocating.

Like a thick fog on a rainy day, it hovers above me, blinding me. It darkens the path in front of me until I can no longer see.

I'm rooted in place, stuck.

Each pull of oxygen burns, and my breathing comes out in ragged bursts.

Faster, faster, faster until I fear I might hyperventilate.

Everything is closing in.

The walls around me, the clothes on my back, everything is tightening to the point of pain. My chest constricts, as a radiating tingle shoots down my left arm.

Where am I?

What's happening to me?

My heart.

Am I having a heart attack?

I'm dying.

"Are you okay?" A voice carries over through my haze. My eyes blink rapidly. "I'm going to need you to inhale, in through the nose . . . one, two, three. Very good, now out through the mouth exhale . . . one, two three."

I breathe in and out.

His voice is steady as he speaks.

"Inhale. One, two, three. Exhale . . ."

My hands shake, and sweat coats my skin. His deep voice continues to soothe me. It lifts me from the darkness and into the light. As reality sets in, I realize I'm in the hospital, kneeling in the hallway outside my mother's room. Peering down, I notice my hands are still shaking. Residual tremors from the attack.

"Is she okay?" another voice asks.

"She will be," the deep voice declares. It's absolute and I believe him.

In, out, in, out.

Still in a daze, I can feel the hand pulling me up, touching my back, guiding me.

"Just breathe. You can do it. Only a few more steps." His soothing voice instructs, calming me down. Making me follow his lead. When we reach our destination, a seat is pulled out and I'm ushered to sit down.

I lift my head and my heart stops then lurches in my chest.

Standing in front of me is the psychologist from the hospital—from *this* hospital. The doctor with eyes so blue, it feels you could get lost in them if you stare too long. Transfixed, I pull in a straggled breath and will myself to calm in front of him. My face turns down and away from his scrutiny. Why did it have to be him to find me? A burning sensation spreads against my cheeks. *I wish I could disappear.* I can't look at him. I need to leave.

"Look at me." With slow movements, I lift my chin up. There is no judgment in his eyes, only concern. Air enters my body as I calm and take him in. I let out another breath.

"Dr. Montgomery," I whisper, more to myself than to him.

He hears me, though, and gives me a nod as his trained eye continues to assess me. I wonder if he remembers who I am. If he remembers that he treated me, or if this look of concern is natural for him due to his profession.

"Yes?" He takes a seat across from me. A small line is present between his brows, making me wish I could hear his thoughts right now, because the way he stares at me is unnerving.

"Do you remember me? I'm—"

"I remember you." He cuts me off with a firm voice, but I

hear a slight hesitation. The expression on his face is one of general concern and it appears he is battling how to respond to me. "Are you feeling better? Are you all right?" His voice softens.

"I'm okay." I lurch forward. "My mother? Where's my mother?"

"She's fine. Still sleeping." With a strangled breath, I finally take in my surroundings. We're sitting in a small room. A fluorescent light flickers above me, making my eyes squint. It's plainly decorated, and appears to be a vacant patient room.

"Why am I here?"

"You were having a panic attack in the middle of the hallway, so I thought it would be prudent to move you somewhere more comfortable and private."

A silence stretches between us. He looks deep in thought and I can't help but wonder what he's thinking about. His eyes are soft. There's something caring inside them, comforting. As if he can feel my pain and there is sympathy living inside the ocean of blue that shines brightly against the early morning light.

With an exhale, he averts his gaze and lets out a breath. His posture becomes more distant, more formal. I bite down on my lip. It feels like an eternity waiting for him to speak.

"Have you had more episodes since you left the hospital?" A burning flush spreads against my cheeks as I tuck my chin down. I feel so small right now. "There's no need to be ashamed." There's softness in his voice that makes the tension building inside me begin to dissipate. "If you don't mind me asking, have you started seeing a therapist?"

"No," I mutter under my breath. He looks as though he wants to say something, scold me for taking such little care of myself, but he refrains.

"Do you still have my card?"

"Yes," I squeak.

"Use it, Eve."

When I finally am able to get up and walk away, all I can do is shake my head. I don't have words to voice how I feel right now. This man has rendered me speechless.

chapter six

PRESTON

I'VE BEEN SITTING IN MY OFFICE SINCE SHE LEFT, STARING AT the goddamn wall. It's been hours since she fell apart in the corridor, and yet I'm still sitting here thinking of her. Her words, her tears, and the look in her eyes play on a constant loop. It takes me back to a previous time, when I had met similar eyes, similar feelings, and similar sadness. An unwelcome feeling I haven't felt in a long time twists its way through my blood stream. A storm. Raging winds are bearing down and I fear I'll be engulfed in the destruction.

This feeling I hide from is a deep-seated guilt. A guilt I thought I had previously eradicated. But these feelings are misplaced. They don't belong to her. No. They belong to someone else. *To the one before.* To the one I never helped. To the one I never saved.

I need to walk away. Cut my ties and pray she never contacts me.

Instead, my words betray my thoughts.

I told her to contact me . . . *again.*

Why did I do that? *Because I'm a fool and was ill prepared to see her.* When I bumped into her earlier, it was as though the universe was playing a sick joke on me. It had been weeks since she was here and she hadn't called me yet. I was okay with that. I had come to terms with it.

I was off the hook.

I rest my head in my hands and pull at my roots until the point of pain.

Fuck!

Now it's all shot to shit. Now I can't bring myself to walk away.

Why does she have to look so much like her?

Is she my punishment?

My penance . . .

chapter seven

EVE

MY TEETH GNAW AT MY LOWER LIP AS I WAIT FOR MY MOM to wake. I pull my legs into my chest, wrap my arms around them protectively, and watch her. *Was she always like this?* Or was there a time when she was young and happy? Was it my father's death that turned her into this? Is this my fate, too? Is Richard's death my own catalyst? Am I destined to become her?

I never understood my mother. It was easier to judge her than be compassionate towards her troubles, but the recent events have been eye opening. Now I know how fast the fear can take over.

Reaching out, I take her hand in mine. *What made you like this, Mom?* It has to be more than simply my dad's death. I wonder if she will ever tell me what haunts her. There is so much pain in her eyes. She refuses to talk about my father's accident. She refuses to talk about anything. I have yet to voice my own fears, my own nightmares, so how can I fault her? How can I judge when I'm walking down the same dark and winding road?

I can't.

My mind drifts to Dr. Montgomery and the way he almost implored that I speak to someone about the issues lingering inside me. There was something in his eyes that made me believe he was more invested than he let on. The circles hollowing his face spoke of sadness—a deep-rooted sorrow, and it made me want to find out about this man. Speak with this man. Learn anything about this man.

A soft groan emanates through the room and pulls me from my thoughts. The muscles in my mother's face twitch as her eyelids flutter. When they finally open, she stares up at me blankly, as if she's trying to understand what she's doing here.

"Oh, thank God," I cry out. Tears spill out through my eyes, rushing forward from my body like rain pouring down in torrents.

I lie on her and weep until there are no more emotions left in my body. Until I purge it all and am so drained I can barely hold my own head up. But I do hold it up, and search her eyes for answers. *Why are we here? Why is she doing this to herself?*

"What's going on with you, Mom?" My words come out on a whisper and her pupils dilate. "Why are you doing this to yourself? You're killing yourself."

"I'm not worth the tears," she mutters. "If you knew, you wouldn't cry." And then her lids shut. No answers, no clarification, no nothing. More confusion is all I get.

Hours must pass, but I have no recollection. I'm so lost in my own grief and concern for her that when the nurse pops in to tell me it's time to leave for the night, I finally peer up and notice through the window that the city is blanketed in darkness. The day has passed and my mom will be okay. Or at least today she will be okay. Who knows what the future will bring.

With a soft kiss on the cheek, I leave her and head home.

I don't stop to talk to Sydney. I'm too tired and drained to deal with any questions she might have for me tonight. So instead, I head straight for the shower and wash off the grime that coats my skin.

I'm spent, burned out, completely depleted.

The pellets of warm water rejuvenate me, and although they cleanse me, they don't wash away the sadness that still lingers beneath my skin.

Once out of the shower, Sydney's open door beckons me to enter and unload all that happened today, but as I peer inside I see her lying down and she appears to be sleeping. I don't disturb her. Instead, I head into my own room and lie on my bed. Letting out all the oxygen in my lungs, I grab my book and try to distract myself from all the day brought.

───────●───────

My body lurches forward.

My sweat stained clothes cling to my frail limbs.

That smell again.

It's everywhere. The smell lingers in the room as if I'm stuck in a nightmare.

Copper. Always copper.

The door slams against the wall, the sound ricocheting through the room. "Are you okay?" Sydney's eyes glow in the dark of my room as she rushes to my bed.

"I . . . I don't know." I wipe my damp cheek with the back of my hand and lean back into my pillow.

The same dream.

Always the same damn dream.

"You were screaming so loudly—it was blood curdling. I was so scared. Was it a nightmare again?"

"Yeah, but I . . . I can never remember the whole thing. Once I open my eyes it goes away. Just pieces and smells . . ." My whole body shakes with the fear of not knowing what is happening to me.

"*Shh*, you're okay," she coos while rubbing my back. "That must have been an awful dream." Her hand continues to run circles over my back as my breathing regulates.

"I wish they would stop." My shoulders sag in defeat.

"Do you think this is because of Richard's death?"

I turn my face so our eyes meet. "Honestly? I don't know."

"Do you want to tell me about it? Anything at all that you can recall?"

"I don't know what there is to say. I can't remember. It is always so vivid, but the moment I open my eyes I only remember the smell . . . and, I guess, the screaming."

"I've got to be honest, every day you get a little worse. Your screaming becomes worse and worse, and all last week at work . . . I could see you were having anxiety. Enough of this shit. You need to see someone. I think you need to call that shrink."

"I can't go to him." I cross my arms over my chest, lower my head and close my eyes.

"Why the hell not?"

I don't answer.

"What aren't you telling me?"

Tentatively, I lift my head and meet her stare. "Well, I bumped into him yesterday at the hospital with Mom," I manage.

"Wait, the hospital? What is your mom doing in the hospital?" She blinks. "Why am I only hearing about this now?"

"I wasn't up for talking about it last night, I'm sorry. I just couldn't last night."

She studies me curiously, then her gaze lowers and I wonder if she's hurt.

"Okay . . ." She lets out air from her lungs, clearly upset that I withheld information from her.

"It's—"

"Well, you need to go to someone else, then." She glances back up, and this time two deep lines of worry appear between her eyes.

"I don't know anyone else." I shudder inwardly at the thought of having to talk to anyone, especially him.

"Listen, I'll ask around, but if I can't find anyone else, just call him."

I consider what she says and reluctantly nod. "Thanks, Syd." My chin quivers. "It means a lot to me."

"Of course. You're my best friend. Like I said, if I can't find you a different doctor, you have to call him."

"Okay, got it. Thanks."

Sydney's eyes dart to the clock, then back to me. "It's almost six. Want to get up and go out for breakfast?"

"You should go back to bed. No reason for us both to be up this early."

She smiles at me brightly. "I'm already wide awake. Might as well grab waffles. You know you want some."

I do want some. I let out an audible sigh and she laughs. "You twisted my arm." I wink.

Hopping out of bed, I head for the bathroom to shower and make myself presentable.

When we finally get to the diner, Sydney opens the door and a chime goes off as we enter. *It's busy.*

"Shit," she says. "Guess we have to wait." Usually neither of us comes this early in the morning, so we didn't anticipate the wait. There's a line right by the hostess booth and as I scan the room I don't spot any open tables. A familiar scent wafts through the air. Confectioners sugar, coffee and the spicy flavor/scent of nutmeg.

Without warning, my pulse picks up as I'm transported back in time to only a few weeks ago. To the last time I was here.

Richard. I was here with him. His presence is all around me. His laugh filters through the space.

"Hey kiddo." He leaned in and gave me a warm hug and a soft kiss on my forehead.

"Richard," I exclaimed through a laugh. *"I'm twenty-four. You can't call me kiddo anymore."*

"Sure I can. You will always be 'kiddo' to me." He laughed this time and my mouth split into a huge smile as I rolled my eyes.

"Fine."

"Plus, I'm not allowed to show nepotism at the office. This is the only time I get to call you that." All I could do was shake my head at him. He was right. He couldn't play favorites, and I imagined calling me nicknames in the office would be frowned upon by the rest of the staff.

"I see you almost every day outside the office, too."

"That you do, but normally when we see each other it's in an office or with your mother. You and I have haven't had time to really talk since you got your promotion a month ago. So, how do you feel about being the point person now?"

"It's a transition. I still get nervous on the initial pitch, and it's a bit hard taking lead on the clients, but I like it."

"Good. You really are a natural, you know." His praise made me smile.

"I don't feel like a natural. It feels like I can barely remember what I'm supposed to say."

"You are, trust me. I have seen many account coordinators transition into account executive. Not everyone can handle the new responsibilities, but you have a knack for it. You'll do perfect on your new pitch."

"How do you know?"

"Because I have faith in you."

I let his words wash over me, they made me believe in myself. They gave me hope that I would succeed.

"Thank you."

"Enough about work. It's Saturday. What do you have planned for the day?"

"Sydney and I are going to the new restaurant that opened up in the meat packing distract."

A small line formed in his forehead. It was almost unnoticeable but I saw it. I wondered what his problem with her was. She was a good friend to me and a fantastic worker. However, Richard always seems put off by her. One day I'd ask him what that was all about. But today was a good day. Mom was in a good place when I called, and I wouldn't ruin my day by asking questions I might not like the answers to.

That was a little over four weeks ago. Two weeks later, Richard suffered cardiac arrest. I never did get to ask him. But I guess it no longer matters.

These swirling thoughts have my hands becoming clammy and my vision blurring as my pulse picks up. I will myself to breathe. To not let the fear win. From out of nowhere, my hand becomes encased by Sydney's warm grasp. She squeezes once, letting me know she has me. Lifting my head, our eyes meet.

Hers are full of love and compassion. She mouths the word "breathe" and I do. I breathe and step forward as the sadness fades away and I'm back in the present.

chapter eight

EVE

BEING BACK AT WORK BECOMES EVEN HARDER AS THE DAYS pass. By the time I return home, I resort to drinking to cope with my days and keep the nightmares at bay. My terrors and anxiety have gotten worse, and I still haven't called the number I know I need to call. I'm not sure what my hesitation is. I guess I'm hoping Sydney finds me someone else.

Tonight I lie in bed sobbing. My bedroom door pushes open and I peer through swollen lids to find Sydney standing in the doorway. I don't speak and neither does she. Her eyes are sunken in from worry as she gnaws at her upper lip.

"This is enough already. You are falling apart and it's breaking my heart. Earlier today I spoke to Natalie."

My mouth opens to object. Natalie works in the office with us. I can't have her knowing that I'm falling apart at the seams.

"Don't worry. I didn't tell Natalie it was you. I told her it was for my younger brother."

My tears dry as I consider this. It would make complete sense. Sydney's brother is a notorious fuck-up in his senior year of some fancy prep school in the city. She's always complaining about him getting expelled.

"She gave me the number of her therapist, Dr. Cole. We're calling her first thing on Monday morning and you're going to see her, understand?"

"Yes." I sniffle.

"Good."

Sydney is right.

Dr. Montgomery is right.

I need to speak to someone.

I need to fix whatever is broken inside me.

And I need to do it before it's too late.

Before I turn into *her*.

———•———

"Are you nervous?" Sydney asks.

Am I? Hell yeah, I am. It's been a few days since she got me the number of the therapist, and when I did nothing with said number for two days, Sydney took it upon herself to call and get me an appointment.

"Wouldn't you be?" I grit out.

"Wait, is this really the first time you have an actual appointment to see a therapist?" I nod. "So, even when you were young and your dad died, you never saw anyone?"

"Nope."

"You would think they would have made you."

"Nope."

She furrows her brows at my one-word answer. A tense silence echoes through the room.

"Do I really have to go?" I finally groan as I bury my head in my hands.

"Girl . . . I love you, but yes, you do. You looked like a walking zombie today at work. If they were planning to sack anyone,

I wouldn't be surprised if you were the first to get the boot."

I pout my lip and roll my eyes. "Fine."

"Good girl," she chides as she throws her coat on.

"Where you going?"

"I'm walking you."

My eyes widen.

"What?"

Sydney tries unsuccessfully to suppress a laugh. Her cheeks puff up until she finally fails and one escapes. "I'm walking you to your appointment." Her lips twitch with amusement as she wraps a scarf around her neck. "What are you still doing lying there like a lump?"

Despite the fact I have no desire to see Dr. Cole, I find myself getting up and putting on my coat. "Lead the way, bitch," I mutter under my breath, eliciting another round of giggles from Sydney.

Dr. Cole's office is not at all what I expected. First off, it's in Alphabet City. Secondly, it's in the basement of a dingy building. Not that I need a fancy Park Avenue location, but this is kind of sketchy.

Sydney chews on her lower lip as she steals a look at the building. "So . . .this looks—"

"Like a dump?" I chime in.

"I was going to say interesting. But yeah, it looks like a dump." She grabs my arm. "Come on, we've come this far. No backing out now."

I follow her into the building and down the steps to the basement apartment. A chime goes off as we enter. When we step in, I know instantly this isn't the right psychologist for me. The place is grimy and dirty. The sound of something shattering has us looking up. A man walks out dressed in wrinkled slacks and there's a stain on his shirt. Not at all professional-look-ing. *Not like Dr. Montgomery.* I can't see someone like this. I wouldn't feel comfortable telling him anything.

"You must be, Eve," he says. His eyes linger on me a second too long, making my back stiffen uncomfortably.

"There seems to be a misunderstanding. I'm so sorry, but we have to go." The words tumble out as I grab Sydney's hand and usher her out the door.

"Well, that was . . ." Sydney trails off, trying to articulate exactly what that was.

"Very unprofessional, right?"

"Yeah, totally. I'll make a few more calls and see who else I can find. But first, let's find the nearest subway and get the hell out of here." She pulls me down the street.

When we're back in Murray Hill, we decide to walk down Third Avenue to find a place to eat dinner. Sydney taps away at her phone the entire meal. By the time we're finished and re-turning to our apartment, she had two more psychologists with spots open for me.

———————•———————

The next few days are a whirlwind of appointments. It feels as if I've seen every therapist in the tri-state area . . . Well, maybe not every one. One was unprofessional, one was an ice queen, and one's voice just rubbed me the wrong way. I couldn't imag-ine seeing any of them. I couldn't imagine being comfortable enough to divulge my life to these people. I *could* imagine each of them judging, criticizing, and in the end I knew none of them would make me feel safe. There was still one I hadn't called and even I was starting to chastise myself for that. What was my holdup with calling him, anyway?

Other than the fact he was handsome, there was nothing else stopping me. I couldn't think of one reason I shouldn't see him as my therapist. I was comfortable with him. He made me feel safe, and he was able to talk me out of a panic attack not once but two times. Both times he never judged me. He had compassion in his eyes and a genuine expression that promised he wanted to help me. The only holdup I could see was his looks, and that was starting to sound like a ridiculous reason even to me.

So what if he's good looking? His looks shouldn't play a part in my treatment.

There's only one choice I can make in this situation . . .

I'm calling him.

chapter nine

EVE

I CALLED HIM.

Well, I called Dr. Montgomery's office.

Despite my hesitation, deep in my bones something tells me he is the only one that can help with my panic attacks. After the last three psychologists I met with, I no longer trust anyone's referral. Truth be told, he was the only one who made me feel comfortable.

He made me feel safe.

His simple breathing techniques have already alleviated the aching pain that presses on my chest when I feel I'm losing control.

"So, what time is your appointment?" Sydney asks as she walks into my room. I've been standing here for at least ten minutes trying to decide what to wear.

"Ten."

"Well, you better get ready, then." A smile spreads across her features as she eyes my outfit.

I look down and survey my attire. "What? You don't think I can go like this?" I wave my hand down my body to emphasize my pajamas.

"As beautiful as you are—and trust me, Eve, you are, I don't think it's appropriate to see your therapist for the first time in booty shorts and a see-through cami."

"Yeah, you might be right. Okay, I'll get dressed. Want to meet after my appointment at Café Europa? We can grab a bite." Pulling out a chambray shirt, I hold it up for her approval, and she shakes her head yes.

"Why don't you text me? I should be able to, but if not, you can fill me in on all the details when I get home later."

I roll my eyes and huff. "This will probably be a waste of time."

"Maybe not. You'll never know until you try." Her shoulders lift as she turns to leave, closing the door behind her.

Once she's out of the room, I strip down and put on a more appropriate outfit. I pair my chambray shirt with black leggings and black riding boots. When I'm fully dressed, I sit on the bed and close my eyes for a brief moment. Seeing him again has me on edge. I have no idea what to expect. The questions play in my mind as my anxiety spikes.

What will it be like to talk to him?

Tell him about my nightmares?

Can I do it?

Will he judge me? *He hasn't yet.*

He's only been kind. Caring.

I breathe in deeply to calm the thoughts in my head. I can't afford for them to drift. I need to be strong and not let my fear win.

My chin chatters from the frigid air as I stand on the corner and wait for the light to change. Cars rush by, but I see no empty cabs. I look down the street and then at my watch. There's no time to wait, so I decide to walk the ten blocks.

With every step I take, I feel the nervous energy within me build. Usually walking calms me, but today it doesn't help at all. As I hurry down Park Avenue, I get lost in thought. My brain can't wrap itself around the reason these nightmares have started, and I'm not even sure what's triggering my recent panic attacks. I assume it has something to do with Richard, but at the same time I'm not sure. *Scary thought.* But as frightened as I am to find out, I'm more frightened to keep on living like this.

I *can't* become my mom.

I *can't* let my fear turn me into a woman who's too scared to live her life.

After ten minutes, I arrive at the address on the card. The building itself is intimating and harsh. It towers high into the sky, the sun gleaming off the walls of tinted glass. With timid steps, I walk inside and immediately notice a broad Lucite desk in the center of the lobby. I head over and smile at the security guard for the building seated behind the surface, thankful he can't see my hands shaking at my sides.

I brighten my smile to hide my nerves. "I have an appointment with Dr. Montgomery."

"And you are?" he asks, narrowing his eyes at me.

"Eve Hamilton."

"Look toward the camera, please." He motions to a small lens protruding from the desk. After the camera flashes once, I turn my attention back to him and he looks down at a screen built into his desktop and starts to type.

"Please proceed to the elevator on the right-hand side of the lobby and press the button for the eighteenth floor," he directs as he hands me my visitor pass.

"Thank you."

I proceed to the elevator and press the button to Dr. Montgomery's floor. Cheesy elevator music echoes through the air. As the elevator climbs, a pulsating knot forms in my belly. The idea of sitting across from this man and airing my dirty laundry is making me feel ill. I'm not sure I'll be able to go through with this, but since I've come this far already, I decide to take the plunge. My lungs expand with oxygen to calm myself. When the elevator reaches his floor, I step out and search for his office. Once inside, a middle-aged woman sitting behind a desk greets me.

"I'm Eve Hamilton. I have an appointment with Dr. Montgomery."

"Yes, please take a seat. He should be with you in a few minutes. I'll need to see a copy of your insurance card. Also, I have a few forms for you to fill out while you wait." Her voice is monotone, as if she's reciting a speech she has repeated countless times.

I grab my wallet and hand her the card. Once she returns it, I take the stack of forms and sit down in an empty chair. I pull out my phone to text Sydney.

Me: Hey, Syd. I'm here and everything's fine so far. I'll text you when I'm headed over to the restaurant.

Syd: Good luck.

Me: Thanks, I'll need it.

My eyes scan the paper in front of me. Seven pages. Seven freaking pages of questions. Starting off with the most mundane information, leading up to . . .

I look a little further down the form and I get to family history. My heart thuds in my chest. Can't he just leave me in my denial and, you know, not make me answer these questions? I feel as though I'll turn the page and there will be ink splat drawings for me to identify.

Describe your personal strengths? *What is this? Am I applying for a job?*

What are your coping styles? *Should I write down drinking?*

Do you experience difficulty sleeping? *I wouldn't be here if I didn't.*

I peer further down the list . . .

Check.

Check.

Check.

What isn't my problem? *Lord, I'm a mess.*

Do you belong to a particular religion or spiritual group? With that, I rise from my seat.

I'm out of here.

This is ridiculous.

Just as I move toward the door, I hear a creak. Looking over my shoulder, my eyes widen as my gaze trails up the man standing in front of me.

How is it that every time I see him he takes my breath away? I've never seen a more beautiful man. He is magnificent. But even that word doesn't do him any justice. He's tall. His strong, lean body towers over my frail one. This man, his presence . . .

It's imposing. As if he alone can make the world shift on its axis.

Dr. Montgomery narrows his eyes as he continues to stare. It's unnerving and exhilarating at the same time. But with a shake of his head, the moment is lost. He pulls his shoulders back and walks toward me.

"Hello, Eve." My name rolls off his tongue like a smooth melody. One only the perfect baritone of his voice can sing.

"Hi, Doctor," I say faintly. His hand reaches out taking mine in his.

"It's good to see you again. But please, I know I'm your doctor, but you can call me Preston." He pauses, almost as if he's unsure. "If that makes you feel more comfortable."

What was I thinking, coming to see this man? I'm desperate to figure out my shit, *but this guy* . . . No. He's too gorgeous. I need to see someone older—much, much, older. Maybe a man in his seventies who wears tiny wire-rimmed glasses.

He gives me a little smile and I swear one thousand butterflies take flight in my belly. "If you would please follow me into my office." His other arm stretches out toward the door adjacent to where we stand. It's cracked open and pitch black inside. *Ominous.*

"Um, okay." My hand feels heavy still encased in his.

My body won't move, though. I'm cemented in place. Ready to dash. To bury my head in the sand and pretend I don't need to be here. I look toward the exit and then back up at him and meet his gaze again.

His full lips turn up into a comforting smile. "It will be okay. It doesn't have to be awkward," he whispers, but not one part of my shaking body believes him.

Peering back to the door, I contemplate my options: walk away and let the fear take over, or follow this man.

Our bodies are close for the few steps it takes to reach his office. He stops abruptly and I almost crash into him as he switches on the light. With wide eyes I look around the office and then at him. His presence fills the small space. He's overpowering and my walls start to close in. How can I speak to someone who has me so unhinged at the mere sight of him? He sucks all the oxygen from the air just by standing here.

My breathing becomes ragged as I cross further into the room. With shallow pulls of air, I try to clear my head. I need to do this. I need to stop the nightmares and this is my only option, so I need to block out my want for this man.

"Why don't you have a seat on the couch?" he says as he walks over to the desk that sits along the far wall and grabs a notepad. I sit on the red velvet couch and look up to see him watching me as I settle myself. His eyes trail my every move as he gets comfortable in the chair across from the coffee table.

Placing the pad on his lap, he reaches up and runs his fingers through his hair. "Okay," he says as if he's collecting his thoughts.

My heart pounds in my chest as I wait for him to speak. With an audible sigh, I breathe through the panic that coils in my stomach, but my face grows hot and a sweat breaks out against my brow.

"Just breathe," he murmurs. "This will be easy. I promise. I'll ask you some very simple questions at first, and take notes about what you say so I can keep it fresh in my memory. Is that all right?"

I bite my lip. "Yes, it's okay."

"Oh, and please feel free to interrupt me at any time, and if you need to stop, we can do that, too." I swallow hard and then nod. "So, let's start off by talking a little bit about when your anxiety began, what brought you to the hospital, and a little about what brings you here today."

"Can't we talk about something simpler?" A nervous laugh escapes me and the right side of his lips turns up at my answer.

A small dimple forms in his cheek. "We could, but what fun would that be for our first appointment?" he jokes and my shoulders relax. "So, how are you today?" I tilt my head and I consider how to answer.

"I'm okay. Tired. Didn't sleep well," I admit on a sigh.

He nods. "I can understand that. Nervous about today?"

"Yeah. A bit, I guess."

"Was there something else that kept you up?"

My upper teeth bite my lower lip and I gnaw on the skin to the point of pain. He picks up his pen and jots a note on the pad of paper. His gaze lifts to mine.

"Simpler?" He smiles.

I nod.

"Have you always lived in New York City?"

"Um, yeah. I mean, I wasn't born in the city, but we moved here when I was young," I stumble out.

"Oh, so then, where were you born?" He leans forward, laying his notebook down and studying me intently.

"I'm from Long Island, originally."

"And do you work? Or are you still in school?"

"I work in marketing at The Stone Agency. It's a full service firm. We specialize in Fashion and Entertainment."

"Very interesting."

"Yeah, it's okay." I shrug with an over the top roll of the eye. I let a small smile form in my cheek and he lets out a laugh.

"It does sound a bit boring. Being a therapist is much more interesting." He winks, lightening the mood, and it works as my own giggle escapes and the once tight muscles in my shoulders uncoil. When my laughter stops, he repositions himself and straightens his back.

"Ready for a tougher question?" he asks and I nod.

"Let's discuss your first visit to the hospital. Is that okay?" The blue of his eyes sparkle at me.

"I guess."

"In order for this to work, you have to trust me. Can you do that? Can you trust me?"

"I'm not sure I can, but I'll try. Well, as you already know I was in a car accident. Obviously, I was brought to the hospital." I'm too embarrassed to tell him about all the panic attacks at home and the nightmares since then, so I grow silent and try to think of something else to say. In the background, I hear the ticking of the grandfather clock.

Dr. Montgomery reaches across the side table and grabs a pair of glasses and puts them on. He adjusts them until they fall slightly down his nose, and then looks down to the paper in front of him. When he looks back up, I swear my heart stops. The look in his eyes, the sexy way he wears those glasses . . .

He's almost too perfect.

He rests his hands on the arms of his chair as he studies me. "You okay? What's going on?"

I will myself to calm, and curse myself for being so blatantly affected by him.

"Um, I'm just nervous. Scared. I'm kind of . . . I don't know. Lost? I'm not sure what we're supposed to talk about or how you'll help me."

"These are all very common feelings to have toward therapy for the first time," he assures me.

"Well, that's good to know. Happy to be somewhat normal," I retort. There's nothing normal about my panic when I think of divulging my nightmares and fears to this man. It was so much easier in the hospital when I thought I would never have to see him again.

"Normal is just a definition we use to place ourselves in boxes, Eve. No normal here." He winks and I'm surprisingly appreciative of the small gesture, because seeing him smile, makes me smile. "So, I think we should start from the beginning. I often find that's where most problems stem from. No response is singular. It's a cause and effect process from where it all began."

"I guess."

"How about you tell me a little about your family?"

Instantly, my muscles tighten. Anytime Mom is a subject, I get a knot in my stomach. I love her, but being her primary caregiver at my age has been hard. "It's just my mom and me." I try to force a smile, but instead my lips tremble, giving me away.

"Where is your father?"

"He died in an accident when I was younger." I want to melt away. Pretend I'm not here. Recede into the confines of my mind.

"How old were you?" The blue of his eyes is soft and sincere.

"Four," I answer before I can stop myself.

"That must have been hard for you."

"To be honest, I don't even remember him. Most of my memories are of my mother and me. And Richard, of course. I can't remember if we spoke about him at the hospital. He was my father's best friend." I take a deep breath. "He was also my boss."

"So you knew Richard well?"

"He basically raised me. It was his funeral I was leaving when I got into the accident." A familiar feeling of dread tugs at my heart. Everything in my body tightens. Soon the back pains will present themselves. My chest will follow shortly. I frantically rub the muscle in my shoulder blade.

"I'm so sorry for your loss. If you don't mind me asking, how did he pass?"

"He had a heart attack. By the time I . . . I found him . . ." I pull my hand from my back and press it to my mouth to hold back a sob.

"I know this must be hard for you. I want you to take deep breaths. Can you do that?" I shrug. "What happened?"

"I remember calling him but he didn't answer. I needed to grab something from him for a work meeting. I was at my mom's. He . . . he lived in the same building as her. When I got there, I found his body. I . . . I remember being in a haze, like my mind faded away and my basic instincts took over. I called 9-1-1. I even went back to my mother's to tell her the news. I was grieving but I was functioning."

"So, when did you stop functioning? What happened?"

I take a slow breath and will myself to not start hyperventilating. "When I saw his body again, in the casket. That's when it happened. I must have been in denial before that moment. Because that's when it finally hit me. Richard was dead." My eyes flood with tears and I swipe them away.

He picks up a pen and scribbles on his notepad. "Was this the first time you attended a funeral since your father's death?" I nod. "I know you were very young when your father died, but do you remember anything?"

"No." He writes again on the pad and I want to lean over his arm and read what he's observed. When he lays his pen down, his eyes lift and his gaze meets mine.

"You said he was like a father figure. Was he in a relationship with your mother?"

"Oh, Lord, no. She can barely function enough to brush her teeth. There was no place in her life for a boyfriend."

"And how is your relationship with her?"

"Strained. Exhausting."

"Do you want to tell me a little about that?"

"Do I have to tell you today?" *Please say no.*

81

"No, you don't." *Oh, thank God.* Hearing I don't have to divulge anything I don't want to has all the muscles in my back loosening. "Is there something in particular you would feel comfortable talking about today?"

"I—No. Not really." I laugh nervously.

"How about we try to talk for a little bit longer? If it gets too much, we can stop."

"Okay," I whisper.

As the minutes pass, we talk about nothing in particular. Nothing as daunting as speaking of my mother or as heartbreaking as discussing Richard. We don't talk of my father. We talk of simple, mundane topics. Topics that make me comfortable. Topics that make me smile. But eventually those topics run out and I notice Dr. Montgomery glance at his watch. Knowing our time is up leaves me with mixed emotions. As happy as I am to be done, a part of me will miss the comfort I felt having someone listen. Someone trained to give me the guidance and advice I so desperately need now that Richard is gone.

This was good. Coming to him was the right decision. A small piece of the weight that has been resting on my shoulders is lifted.

"You did a great job today. You did really well. The hardest step is coming in. You've got this." He smiles and picks up a black leather journal from the side table. When I lift my hand for it, our fingers touch. The soft skin of his thumb brushes against mine and my cheeks heat as he hands it to me.

"I have a little assignment for you."

"An assignment?"

"Yes, I want you to keep this notebook. Journal how you're feeling. If a panic attack starts to form, write down the triggers. No matter what you are thinking or how you feel, I want you to journal it, okay?"

"Are you going to read it?" *Please say no. Please!*

"I will ask you to tell me what you wrote so we can pinpoint your triggers, but no, I don't have to read it."

I can work with that. As long as I know that I can pick and choose what I tell him. "Okay. I'll do it."

"Great. Also, I'll email you some techniques for when you feel an attack forming."

I laugh at his suggestion. "I'm just imagining the crazy new age junk you're going to make me do."

"No, nothing like that." His mouth begins to split into a grin, but before it forms he rights himself. *Professional mask back on.* No matter how small . . . I miss the grin already. "More like breathing techniques and visualization exercises. I'll also send you information about a few support groups you can attend if you feel up to it. Believe it or not, there are many people who suffer from anxiety and grief. You might find it comforting to speak to others who have gone through it." He stands and heads over to his desk. I watch as he scribbles on the back of a business card and lifts it up to me to take it. "And if you need me, I'm giving you my direct number. Please feel free to call me."

Having his number is dangerous. The idea of having him only a phone call away . . . I can never use it. Once I do, I fear I'll never want to stop. "I wouldn't dream of doing that, Dr. Montgomery."

"You might not now, but the time might come when you will need it."

I pray he's never right.

I try texting Sydney as soon as I leave, but she doesn't answer so I head home.

"How was it?" she shouts from the living room as I shut the door.

I drop my keys on the console table and head toward her voice. When I step into the living room, she drops the magazine she's reading and leans forward, obviously waiting for me to spill.

"Fine," I mutter.

"You have to give me more than that. Did you figure out what the nightmares are about?"

"Syd, it was my first session," I deadpan. "Do you really think we figured it out that quickly?"

She frowns. "Well, what did you talk about, then?"

"He asked about my job. I told him about my mom—"

"You told him about your mom?" Her eyes look huge with shock.

"Well, I told him it was just me and her, that's all."

"Oh."

"It was weird, Syd. Telling someone my problems."

"Anything else?"

I let out an audible groan. "Oh, my God, Sydney, I have barely shut the door and you're already giving me the third degree." I take a seat next to her on the couch. "I'm starved. Want to order in?"

"Yeah, sure."

"What should we order?" I pull out my phone and start looking up delivery numbers saved on my phone. "Pizza?"

"Pizza is fine. So, that's all I'm getting? Weird?"

"Yes. You know, like not knowing what to talk about or what to expect, weird."

"So, basically your session was like the first awkward get to know you date, right?"

"That's exactly what it was like." And oh, was it ever. That awkward date in which you stare at the guy and think *Lord, is he beautiful* the whole time. Except it wasn't a date. He's my doctor, so these thoughts are not okay right now.

"Speaking of first dates . . . Is he still as hot as before?"

"Oh, my God, Syd! Leave me alone!" I laugh and throw a pillow at her.

She pretends to huff. "Fine, I'm going to take a quick shower."

"Okay, I'll stay here and listen for the pizza."

She blows me an air kiss. "Thanks." She starts out of the room, then looks over her shoulder and opens her mouth to say something but I stop her.

"Go shower. You smell." I laugh.

Once she's gone, I settle back into the couch and my thoughts drift back to my therapy session. *God, I hope it helps.*

Reaching into my purse, I pull out the notebook and squint my eyes at it. *Here goes nothing.*

Journal Entry

I hate that I have to do this. Not sure what it will actually accomplish. Well, I haven't had a panic attack since I received this journal a few hours ago. So instead, I'll write about my first time. Oh, shit, that didn't sound good. Thank God, Dr. Montgomery doesn't have to read this.

First attack. I had my first anxiety attack at Richard's funeral. I have no idea where it came from. One minute I was there and the next I hyperventilated to the point of making myself crash. I remember little things.

I remember my rapid heartbeat.

I remember the cool sweat breaking out against my brow.
I remember being lost in my thoughts.
Then I remember nothing.

Laying my notebook down, I look over the words I wrote. Jotting down my feelings is somewhat comforting. Like I own the feelings. *They don't own me.* Dr. Montgomery is obviously more than just a pretty face. He knows what he's talking about.

Maybe weekly sessions with the doc won't be so bad after all.

chapter ten

PRESTON

WHAT THE FUCK AM I DOING? I SHOULDN'T BE SPEAKING to this girl, let alone treating her. I knew it was coming; I tried to prepare myself but nothing could prepare me for how it felt when she sat across the room from me.

It was as if all the oxygen from my lungs was drained. I knew right then and there that this wasn't fucking normal. The very second our gazes met, I knew I needed to tell her to leave. To go and never come back. She looked too much like Sloane and yet she was nothing like her. Every second she spoke, it became more apparent how different they were. Sloane was weak, but this girl . . . Eve Hamilton . . . She might not see it, but she is one of the strongest people I have ever met.

Looking toward the window, it appears snow is collecting on the surface. Bleak and depressing. Although I can see the outside, it feels as if the walls of my office are closing in. Familiar weaknesses are resurfacing. I grit my teeth. These are the feelings this girl brings out in me. She makes me remember. She reminds me of all my failures, shortcomings, and faults, but most of all her simple presence reminds me of all I lost.

The phone ringing on my desk pulls me from my inner

turmoil. The Caller ID shows it's my older brother. I wonder what he wants at this time of day. Usually he's too busy to talk when he's working. I pick up the phone but don't even have time to speak before he utters one sentence that lands a punch in my gut.

"I need you." *Fuck.*

"Why?" I answer. "What's wrong?"

"Oh, God, nothing like that." He laughs through the line. "It's our anniversary and I've been so busy at work, and, well, I forgot."

"Wow, you forgot your anniversary? That's pretty low, even for you."

"You don't need to remind me what a fuck up I am. But the good news is she'll never know. I've been working all day to plan something. I just need your help."

"So what can I help you with?"

"I'm surprising her with a trip next month."

"And?"

"I need you to watch the kids. Can you?" He lets out a long sigh.

"Whatever you need. You know that."

"Yeah, I do. Thanks, Pres."

Hanging up the phone, all I can do is shake my head. I'm shocked that he forgot. That wasn't like him at all, but I can't help the smile that spreads across my face knowing how hard he worked to right his wrong. Since Sloane, there's been no one to make me feel that way. No one worth risking my heart for. *Again.* This kind of love gives me faith that maybe one day I'll find someone worth risking it all for.

chapter eleven

EVE

Journal Entry

Everything felt wrong. My heart was beating erratically in my chest. I had no control over it. No power over my body. My heart was seizing. I felt tears welling in my eyes.

By the time I made it to the bathroom, my breathing had become shallow. Every time I imagined what I would say if I bumped into someone, I lost my words. My fear dried my mouth . . . cemented my tongue. All I could do was wait for the lingering effects of the attack to pass.

I sit in the waiting area after a stressful day of work, watching the door for a sign of life. *Will this ever get easier?* It's been one week. One week since I found the strength to walk into this building and figure out what is going on with me. One week since I welcomed Dr. Montgomery into my life. Unloaded my burdens and began to purge my soul. As the seconds pass and my thoughts continue to drift, I can't help but wonder about my new psychologist. Who is this man? What makes him tick? When the familiar knots start to form, I shake the thoughts away. Just thinking of him and the beginning of our session ties me in knots.

"Ms. Hamilton, the doctor will see you now." I peer up at her and she points in the direction of his office. "He said to show yourself back."

With one hand tucked into my coat pocket, I make my way to Dr. Montgomery's door and push it open. He's just finishing up a call and motions to me to take a seat on the couch.

"Okay, sweetie. Of course I'll be there. I wouldn't miss it for the world." He has a smile on his face—one that doesn't only touch his eyes, but also touches his soul. "Love you too." Hearing those words leave his mouth has me feeling the strangest sort of feeling. Almost like jealousy, *but it can't be that*. I don't know this man well enough to be jealous.

No, what I'm jealous of is that feeling. To have someone love you, to belong to someone, to have your soul attached to someone else's.

As he hangs up the phone, his eyes are still filled with a look I miss.

Unconditional love.

"Sorry about that. It's my niece's birthday today. Her party is this weekend." *His niece*. The oxygen I didn't know I was holding expels from my lungs.

"Lucky girl to have an uncle like you."

"I'm the lucky one." The warmth of his smile echoes in his voice, and at that moment I see a different side of him. It makes me trust him further. It makes me like him even more. "So, how are you today?"

"I'm okay. Work has been rough. Things with my mom have been tough. I guess everything has been hard," I admit with a sigh.

"How so?"

I proceed to give him an update of everything that has happened since I was last here. For some reason, I leave out the nightmares. I'm just not ready to tackles those yet when I have so many other issues going on. He listens with undivided attention. Once I'm done, he sets his notebook down and peers up at me.

"Let's talk about Richard. Can you do that? Or do you need a minute?"

I consider what he's asking of me. "I can do it."

He lets out the breath he must have been holding as he waited for my answer, and then leans forward.

"You said Richard was your father's best friend. Was he always a part of your life?"

"As far back as I can remember, it was Richard." My heart thuds in my chest, but every time I feel myself falling, I concentrate on Dr. Montgomery's broad shoulders that move slightly as he breathes and it anchors me.

"How so?"

"My mom . . . Well, let's just say she didn't handle Dad's death well. Richard stepped up to help with me." My voice is low.

He cocked his head. "I'm going to need you to elaborate on your mother a bit."

A flash of grief rips through me. My mouth trembles as I speak. "She lost it. But this is the only way I know her. She's always been this way to me. Does that make sense?"

"It does. What was your mom like? Before your dad's accident."

"People don't really talk about that, but I saw pictures of my parents from before I was born and she looks like a totally different person. Her eyes were bright and she always had a smile.

She was young, pretty. She looked carefree and in love."

"And that's not the mother you know?"

"Oh, God, no." I shake my head vehemently. *My mom has never been that mom to me.* The tears I've been holding back force their way out at the thought.

Dr. Montgomery's hand reaches out. When he speaks, his hand encases mine. "Tell me about the mom you know." He gives my palm a squeeze and I look down at our connected hands. His grasp is strong. It comforts me. It gives me the reassurance I need.

Dr. Montgomery pulls away, and my body grows cold with the loss. I peer up at him and find his brow furrowed. "You can do it," he encourages, while reclining back in his chair. With the new distance between us, I shift uncomfortably. Suddenly, I feel awkward.

"My mom . . . My mom is a hypochondriac. For as long as I can remember, she's been popping pills for some imaginary ailment. She barely makes it out of bed half the time. She's always ill. She doesn't do anything for herself." I let out a deep breath, my whole body shaking as I purge the memories from my mind.

"She gave up driving because she wouldn't get in a car. She wouldn't leave our house, so we never went anywhere. That's why we moved to the city. When Richard found out, he made us give up our house and move to the vacant apartment near his."

"That must have been hard for you."

"Maybe. As I said before, I don't remember much from my childhood." *Sometimes I thank God for that.*

"What was she like once you moved to the city?"

"Richard hired us a full-time caregiver who also cleaned

cared for me. Loved me. She was a mom to me.

Not long enough. "Almost ten years, and then one day she
wasn't."

"What happened?"

She left me. "She had to go back to Brazil because her mother got sick. It was a little shy of my thirteenth birthday."

I still feel the pain from when she left. Sadness courses
through my veins at the memory, like a caged animal threatening to break loose. A glossy sheen coats my skin. Every muscle
feels tight, as if I'm cemented in place.

"It's okay. Breathe."

In. Out.

In. Out.

"She left right before my birthday. I remember because
Mom was too "sick" to do anything special, but I could always
count on Richard."

"What did he do?"

"What didn't he do? He was there for everything. As I said,
Dad was his best friend. They grew up together. They were sup-
posedly as close as brothers. When my father died, I became
Richard's surrogate daughter. Although he had been previously married, his wife never wanted children, and once they di-
vorced he had no interest in remarrying, so mom and I were,
for all intents and purpose, his family. He was the one with me
when I broke my arm and had to go to the hospital, the one
who came to the school for parent teacher meetings. He was
the one who brought me medicine when I was sick, not Mom.

93

She was too scared she'd catch something, so she stayed in the apartment, and if I was there she stayed in her room." I clamp my lips together, but the sob breaks out anyway.

"I'm so sorry." The blue of his gaze glistens with emotion, so sharp it sears me.

"It was exhausting. It *is* exhausting."

"Do you need a minute?"

I shake my head. I need to get this over with. To tell him everything, expel it. Then it will be done.

"What is your relationship with her like now?"

"She needs me all the time. My phone rings all day, every day. A new ailment. A new diagnosis. A new second opinion."

"So, basically you have become the mother?"

"Yes."

"And who takes care of you?"

"Richard did."

And with that, I let go. I let it all go. Every tear pours out with strangled breaths and a broken heart.

The tears of a child who grew up too fast.

The tears of an adult who lost too much.

chapter twelve

PRESTON

S HE'S BROKEN, AND ALL I WANT TO DO IS MEND HER.
        Each tear she sheds rips a little bit more of my already tattered soul. Hearing about her childhood is almost too much to bear. She's lost, wandering alone in this world. I try to open my mouth to comfort her, but I remind myself I'm here to listen. Not to take her in my arms and hold her. *But I want to.* I want to tell her it will all be okay. That every bad thing that happened turned her into the amazing woman she is today. I don't know her well, but I can already tell. She's so much more than she lets on. So much more than she gives herself credit for. She's strong and loyal, and she's beautiful. *Inside and out.* I shouldn't think these things. I shouldn't look at her in this light, but I can't help it.

As she tells me her story, foreign feelings invade my bloodstream. What type of mother would abandon her child like that? What kind of mother forces her child to be the parent? Sadness, outrage, and disapproval flows through me. Judgment clouds all reason, making me a completely biased voice. I'm judging this woman I don't even know. Condemning her.

God, my head's a mess. I can't think things like this. I need to be impartial. But I'm so angry for her. I'm not objective and I shouldn't continue to treat her. Hell, I'm not even sure I should be in the same room with her.

It takes every bit of my energy to not reach out for her. Not to grab her in my arms, pull her into me and never let her go. To tell her she'll be okay and I would protect her. But instead, I straighten my back and tighten my jaw. She might think I'm cold. I might seem stiff, but it's the only way I know. It's the only thing I can do to not comfort her.

chapter thirteen

EVE

'M FREAKING TIRED.

So tired I can barely make out the words I'm typing on my keyboard.

Needing a pick-me-up, I head to the coffee room. Surprisingly, no one is in here, but I welcome the silence. As much I've always enjoyed the energy coursing through the office, my heart isn't here anymore. These last few weeks, I've been coasting. Basically pretending to work as I attempt to keep my mind and emotions at bay. Thank God no one has asked what I've been up to because the answer would be nothing. I haven't contacted any new leads. I haven't called any of my clients. I've done nothing.

As the Keurig roars to life and steam from the machine fills the air, a presence looms behind me. Looking over my shoulder, I see Barry standing close. I narrow my eyes at him.

"Can I help you?"

"Nope. Just grabbing coffee."

The heat of his body tells me he's standing too close. "Barry? Do you mind giving me some space?" He shuffles a step, but he's still too close.

"So . . ." He leans in to speak and the closer he gets, the more I feel as if I'm being suffocated. "Did Richard ever tell you his partner's name? Or better yet, has the lawyer for his estate contacted you?"

Even though I do know, I'm hesitant to tell anyone. It was bad enough for me to be Richard's favorite, but if the staff knew my mom was the silent owner, it would make working here even more complicated. I don't owe Barry an answer. The silent partner is a non-entity. Apart from providing capital, she has no interest in becoming involved.

"No, Barry. I don't," I manage, but the more we talk of Richard, the more my heartrate accelerates. Without saying another word, I jet down the hall and into the bathroom.

Once there, I throw myself into a stall and dry heave into the toilet. This is bad. So fucking bad. I swear I'm dying. This can't be normal. It can't. Pulse racing. Heart pounding. Sweat and dry heaves.

I'm having a heart attack. No. It's just panic.

Inhale. One. Two. Three.

Exhale. One. Two. Three.

I can get through this. Think of the breathing techniques.

It takes me sitting on the bathroom floor for an hour before I have the strength to get up and pretend to function.

But eventually I get through.

———————•———————

This will be my sixth session seeing Preston Montgomery as a patient. I can't believe six weeks have passed since the first time I sat in his waiting room.

The creak of wood causes my back to straighten.

"Hi. Sorry, I'm running late today. How are you? It's good

to see you again." He seems so relaxed and carefree.

"I'm good." I smile tightly, but I don't think he senses my unease. He turns to his previous patient and says his good-bye before returning his attention to me.

"Would you please see yourself to my office? I need to check my messages."

"Of course, no problem."

As he peers at me, something inside me stirs. A feeling I haven't felt for a while—comfort. He sees me and understands me. It's amazing. It's all encompassing. His eyes blink rapidly and the moment is lost. Shaking my head, I make an effort to no longer gawk at him and head straight into his office.

When he walks in a few minutes later, our eyes meet and a strange feeling lingers in the room. I find myself anxious as I wait for him to speak from across the coffee table.

"Hi."

"Hey, Doc," I say and he shakes his head at my moniker.

"You seem in good sorts today."

"I am now, but I wasn't before."

And it's true. For weeks I've been off, but being here—it's like sunshine after a stormy day. I want to bask in its rays. Feel the warmth on my face.

"What happened?"

"I had an awful panic attack at the office. But I've just been off in general. Like my chest is heavy all the time." *Except when you're around.* "Does that make sense?"

"It does. Have you been practicing the breathing techniques?"

"Here and there." I look down at the floor, not wanting to make eye contact with him. I know he will see I haven't been following his numerous suggestions. Only the ones about breathing.

"That's really good." He either doesn't notice how evasive I am or he's giving me a pass. "And how has that been working for you?" He smiles and I know it's the latter.

"It did calm me," I admit on a sigh. "Not so much when I had the full blown attack in the office, but when I felt another one creeping up, I was able to pull away."

"So, you found the breathing helped you distance yourself from the fear?"

"Yes."

"Okay, good." He leans forward in his chair. "How about you tell me a little about what triggered your last attack?"

"I was at work. A coworker was bombarding me with questions about the company. Most of my attacks happen at work, which, of course, is not ideal. I had one that was terrible this week. I felt like I was dying. Like I was having a heart attack right there in the office bathroom." My eyes flutter closed as I shudder inwardly at the thought of every attack I've had at work. It's debilitating.

"Okay." He pauses and I hear the sound of his pencil scribbling against the pad. "Tell me about your job. You said you work in marketing, but what are your daily activities?"

Opening my eyes, I stare up at him. "It depends. I find leads, contact them, and then pitch them. I wine and dine them. If I land a client, I come up with a strategic marketing plan to fit their needs. That's about it."

"I'm sure there's a little bit more to it than that?"

"Yeah, I guess, but I don't want to bore you with the details."

"Can you talk to me about how you like working there?"

"I used to love it, but it's just not the same anymore," I huff out. Suddenly, talking about work is suffocating.

"How is it not the same?"

It feels as if ice is spreading through my veins as I try to reel in my emotions. He nods to me with encouragement. I exhale and press through.

"Go on, Eve, I'm here for you." He reassures me.

"I'm there because of Richard. He gave me the job. He trained me. He taught me the ins and outs. He encouraged me. I just can't be there without him. It feels wrong." Tears pool in my eyes and I think I might break down, but when I catch Dr. Montgomery's eyes, there is so much compassion and understanding in them. They hold me together. They make me stronger.

"I know this is difficult for you, but I think we are getting somewhere. Have you noted when this heaviness presents itself?"

"I have."

"Would you like to share?" He smiles.

"Not particularly." I laugh. "But if I have to." He purses his lips and I laugh some more as I reach for my notebook. "Fine." I scan the pages, one after another. Note after note, until one thing becomes clear. I furrow my brow.

"I see you found something. The common denominator?"

"From the look in your eyes, I believe you already know, doc."

"I do." He looks at me with an expression full of understanding and something else, something I can't put my finger on. I feel as if he wants to close the gap and reach for me, and then just as quickly it's gone. "Go on."

I take a deep inhale then let out an audible breath. "Work. It's almost always at work."

"Why do you think that is?"

"If I knew the answer to that—"

"I know you don't, but that's why we're here. We'll figure this out together."

"Can't you just tell me?"

"I can tell you my belief, but until you figure it out for yourself, you won't learn. It's like a plant. You drop a seed into the dirt, pour a little water, but in the end, the seed needs to learn how to grow by its self. All you can do is give it the tools it needs."

"Fine. Don't tell me," I huff out and he laughs again. It's a beautiful sound.

"Tell me some of the things Richard did for you in the office and outside the office. You told me he was always there for you in your personal life, and that at work he helped you with your training. What else did he do?"

"He gave me encouragement."

"Does anyone else give you that?"

"No." He cast his eyes down and his jaw tightens. My answer seems to sadden and anger him at the same time.

"So, now when you're working, you no longer have reassurance that you are doing a good job?"

My mouth drops open. *Is that it?*

"What are you thinking?"

"It's more than the encouragement. It's the approval, right? The acknowledgment?" He nods as I work it out. "And it's because of what?"

"Growing up, who gave you encouragement?"

"No one. Well, no one but Richard."

"So, your belief in yourself is dependent on him?"

"Yeah, I guess."

"And how do you feel now at work?"

"Unmotivated. I have no idea what I'm doing. I can't see the correct path for anything. It's as if I can't do it anymore. It's as though I don't know what I'm doing now without him there. God, I miss him so much."

"And what do you think Richard would say to that?" I close my eyes and hear his words in my head.

"He would say that notion was ridiculous. That I'm an amazing woman and I can succeed in whatever I put my mind to."

"So, here's what I think. Richard was a father figure and a mentor for almost your whole life. I think the reason your panic attacks are mostly triggered at the office is because your need for approval was always fulfilled by him instead of your parents, and now his absence is a giant void that's manifesting itself into anxiety."

I consider his words and they make so much sense. How had I not seen it? Was I so blinded by my grief that I couldn't see what was so blatantly in front of me? He was my father, my mother . . . my mentor.

"So what do I do?" I mumble.

"You do what he would have advised. You take one day at a time. Every time you start to panic, when you start doubting your ability to do your job—when you're questioning your decisions—you visualize Richard. You think of him and the lessons he implemented all your life. You remember his words. You replay them and you live them. He was your champion. Now you need to learn to be your own champion, Eve."

"I don't know if I can."

"You can." His voice is so assertive. So sure.

"How do you know?"

"Because I have faith in you." Warmth spreads through me at his words. Familiar words Richard once said. They make me believe.

chapter fourteen

EVE

3 WEEKS LATER . . .

Journal entry

Ever since we figured out why work was a trigger, the panic has lessened. It's crazy how the techniques he was so adamant about using seem to work.

The only thing that hasn't gotten better is my nights. I still suffer from anxiety over the idea of sleeping. I'm not sure why I don't tell him. Okay, that's a lie. I'm too scared to acknowledge them. Afraid that finding the catalyst of them will break me and swallow me whole. Instead, every week I sit on the couch in front of him and pretend they never happened.

The desire to sneak out of the apartment before Sydney wakes is encompassing. It's been a long, grueling week, and I need a minute to myself. I want to go grab breakfast alone but I have to do the right thing and at least ask.

"Syd? You want breakfast?" A groan emanates through the door separating us. I pop my head in. "Syd?" She's still lying in her bed, and she's submerged under the blanket.

"Too early."

"It's actually not."

"Why did we drink so much last night?" She buries her head under the pillow and I force back a laugh.

"Because you said, and I quote, 'Guys get cuter when we're drunk.' Is that a no to breakfast?" She doesn't answer, so I assume the answer is no.

"Text me if you want me to bring you back something," I yell on my way out.

Throwing on my coat and scarf, I head out into the winter air. The wind bites my skin. It causes my eyes to water. Bearing down against the elements, I push the door open to the diner and step inside.

What the hell?

What is he doing here? Standing in the corner is Dr. Montgomery, and he's with two small children. I can't let him see me.

Quickly, I attempt to turn around. Bumping into your therapist over waffles could definitely get awkward.

"Eve?" His face blanches and he straightens his back. A strange look passes over his features. Maybe he's shocked to see me, too.

He's dressed casually today. So casual I might not have recognized him if not for the mesmerizing eyes. He's wearing a tight grey thermal, distressed jeans, and Chucks. It makes him appear younger than usual, but the fine lines along his forehead lead me to believe he's in his mid-thirties. My eyes follow a path to survey him in his entirety. He's tall and lean, and towers over my five foot four frame. His chocolate hair has streaks of blonde as if it's been sun kissed. It looks as though he recently ran his fingers through it because it has that perfectly tousled look to it. And his bone structure is striking.

"Uncle Preston, Uncle Preston." A little girl tugs on the hem of his shirt and brings me out of my haze.

"Yes, sweetheart?" he coos at her, his lip tipping into the first genuine smile I have ever seen on his face. It's a beautiful smile. A caring smile. One that says he adores this little girl and would do anything for her. A caring protector who would lay down his life for her happiness. It reminds me of the way Richard used to smile at me. It makes my heart lurch at the thought, but it also makes me want to get to know him better. It makes me want to get to know this side of him.

"Who's she?" she blurts out in a small voice and he lets out a laugh.

"This is Eve, she's a . . ." He pauses, his lips pinching together as he considers an appropriate title for me. "A friend."

"A girlfriend?" she teases and I feel my whole face flush.

"No, Avery. She's not a girlfriend."

"You're really pretty. You should be his girlfriend," she teases in her little squeaky voice and I wonder how old she is to have so much sass. "You look like Elsa. Are you Elsa?" I can't help but stifle back a laugh.

"No sweetie, I'm not."

"Oh." She lets out a huff and turns around, no longer impressed by me. My lips part in a smile and I catch Dr. Montgomery suppressing his own smile as well. All of a sudden another face pops out from behind him. This time it's a little boy. He looks to be the same age as the little girl, Avery. Their features are similar. Both have crystal blue eyes and small button noses. Their hair has the same golden brown color with streaks of blonde.

"Hi, and who is this?" I say looking straight at the little boy, still hiding behind his uncle's leg.

"This is Logan. Logan, can you say hi?" I see Dr. Montgomery gently embrace him, encouraging him, letting him know he's there for him if he needs him.

"When I was his age I was shy, too. He doesn't have to say hi." I turn my attention to the little boy. "It's okay, sweetheart. You don't have to if it makes you uncomfortable." Trying to think of something to say to put him at ease, I notice his T-shirt has a familiar cartoon on it. "Do you like Cars?" He gives me a timid nod. "I have seen the movie a million times." His pupils enlarge at my words. He looks awestruck.

"Hi, Eve," he whispers out and a part of me melts. This child reminds me so much of me as a child. I want to hug him and tell him there is nothing to be scared of.

From my peripheral vision, I see the doctor staring. His blue eyes pierce the distance separating us. They search my own as if trying to hear my thoughts. At first they are sharp and accessing, but as each second passes between us and Logan moves further into the room, no longer hiding, they soften. They are kind and tender and say thank you.

"Are you going to see the new one in the theater? It just came out," I ask Logan and by this point he's no longer hidden at all. Now he stands right beside me. A giant grin lines his face. His eyes are alive and dance with wonder as he turns and bounces with excitement.

"Can we? Can we?" He tugs on his uncle's coat, and with that Dr. Montgomery lets out a laugh. He looks gorgeous when he laughs.

"Maybe after breakfast."

"That would be super fun. Do you have all the toys?" I turn

my head back to Logan and reach out to have a look at his car.

"I have every single toy. Uncle Preston got me a ton for my last birthday." He reaches into his little pocket and pulls out car after car.

"It was your birthday? How old are you?" I ask.

"I'm five." He stands proud.

"You are? Wow. You're so big." Avery steps forward with her little hand on her hip.

"I'm older." Dr. Montgomery's lip turns up as he shakes his head.

"She's five minutes older than Logan," he clarifies.

"I'm still older, Uncle Preston." He places his arm around her and gives her a little squeeze, all while smirking. This is a totally different side to him, so unlike the stiff professional version I'm met with at my sessions. I like seeing this side. It makes him seem feasible. Like us sitting together at a table with his niece and nephew makes sense. I feel a tug on my shirt and I look down to see Logan standing directly beside me.

"This one is from the first movie and this one is the bad guy." The tiny features of his face grimace as he holds the mean car up to me.

"I know. He's really mean."

"Yeah, like my sister." He laughs. I glance up and Dr. Montgomery's watching me intently. His eyes shimmer, silently saying a million things. So many unspoken words behind them, words that I'm desperate to hear. His lips part in a half smile and then he peers back down to his nephew.

At that moment the hostess walks over with three menus.

"It was good seeing you," Dr. Montgomery says to me as he ushers the kids away from me. But Logan doesn't move. Instead, he holds steadfast and pouts his lip.

"Can she eat with us?" Logan asks him.

"I don't think so," I say, but I wish I could. I'd do anything to be able to stay and spend more time with them.

"Oh, come on, Uncle Preston. Please, please, please," he whines, and Avery turns back toward us and starts to chime in with her own chant. A strange, faintly eager look flashes across his normally professional facade. An array of emotions plays out on his features, but the one that stands out the most is a plea . . . A plea to make this little boy and girl he obviously cares deeply for happy. I smile down at the tiny faces below me.

"Of course I will." I lift my gaze and I'm met with mesmerizing blue. He mouths a thank you and I give him a sincere smile in return.

As we start walking toward a big booth, Avery and Logan are lost in an argument about his cars being cooler than her Barbie dolls. I feel a soft touch on my shoulder and turn to find Dr. Montgomery staring back at me.

"Thank you, Eve. I know this isn't how you planned to spend your day. Having you join us is against the rules—you being a patient and all—but these kids . . . they're everything to me, and Logan's going through a tough time right now. So, even though it's wrong . . . Thank you." The sadness in his stare is palpable. It breaks my heart into a million pieces.

"What's going on?"

"He's just really having a tough time in kindergarten. It's hard for him to adjust. He's not fitting in, and getting along with his peers has been a struggle. He's shy, introverted and some of the kids have been teasing him. So to see him . . ." He pauses to inhale deeply and calm his emotions. "To see him so comfortable with you, it really means a lot."

"They're really sweet kids. Having breakfast with you is a

pleasure. You have nothing to worry about."

"Come on, they're almost at the table." Dr. Montgomery places his hand on the small of my back to let me lead the way. The contact causes my skin to prick with goose bumps. When the four of us arrive at the booth, I find myself sandwiched between the children and all I can do is laugh.

"So, what's everyone having?" I ask as I look from right to left at both kids. In unison they both answer, "Chocolate chip waffles."

"I see you've been here before." Their little heads bob up and down.

"We come here all the time with Uncle Preston," Avery declares and I lift my gaze to catch my doctor's eyes.

"What will you have?" he inquires.

"I'm having the same. What about you?"

"Same. It's my weekend staple."

Interesting. "That's funny. I've been coming here for years and I've never seen you before." Small lines etch away at his features and his pupils appear to grow larger, but he quickly masks the change and smiles.

"I'm usually here a bit earlier than this, but with the kids today . . ."

The waitress comes over and he orders the famous chocolate chip waffles with whipped cream for all of us. When she steps away, I turn my attention back to Logan on my right hand side who is racing his cars across the table in front of me.

"Who's winning?" I ask.

"Lightening McQueen," he exclaims and the excitement in his little voice fills me with excitement, too.

"Of course he is."

"So, do you guys live around here?" I'm looking at Logan

when I ask this, but the truth is I'm secretly hoping for an answer from his uncle. The desire to know more about this man is all encompassing.

"Not us," Logan replies as he pushes the car back and forth, the little tires scratching at the wood of the table. "But Uncle Preston does." I look up.

"Where do you live?" He fidgets in his chair before answering.

"Lexington and Thirty-Fifth."

"Oh? I'm on Thirty-Third and Third." He nods but doesn't reply. Instead, he reaches across the table for the rogue car that Logan has rolled his way and proceeds to enter the race.

I watch him for a moment. I watch sun stream in through the window and blanket him with a glow. I watch the love that pours from him toward the kids. This is a man I want to know. A man I could be friends with. It's the first time in a long time that I wish time would cease, but instead, it seems to pass faster than normal. There's never a lull in the conversation between us. The kids tell us stories all about kindergarten and their friends and all the mischief they get themselves into. The waitress returns with our breakfast and the table is filled with sounds of food joy.

I lift my fork and take another giant mouthful, this time scooping up extra cream.

As I enjoy and savor the flavor, I hear a round of giggles echoing through the air.

"What?" I lift my eyebrow and from across the table Dr. Montgomery leans forward. Time stands still as his hand reaches up.

"You have a—" His finger wipes my lip and it causes my breath to hitch. Our eyes lock. The intensity of his stare sears me. Every ounce of oxygen leaves my body, but then his blue eyes widen in shock as he realizes what he's done. His hand jerks back, as though burned.

"You had something . . . I'm sorry. I shouldn't have done that," he stammers.

"It's okay." I try and shake it off, but I still feel his finger on my skin.

"That was funny. It looked like you had a mustache." Logan laughs. Then Avery joins in and pretty soon the tension has dissipated as we all begin to laugh. Through our laughter, I notice the waitress deliver the bill and I reach into my purse, but I'm met with Dr. Montgomery shaking his head at me from across the table.

"My treat."

"Thank you, I had such a great time with you guys today." Logan grabs my hand. His little fingers are sticky to the touch.

"Do you want to go sledding with us?" he asks and I glance out the window. This morning when I left the apartment, I hadn't noticed how perfect it was outside. But now sitting here, I see that it's a beautiful winter day. The streets of Manhattan are blanketed with freshly fallen snow. It's still clean and glistens into a beautiful crisp white.

"You guys are going sledding?" My right eyebrow rises in question and Dr. Montgomery's lips spread into a large grin.

"It's on the list of cool uncle duties."

"Oh, you're the cool uncle?"

"You bet."

"I can totally see that. So, sledding. That sounds like fun." I can imagine him running with kids in Central Park, sled in tow. *What I would do to see that.*

"Come. Please, please, please!" Avery chimes in with her

own little pleas. Dr. Montgomery is deep in thought, but when our gaze catches, he exhales.

"You could join us if you want?" His lips turn up. It's a different smile and so unlike all the other smiles I've now seen from him today. It's not the smirk, nor is it the mesmerizing one where his eyes twinkle. It's not the one that he gives his niece and nephew either. No, this smile says he's unsure. That he wants me to come, he just doesn't want to blur the lines anymore then he already has. This smile makes me beam up at him. But then my lips purse because I can't go. I need to check on my mom.

"I can't, guys." Both kids pout. "I already have plans. I wish I could say yes, but unfortunately, I can't. Maybe next time." *Please, God, let there be a next time.*

We all go awkwardly silent for a minute, the kids silently sulking. When the waitress returns with his change, we stand.

"Can we see you again?" Logan says to me.

"Of course. I would love that."

"It was good seeing you, and thank you for being so good with them," Dr. Montgomery says. Both kids run up to give me a hug and as I hug them back I give them all a small smile and turn to leave.

I'm off to my mom's and they're off to have a perfect day, one I wish I could have with them.

I exit the restaurant and decide to walk the distance to my mother's apartment. My feet slip into a slow, sluggish rhythm as I make my way down the sidewalk. I'm procrastinating. That much is obvious. There are a million things I would rather be doing than heading uptown to take care of my mother. One of them is sledding. I yearn to be silly and normal and to enjoy myself. But instead, I find myself standing on the corner, waiting for the light to change.

A knot is forming in my stomach from worrying what I will find when I arrive. No, I can't let my brain go there right now, not after my wonderful morning. In place of the dreary thoughts looming over me, I think of the kids and Dr. Montgomery. Today I saw a different side of him, a playful side. I'm not sure that's the kind of thing I should know about my doctor. I'm already attracted to him physically, and seeing him like this . . . It's confusing. He's not like this in his office. I'm not sure how I'm supposed to act now.

A memory flashes before my eyes. His finger. The feel of his skin on mine as he slides away the cream that collected on my lip.

Shit. This just got a whole lot more complicated.

———— • ————

As I peel the clothes off my body hours later, my cell phone rings. I'm not sure who it could be, but I tense when I see it's my mother. Panic sets in. I was with her earlier today. *This can't be good.*

"Hey, Mom. Are you okay?"

"I'm dying." *Shit.*

"You're not dying, Mom." Nervously, I pace my room. This can't be happening right now. I want to scream.

"No, I am. This time for sure."

"Why do you think that?"

"My head is killing me and I have this weird rash on my arms. I know it's spreading. I can feel it."

"Can you, or is it in your mind?"

"I resent that you think that way. Of course it's not in my mind. I need you to take—"

"Mom, I was there all afternoon and you were fine. I'm not coming back to your apartment to take you to the hospital over a headache."

"But it could be anything! I could have a tumor. It could be cancer. I could die. You have no idea. I could be dying," she screams over the phone.

My entire body is tense, as if I'm glass and one wrong word will send me crashing into a million pieces. "Okay, Mom. I'll be there in fifteen minutes."

And just like that, I fall to pieces.

chapter fifteen

EVE

SOFT KISSES FAN MY SKIN. THEY TRACE MY COLLAR TO THE *hollow my neck. My fingers thread in his hair. A soft, desperate moan escapes me. I want him so much. Right here, right now. He trails his hand downward. Tingles spread across my body, lower and lower until he's teasing my entrance.*

"Preston."

I shoot forward. My breath is uneven and ragged. I try to gain my composure, but it's virtually impossible as I'm brought back into the first dream I've had in weeks. I exhale a shallow breath.

What the hell is going on with me?

First, disturbing nightmares filled with blood, and now, sexual dreams about my therapist. I'm starting to think Preston—Dr. Montgomery—should give me a referral to a doctor who can medicate me. I'm obviously crazy.

Needing an outlet for my pent up frustrations, I pick up my journal and start writing.

Journal Entry

I thought of him all day. I dreamt of him all night. I dreamt of how his hands would feel while he rocked me.

With every minute that passes, I wonder how his lips would taste. For some reason, I want to tell him everything, and I want him to hold me in his arms as I confess the demons that lurk inside.

By the time I calm myself enough to look at the clock next to my bed, the damn thing starts blaring with upbeat tunes. It's after six in the morning. When I enter the kitchen, I find Sydney already dressed for work.

"Good morning, sunshine. Where were you yesterday?" she asks from her perch on a stool at the kitchen island.

"After breakfast, which you were too hung-over to attend, I went to my mom's. You were sleeping by the time I got home . . . or were you *still* sleeping?"

"You know, if you had woken me I would have joined you for breakfast."

"Um, I did try to wake you. We had a whole conversation, you don't remember? How drunk were you?" I chide, but secretly I'm happy she was holed up in bed yesterday. My cheeks warm and a flush spreads across my body.

"Why are you turning bright red? Did something happen?"

"Um, no." It's no big deal, but I doubt she'd understand my schoolgirl crush. I have it completely under control. Nothing is happening. Nothing *will* happen. It's completely innocent. Just because he unnerves me, comforts me and makes me feel stronger, doesn't mean . . .

Fuck.

God, why does he have to be my therapist? Why did I have

to see the other side of him? Why does he have to take my breath away?

Fuck. I'm screwed.

Yeah, no way can I tell Sydney anything.

—————————•—————————

Monday comes before I know it.

Then Tuesday.

By the time Wednesday arrives, I'm ready for the week to be over. The clock on my desk says its only three p.m. *Two more days to go.*

The phone rings on my desk and the light for my line rings. "The Stone Agency. This is Eve."

"Eve, it's Michael."

"Hi, Michael. How can I help you?"

"When you have a free minute, can you come to my office?"

"Yes, of course. No problem."

What could he want to talk to me about? Maybe he's noticed my lack of work, or maybe a client complained. Maybe he's noticed my attacks? My heart pounds and my hands shake at my sides as I approach his door.

When I walk into his office, he motions for me to close the door and take a seat. If my heart rams against my ribs any harder, it might pop out of my chest. He looks tired as he continues to study me for a few more minutes before he exhales.

"How are you?"

"I'm okay."

"I've been meaning to check on you. Richard would have wanted me to." I recognize the remorse in his voice.

My lips part slightly. "There is no obligation, Michael. It's okay."

"I'm not sure you know this, but Richard and I were really close. I started working for him straight out of college. Your father had just passed." He bowed his head before looking back up. "He was hurting. He had lost his best friend. I understood his loss. I had lost my older brother to drugs. I guess what I'm trying to tell you is, I know how close you and Richard were. I know how much he loved you. You were for all intents and purposes his daughter, and if there is anything you ever need, I'm here for you. I'll never be Richard. I wouldn't try to fill his shoes. But I can be your friend when and if you need one. I would consider it a great honor to be a part of your life."

"Thank you, Michael. I'd like that." His lips turn up and his eyes crinkle, aging him.

We sit in silence for a moment and then he coughs, clearing his throat. "Oh, I forgot to mention earlier, but the lawyers are coming at the end of next week to go through the paperwork in regards to the company. Can you mark it on your calendar?"

"Okay. Sure. No problem."

"Great, well, I'm sure you have much work to catch up on, so I'll speak to you later."

If he only knew how much . . .

chapter sixteen

EVE

Pacing back and forth in my room, I'm debating whether I should pour myself a glass of wine. I shouldn't. My drinking only puts a Band Aid on the issue . . . my damn nightmares. I'm just so goddamn scared to close my eyes without its security.

My anxiety feels like an all-encompassing disease.

It coils inside me like a venomous serpent.

Its bitterness slowly infects me.

Until one day it takes over everything.

My hands start to sweat. My muscles start to tighten. Pure panic fills me fast. It feels as if every last breath has been extracted from my lungs. I grab at my arm, pressing my index finger to the pulse in my wrist. It beats erratically. Pain radiates down my left arm as all the muscles tense, and tears pour down my face. I grab my phone and call the number on Dr. Montgomery's card.

Ring. *Inhale.*

Ring. *Exhale.*

Rin—

"Hello?"

My body stiffens at the sound of his voice. I didn't expect

him to answer, and now that he has I don't know what to say.

"Hello, is anyone there?"

"Dr. Montgomery?"

"Eve, is that you?"

"Yes," I squeak.

"Is everything okay?"

"Yeah, I'm so sorry. I didn't mean to bother you. I didn't think you would answer."

"You're not bothering me."

I let out a chocked sob.

"*Shh*, you're okay. *Shh*," he coos in the phone. "Take a deep breath in. Now exhale. Can you tell me what's wrong?"

"I'm scared," I whimper.

"What are you scared of?"

"Everything."

"I've got you. I'm here, okay? Can you tell me what set you off tonight?"

"I'm afraid to fall asleep." It sounds so ridiculous, even to my own ears. But the fear is real.

"How long has this been going on?"

"I'm sure you're busy. I'm okay now." I evade his question. Calling him was a mistake.

"Eve." His voice is authoritative. "Please, speak to me."

I can't help but concede. "I have nightmares." Once I purge the words I purposely withheld for so long, it feels as if a small weight that I carry in my heart is lifted.

"What are they about?" I let out an audible sigh.

"I don't know."

"You don't remember your nightmares when you wake?"

"Not really."

"Is there anything at all that sticks out?"

"The smell of blood."

I hear the steady rhythm of his breathing through the line. "Do you want to meet me?"

"Meet you?" I look at the clock. It's after nine pm.

"Yes, come to the diner." He's not asking me to meet him, he's telling me, and something inside me stirs. The idea of seeing Dr. Montgomery again outside the office has my pulse racing, jumping out of my bed and searching for clothes.

"Okay, give me thirty minutes," I reply

"See you then." He hangs up, leaving me in a ball of nerves. *Shit.*

I throw on a cute pair of leggings, an oversized button down, and my boots. Then I stop in the bathroom to brush my teeth, fix my hair and put on a light dusting of makeup. I want to appear as if I just rolled out of bed, not that I'm "trying." Even though I am. I should probably find a new doctor, one who doesn't have me running around like a crazy woman trying to look pretty for. But I can't make myself do that. When I'm with him, I feel normal. I probably shouldn't since I talk to him about my deep secrets and neuroses, but I do.

Grabbing my pea coat, I make my way to the elevator and then down to the lobby and into the frigid air. It's a cold blast that has my teeth chattering as I walk to the corner of Thirty-Fifth and Third, but luck is on my side as it only takes me a few minutes to get there. Not seeing him, I step further into the room and go to wait by the wall. After a few seconds, I sense a familiar presence beside me, and my heart hammers in my chest.

"Eve." Slowly, I turn my face up and I meet shimmering blue eyes.

"Oh, hi. Have you been here long?" I ask.

"No. Just got here. Ready to sit?" I nod and the hostess leads us to an empty table in the corner. After we sit, Dr. Montgomery cocks his head to the side. Surveying.

"You okay?"

"I've been better."

"Why didn't you tell me you were having nightmares?" I was right. Before, he was hurt. Now, sitting across from him, it plays clearly over his features. His brows are knit, his teeth are biting his lower lip, but really it's the eyes that give him away. They look hollow, sad, and concerned.

"I was embarrassed." My cheeks grow warm from the admission.

"You never have to be embarrassed in front of me. I won't judge you." His statement is true. There isn't an ounce of judgment in his voice. "Do you want to tell me about them now."

I shake my head.

"I understand."

We sit in silence for a few seconds. The waitress comes over and he orders a milkshake and a burger. When she turns to me, I reply that I'll only have water.

"You have to get something." Dr. Montgomery says as the waitress walks away.

"I already ate dinner."

"So get dessert." *I'll have you for dessert.* Thank God he can't hear the dirty thoughts playing through my mind.

"It's too late to eat dessert."

"It's never too late for something sweet." With that he smiles, and a part of me melts, right then and there at the table. His lips turn up a fraction and I blush.

"Why are you eating so late?" I blurt out, trying to right my improper thoughts.

"I went downtown to see a movie right after work."

"Really? That's cool that you got to go out after work. I have too much to do this week, but on Friday, Corner Bar here I come."

"Yeah, normally I don't go out during the work week, and on the weekends I go to Oak. But whenever a new foreign film comes out, I go to the afternoon or evening show on release day," he admits and I can't hold back the giggle that escapes. "Hey, are you making fun of me?" He pretends to pout.

"Sorry, that just slipped out. I totally didn't expect that. Once again, you caught me off guard. Sledding, foreign films— you're the most interesting person I know." *Did I just say that out loud?* "So. Um. How did you get into watching them?"

"So, I went to NYU. Well, at the time my girlfriend and I were both film majors. She loved foreign films, every time a new movie came out, we had a tradition to see it on opening day during the afternoon to avoid the crowds."

"And you still keep this tradition?"

"Yeah."

"And does she?"

"She's dead."

My mouth drops open at this information. "Oh."

"A new film came out today so I went."

Running my hands through my hair, I try to come up with any response. "Okay, cool." *God, I'm lame. He tells me his ex-girlfriend is dead and all I can say is, "Okay, cool."* I study him for a minute. "Actually, you do seem like the type to watch foreign films."

"And what type is that?"

"The deep, dark, and brooding type."

"Wait, do I really seem that way?" He grimaces.

"Kind of. You're pretty serious all the time."

He looks down at his hands on the table, then lifts his eyes to meet mine. His usual pale blues appear flat and lifeless. "I'm only that way with you." His tone is low and he sounds apologetic.

I don't speak for a moment, trying to absorb what he just said. "Oh."

"I didn't mean it like that."

Uncomfortable, I shuffle in my seat. "How did you mean it?"

"You're my patient. I have to act that way."

"But why? We're just two people drinking coffee and having a conversation."

"No matter where we are, we'll never be just friends having a cup of coffee."

"I-I don't understand." My voice rises louder than I intended and he peers around the room before leaning into the table and answering me in a whisper.

"As your psychologist, there is a trust level we have to have. Our relationship is about you. If it starts to be about me, then lines have been crossed."

My chest hurts. I hate this. "I don't think it's that black and white."

"It has to be. This . . . Me eating with you . . . Even this is frowned upon."

"Then, why are you here?"

He shakes his head and bites his lip. "I needed to see you. Make sure you were okay. I guess I can't stay away." A muscle in his jaw twitches and I know he wants to say more but doesn't.

"I don't want you to. I feel comfortable with you, and I

don't normally—" My voice shakes as my lips tremble.

"You shouldn't feel comfortable with me. Being friends . . . We're asking for trouble."

"I don't care, so why should you?"

He looks down and lets out a sigh. His gaze lifts again. "It's not me who cares. It's the APA." My eyebrow lifts in confusion. "The American Psychological Association. They care," he clarifies.

The thought rips me apart.

I want to continue to argue that it's okay, but I know he won't concede. I don't want to lose this, so I release an exhale and put on a fake smile. "So, tell me about this film," I say, essentially changing the conversation. If this is all I get, I refuse to waste it talking about why we can't be friends.

Once we're done and Dr. Montgomery pays the bill, we both get up to exit the restaurant. As we approach the door, he holds it open and allows me to exit first. When I pass through, he places his hand on the small of my back, and my body tenses as electric currents tingle from where he touches me. Reality starts to blend with this fantasy bubble of two friends having a late night bite together in the city.

"My place is this way," I gesture in the direction of my apartment.

"I'm in the opposite direction, but I'll walk you back." He shifts his weight back and forth on the balls of his feet and I think he's not ready to part ways, either. "You're on Thirty-Third, right?"

"Yeah, the high-rise on the corner. But you don't have to."

"I want to." He becomes quiet as his eyes roam over me. *They're beautiful. Were they always so clear?* What the fuck is wrong with me? I need to get out of here. I need air and distance from this man who's clouding my better judgment, because right now I don't give a damn about the APA or whatever it's called. All I want is to have him stare into my eyes and smile.

"When you get home, I want you to practice your breathing and visualization. I would also suggest running a bath."

"Okay," I squeak. The idea of him knowing I'll be lying naked in a bath has my cheeks going warm.

"Okay, great. I think that should really help tonight, but if it doesn't you can call me, and we can talk through it before we meet on Friday."

Neither of us speaks the rest of the way to my apartment. When we get to my high rise, I turn to face him and accidently lose my footing. My body lurches forward. I'm about to collide with the cement when two strong arms catch me. He pulls me toward him and holds me in his arms.

Looking up, our eyes lock. I get lost in his mesmerizing blues, never wanting to leave the comfort of his strength, but then I see his cheeks pale and a curse pours from his lips. He presses his lids closed for a moment before reopening them and pulling away from me. I don't know what to do or how to make the moment right, so I reach forward and my hand touches his.

Gently . . .

Softly . . .

I hear his inhale of oxygen as the pads of my fingers press against his skin.

"Thank you, Dr. Montgomery."

He exhales.

"Please, call me Preston. After waffles, late night calls and saving you from falling. We can be on a first name basis." He laughs to make light of the situation, but it makes my whole body warm.

"Goodnight, Preston." His name rolls off my tongue like a dirty secret. Like forbidden fruit. Like something I want to say over and over again but shouldn't.

"Goodnight, Eve."

chapter seventeen

EVE

I DASH INTO THE OFFICE ON FRIDAY MORNING WITH A MINUTE to spare, but it wouldn't matter if I were late. Most of the staff works from home anyway. The beauty of marketing is you can do it from anywhere, which has been great for me since the funeral and the start of my panic attacks. But unfortunately, with the new project I'm working on, I need to meet with Michael every day, so working from home isn't an option.

My eyes roam the room and I wonder if Sydney is here yet. She left the apartment early this morning and I didn't see her. While I search for her, I notice Barry standing by the windows. When he sees me, his pupils grow and he moves in my direction. Not in the mood to deal with him, I look for an escape. With steady steps, I head to the break room and as if I conjured her, Sydney is by the Keurig.

"Hey, you," I say as I step into the room and reach for a mug.

She peers over her shoulder and smiles at me. "What up? God, am I tired." My stomach tightens. I wonder if she's tired because I kept her up last night with my nightmares. Or worse yet, that I've been keeping her up for weeks with my nightmares.

"Where were you this morning?"

"Oh, I had to pick up a banner I ordered for a client." The machine roars to life and she leans in closer to speak.

"This new presentation is kicking my ass. What's going on with you? I never see you anymore. You're always off running around, and when you're home, you're holed up in your room. You doing okay? Did you get any sleep last night?"

"I guess, kind of." I smile through a yawn.

"How's therapy going, by the way? Figure anything out yet?" Her eyebrow rises and I laugh.

"It's not like that, Syd. I'm pretty sure it will take more than a handful of sessions and one phone call to fix me."

"A phone call? You didn't tell me that?" *Oops.* "Did something happen?" Her eyes go round as each word she says raises an octave.

"I kind of freaked out a few nights ago," I mutter out, knowing full well she'll want details and I'm too tired to give them right now.

"What do you mean?"

"I had an attack." A crease appears between her brows at my admission.

"Why didn't you come to me? I had no idea. I'm right down the hall."

"I know. I just feel like such a burden lately. My problems—" She lifts a hand.

"Are my problems. We are more than just roommates, Eve. You're my friend. You're like a sister to me. You can tell me these things."

"I know. I just—"

"Please, next time can you come to me? I want to be there for you."

"Okay." I nod.

"I really care about you, and I—"

"I know, and I'm sorry. I promise." I give her a small smile. "I have so much work to do today. Lunch?"

"Sure."

"Sushi?"

"Sounds perfect."

I head back to my desk. As I stare aimlessly at the papers in front of me, a restless feeling gnaws at me from the inside out. When will the pain go away?

chapter eighteen

PRESTON

T*AP*
    Tap
Tap

The pen in my hand drums against the surface of my desk. For the last two and half months, the highlight of every week is our sessions together. *Where is she?* Why isn't she here yet? Glancing across the room to the clock on the wall I take in the time . . . She's officially fifteen minutes late. I'm going to call her.

My fingers scroll through the contacts until I reach her name and I press send. The phone goes straight to voicemail. *Shit.* I would be lying to myself if I didn't admit I was nervous. After seeing her a few days ago, I know she's been having a rough time, and the fact that she's not here at her scheduled appointment isn't like her. I want to make sure she's okay, but other then calling what can I do? *Nothing.* So I'll just have to wait. I'll give her five more minutes.

The time I've allotted has come and gone and her phone is still sending me to voicemail, so I decide to head out for the night. Eve was my last patient for the day and since she's not here I'm going home.

When I'm almost to my place, my stomach growls. Fuck. I have no food at home. *What's fast and won't take too long?* Pizza. I'll just head over to Pizza 33 and grab a quick bite. I'll be in and out in five minutes, then I can head home and go over my patient notes for the day.

Walking down Third Avenue, I get to the corner and wait for the light to change so I can cross. With a slight turn of my head, I see the sign for The Corner Bar. Looks pretty empty for a Friday happy hour. My eyes squint as I peer inside and then I stop dead in my tracks. *There she is.* Standing at the near empty bar as clear as day. Why is she here when she's supposed to be in my office? I watch as a young bartender hands her a shot and she takes a swig. She leans over the bar suggestively and my blood starts to boil. I head toward the door.

A part of me wishes I were strong enough to keep walking, ignore what I see. But as the distance between the door and me gets closer, I know I'm only fooling myself. I need to go in. *I have to.* It's as if a crazy beacon is going off alerting me that I have to, and for some reason I can't will myself to not.

chapter nineteen

EVE

INSTEAD OF GOING HOME, I HEAD STRAIGHT TO THE BAR under my building. I'm three tequila shots in when my eyes focus on the large window facing Third Avenue. I spot a man in a well-tailored suit. I can only see his profile, but he looks a lot like Dr. Montgomery. Lord, I must be drunk. No way is he here. I look back down at my empty glass and then back at the stranger, he's nowhere to be found. Great, now I'm seeing shit, too. I let out a loud laugh.

"What's got you laughing?" Austin leans on the bar, his shaggy blond hair lying over his forehead. He combs it back and it showcases a pair of deep, warm brown eyes. They twinkle with mischief. I know I fled his apartment a few weeks ago, but he's cute and a much better idea than daydreaming about Preston. I lean forward seductively as I answer his question.

"Nothing." The tequila is warming my body and I feel good.

"Eve."

Turning around, I blink my eyes a few times. He's here. *What is he doing here?* He seems larger than life towering over me.

Overwhelming me.

"It's youuu . . . Preston."

"How many have you had?"

"Just a few, but that can change." I smirk. "What are you doing here?"

"You missed your appointment today." *Wow, he sounds pissed.*

"Oh, shit. I totally forgot. Did you come here looking for me?" His eyes turn hooded.

"No. Although I was worried about you." My breath catches in my throat. *He was worried.*

"Why?"

"I know how you've been struggling, and then you didn't show up today after work . . ."

"So why are you here?"

"Well, I was walking past the bar to grab takeout from Pizza 33, and lo and behold, who did I see through the window. Throwing back shots none the less." His words now have a little bite to them but as he stands there glaring down at me it's impossible not to get lost in his blue eyes.

"I guess I had a lot on my mind," I mutter and his eyes soften.

"It's okay. I understand." He raises his hand and runs it through his hair. He seems uncomfortable now, and I have liquid courage, so I step closer to him. Every cell of my body tingles with the proximity of my body to his.

"It's not. But I promise never to do it again." I place my hand on his arm.

His eyes narrow slightly as he takes a deep breath and lifts my hand off him. "Eve." His voice is almost a whisper as his eyes lock on mine. For a moment I think his eyes mirror my want.

"Another," I shout across the bar at Austin, but he doesn't

hear me.

"You should stop drinking. You're drunk."

"I'm not drunk." *How dare he think he can come here and tell me what to do?* This isn't his office and he's not in charge of me. "And if you're not planning on having a drink with me, please leave and let me have fun with Austin over there." I turn my back to him and wave Austin back over.

"Eve."

His voice holds warning, but I don't heed it. I lift up on my tiptoes and stick my butt out. Trying to be sexy, I lean over the bar, and with my luck, I lose my footing and stumble backwards instead. Out of nowhere, Preston's arms reach around and catch me. My eyes meet his and his gaze sears me. The way he looks at me is almost predatory.

"You're going home." He pulls a credit card out of his wallet and hands it to Austin. "Close out her tab, she's leaving." His jaw is clenched tight as he speaks, so I don't argue. I just nod at Austin.

Once the bill is paid, Preston ushers me out of the bar and we turn the corner to the entrance of my apartment building. He doesn't speak.

"This is me." I point to the door right in front of us.

I don't want him to leave.

"You're drunk, I think—"

"I'm not sure I'm interested in what you're thinking," I step closer, my hands resting on his chest. "That is, unless you're thinking of coming up with me."

I meet his gaze. His eyes are dark against the black of the sky. His breathing quickens. His chest rises and falls with each inhale of air. *He wants me. I can see it.*

A couple walks past us, forcing our bodies closer together.

If I reach up, I can run my hands his through his hair. *I wonder what it feels like?*

I wonder if it's as soft as I imagine in my dreams.

Slowly, as I study his features, I step to my tiptoes, and my body pivots forward. We are so close, too close. I can almost taste him.

I want to drink him in.

I want him to devour me, consume me.

He takes a step in, closing the distance. There's something thrilling in the way he looks at me, to the way his gaze sears me. It makes me tremble. It makes me almost faint. The cadence of my heart picks up and warmth spreads through my body.

Then it happens . . .

Lips touch.

Gasps and pants.

Breathing each other in.

With his mouth pressed against mine, I moan into his kiss.

A forbidden kiss.

A stolen kiss.

With a sharp jerk, he steps back, turning his body away from me. A deep line mars his perfect face right between his brows. Embarrassment settles in when I realize he pulled away.

I'm mortified.

"I have to go," he mutters more to himself than to me. His dazzling blues now seem lifeless and hollow. "Call my office to schedule an appointment." *No!* I want to shout back. *Look at me. Talk to me.* But I don't.

Instead, without even a backward glance, I turn and walk into the building. He waits for me to enter, and then he leaves. Once he's out of sight, I release a large exhale. I square my shoulders and walk right out the door and back to the bar.

Austin is preparing a martini. When he lifts his head, our eyes lock and a wide grin spreads across his face.

"Back so soon? Fight with the boyfriend?" His eyebrow raises and he purses his lips as though he caught me in something.

I let out a bitter laugh. "He is not my boyfriend."

"Didn't look that way to me." He cocks his head and I just shake mine.

"Trust me. He's not." I give him a dismissive wave of my hand, which elicits a chuckle from him.

"Well, then, he wants you." *Maybe so, but not enough.* He lifts his shoulder in a half shrug. "I'm a guy. I know this shit." My eyes roll at that. "So, what can I get you, darling?" His cute twang brings a smirk to my face.

"A shot."

My eyes are heavy as I make my way to my apartment and into bed. The last shot of tequila is taking effect, but from across the room, I see the journal. Stumbling, I grasp it in my hand.

Journal Entry

He kissed me and then he walked away. He left me there, standing on the sidewalk in a cloud of confusion. How can I face him again? I can't. But then again, he kissed me. As mortified as I was, I was also right. He wants this, too.

Once I'm done, I throw it across the floor. The sound echoes in my ears. Without taking off my clothes, I crawl into bed. The tequila coursing through my blood.

I'm lulled to sleep reliving the kiss over and over again.

It's official, there's a jackhammer in my skull. My whole body aches and I feel like shit.

Remorse runs through me as last night plays out in my head. I wish I could wake up this morning and not remember what happened, or rather, what *I* instigated. But unfortunately, the memories are there, and they're screaming at me. My stomach turns when I think of his rejection.

How will I face him?

I bury my head in my pillow and pretend it never happened.

"Hey, sleepyhead."

I let out a groan at the sound of Sydney's voice.

"Hungover?"

"No." I reach for my pillow and place it over my head to block out the sound.

"Well, you look hungover."

"I'm sick," I mumble. I'm never leaving my bed and facing the world again.

"What's wrong?"

Groaning again, I continue to hide and not answer.

"Get out of there and look at me," she scolds.

"No."

"What are you? Five? Get your head out from that pillow and tell me what's wrong."

"Sick."

"So, now you're your mom?"

Low blow. No way did she go there. I throw the pillow at her across the room, and it lands on the floor with a thump. Peeking up from the bed, I narrow my eyes at her.

"Not cool."

"It got you out, though." She gives me a coy smile and I wish I had another pillow to throw at her head. "Seriously, though, what's going on? You've never slept this late. Not even when you're hungover."

I look her dead in the eyes. "I told you. I'm sick."

"You don't look sick," she retorts. "Saying you're sick when you're not is something you hate, so why don't you man up and tell me what's going on?"

This is why I both love and hate Sydney. She always calls me on my bullshit. "Fine, I'm hiding. Okay? You happy now?"

She nods and her lips tip up into a smile. "Kind of. What are you hiding from?"

"Life."

"You need to be more specific."

"Preston—I mean Dr. Montgomery. I mean . . . I don't know what I mean."

Her eyebrow rises. "I don't get it. I feel I'm missing some crucial info."

I bite my lip and conjure up the courage to tell her about my massive faux pas.

"Um, I might have gotten drunk . . ." She waves her hand to get me to continue. "I might have gotten drunk and madeapas-sathim," I rush out in one syllable before I chicken out.

Her mouth drops open, her eyes wide.

"Oh. What did he say?"

"He kissed me. And then he pretty much ran away."

"He's your therapist."

"Yes, thank you, Captain Obvious. Why do you think I'm hiding?"

"You know what? Fuck it. You're both adults, shit happens. Don't beat yourself up over it. How are you planning on handling it from now on?" Her eyes soften as she sits on the end of the bed.

"I don't know. What do you think I should do?"

"I can't tell you what to do, but you're making such great progress I'd hate for you to start over from scratch. Why don't you clear the air?"

"You don't think I can just ignore it and pretend it never happened?" I don't want to ignore it, but I know the truth and that he regrets it.

"Yeah, no." She breathes in and then lets out an exaggerated breath. "Maybe you should call his office and speak to him. If you show up to your next appointment feeling the way you do, it will be all kinds of awkward."

I shrug. "Maybe. I'll think about it." She stands and walks toward the door. "I'll make us some greasy breakfast. Get your ass up and stop wallowing, you little wench."

I give her a little shake of my head and then I lie back down, considering what I should do.

I grab my journal.

Journal Entry

I'm a fuckup. Shit! What the fuck am I going to do? He'll never want to see me again. I know it sounds crazy but he makes me feel. I've never had that with anyone before and it scares the life out of me. I used to laugh when I heard women talk like this but now I'm living it and it's not so funny.

He's brought me such clarity in the last few weeks. I can't risk losing him. Not for a passing crush, because that's what this is. It's only a crush.

It's only a crush.

I tell myself this over and over again. As if I say it enough it will make it true.

But I don't believe it.

And I'm afraid if I lose him, I'll lose what I've gained.

I'm afraid I'll lose me.

I pick up my phone and fire off a text.

Me: I'm sorry.

I'm not even sure what I'm sorry for.

Missing the appointment, getting drunk, pushing my body to his, tempting him?

After putting the phone down, I try to busy myself so I don't check my phone. Eyeing the frame I bought the other week, I decide to put a picture of Richard and me in it and add it to the wall collage hanging above my desk. *Where is my tape measure?* It's not in the desk drawer. It's not under my bed? I head into Sydney's room.

"Hey, do you have a tape measure by any chance? My tape measure?" I smirk.

"Actually," she grimaces, "I think I do. Hmm, I think it's in the closet in the very back. There should be a storage box. It might be up top, actually."

As I rummage through her closet, I spot a familiar shirt buried in a pile of clothes. My eyebrow rises as I look at it. Turning it over, I examine the cuff. Embroidered in red, I see a familiar monogram.

RDS.

Richard David Stone. *Why is this in her closet?* Why would she have his shirt unless . . . my breath leaves my body and I can feel the blood throbbing inside my veins. *She has Richard's shirt.*

"Where did you get this?" My words are sharp. Confusion, anger, and betrayal hang on every syllable.

"Get what?"

"This," I lift the offending shirt up. *The evidence of her lie.*

"What are you talking about?" She turns around to look at me and her face is guilt ridden.

"This was Richard's." I bite out.

Silence. She doesn't say anything and it infuriates me.

"This shirt. This shirt was Richard's. I should know. I bought it for his fiftieth birthday, three years ago."

"It happened before I knew you." Her hands reach up. "Months before I knew you."

"Just say it." I pace back and forth, my body not knowing what to do with the nervous energy coursing through me.

"I slept with Richard. I had a fling with Richard."

Everything inside me seizes. A fling. *A fling means more then once.*

"Before you started working at the company, we were at the company holiday party, and one thing lead to another. We started sleeping together. No one knows."

"You were *with* Richard?" Were they in a relationship?

"It was just sex."

Even though she speaks and I hear her words, it's as if I don't understand what she's saying. *None of this makes any sense.* They were together more then once. How did I not know this?

"You were with Richard. My Richard."

"It was before I knew you, and he broke it off with me when you moved in."

"He broke it off?" Her head bobs up and down.

"Why didn't you tell me? I don't understand."

"I just couldn't. What did you want me to say? Hi, move in with me but F.Y.I., I slept with our boss, who also happens to be your family friend. My relationship with Richard was purely physical. Just sex, no strings attached, no promises of devotion and happily ever afters."

"He was more than my family friend and you know it."

"When I asked you to be my roommate, I didn't know that, and by the time I found out, it was too late. I didn't want to risk our friendship. I'm sorry. I never meant to upset you but—"

"But what? You lied to me."

"I never lied to you. I just omitted the truth."

"Well, that makes it so much better. You should've told me." I run my hands through my hair. Outrage runs through me. "I have to go."

"Can we talk about this?"

"There is nothing you can say right now that I want to listen to. As much as it repulses me that you slept with Richard—my Richard—it was before you knew me, so that I understand. What I can't get over is that you never told me."

"How could I? *God!*" She groans, burying her head in her hands before looking up. "I was embarrassed. Don't let this destroy our friendship, Eve. Please. You're like a sister to me."

"Yeah, I imagine you would be . . ." As the words come out of my mouth I realize what a hypocrite I'm being. She slept with her boss and I want my psychologist, but it doesn't change the hurt I feel.

I need to leave. I need to get out of here. I need air.

Without looking back, I grab my coat and head out the door. I welcome the breeze that gently cools the flush on my cheeks. I don't know where I'm going or what to do.

Out of nowhere, the phone rings in my pocket and my whole body seizes when I see the name on the screen. *Preston Montgomery.* Shit. What do I do? Do I answer it? I have to. But what do I say?

"Hi," I answer, almost on a whisper.

"Hello." I want to apologize for my behavior and just hang up the phone. I can't talk to him now. Not when I'm on the verge of losing it. *Of falling apart.*

"I-I'm really sorry about last night," I stammer.

"Listen, what happened last night can never happen again." An uneasy feeling passes through my body. *You can't risk losing him. Just agree and get off the phone.*

"Yes, I understand."

"I was wrong to do that. I don't want to stop treating you, but if anything like that happens again I won't be able to continue our sessions. You will have to find another psychologist." His voice is cold, professional.

This is not Preston.

This is all Dr. Montgomery.

I bite my lip and carefully choose my words, willing my voice not to give away my hurt.

"I understand, and it won't happen again. I promise."

"Okay. Then I will see you at your scheduled appointment this week."

His cold tone finally has me snapping and falling apart. I start to sob uncontrollably in the phone.

"Eve, please don't cry. I didn't mean to make you cry." The sobs come out in heavy broken breaths. "*Shh.* It's okay, you're okay. Please calm down. Where are you?"

"What?"

"Where. Are. You?" His voice leaves no place for argument.

"By my apartment."

"Meet me."

"But you just said—"

"Forget what I said. None of that matters right now. Meet me."

"I can't, I'm a mess."

"I don't care, and you could never be a mess. I'll see you in ten minutes. I'm on Thirty-Fifth between Park and Lexington. Number 115."

My brain and my heart are at war. I know I shouldn't go, but there's no one I want to speak to about this but Preston.

chapter twenty

PRESTON

WHAT AM I DOING? WHAT THE *FUCK* AM I DOING? I JUST told my patient to meet me for the second time in a matter of days. Talk about crossing into completely unprofessional territory. But fuck, when I heard her crying she broke me. She's cried before, but that was when she was just my patient.

Ever since the day with the kids, I'm having a hard time distinguishing the woman who sits in front of me week after week from the woman at the diner. I knew she was strong. I knew she was caring. But the side I saw . . .

She is special. The kind of special that makes you question everything you believe in or everything you *thought* you believed in before *her*. I know I'm doing something I shouldn't, and in the past that would have mattered to me, but hearing how distraught she was . . . something inside of me snapped. This can't wait until next week to get fixed. *I* can't wait. I need to help her. I need to take her pain and make it mine. I need to see her now.

So what am I doing?

I'm now pacing my apartment thinking I might have made the biggest mistake of my professional life. I invited Eve Hamilton into my house, and by doing so I invited myself into her world, and worse . . .

I invited her into mine.

I take a swig of my scotch. The amber liquid coats my throat and burns, but I need it. I need to drown the voice inside me. The one telling me to call her back and say I'll see her on Friday, but instead I throw back another shot. I need to see her and make sure she's okay.

Even if her presence consumes me.

Even if seeing her destroys me.

chapter twenty-one

EVE

A S I TAKE A STEP TOWARD THE LARGE WOODEN DOOR. IT swings open. *Preston* is standing there. The moonlight peeps out from a cloud and bathes him in its glow. I suck in a breath. He's beautiful, mesmerizing, consuming. I feel bare before him. Being here, standing at his door feels so right, yet wrong at the same time.

"Are you okay?" he asks as I move closer to him and he ushers me inside.

"No."

"Come in. Come on, I got you." He takes my hand in his and I'm instantly warm.

"I feel betrayed. They betrayed me," I blurt out, and I can tell by the look in his eyes he has no clue what I'm talking about.

"What happened?"

"Richard and Sydney had sex," I huff out on a sigh.

"Can you please start from the beginning? So I can understand."

"I found a shirt I bought for Richard in her closet. I con-fronted her. Apparently they had a relationship. It happened before I started to work at the company, and it ended when I moved in with Syd, but neither of them told me. I mean for crying out loud. I always knew he was weird about me living with her, and she was always weird about him, but neither of them said anything."

"I understand why you're angry. I really do. But I think if you sit for a minute and take a step back, you might see that this is not so black and white."

"What do you mean?"

"I think right now you're feeling blindsided by Richard. But since he's not here to explain himself, you're lashing out at Sydney because you're hurt. You feel Richard betrayed you, but did he? Furthermore, did Sydney? They were both consenting adults, and Sydney didn't know you. So, I believe your real problem is with him. You're afraid the Richard you knew might not necessarily be the Richard everyone else knew. But you need to realize and accept that that's okay. He didn't love you any less because he had a clandestine relationship with her. He just put you in a bubble and as your "father", he didn't want you to see him as anything other than perfect. This isn't really about Sydney at all."

His words seep into my soul. He's right. I know he's right. I just wish Richard were here. I wish I could talk to him one more time. I wish I had a chance to say good-bye.

My tears flow again and this time, Preston pulls me close to him on the couch. I turn my face toward his body and bury my head in the crook of his neck. Needing comfort, needing him to hold me. Needing more of him.

He does. He holds me until every tear is expelled from my body. When I have no more tears left in me, I peer up. He's looking at me in a way that makes my body quiver. That makes me want to close the tiny distance between us. Effortlessly I inch forward.

"Eve," he groans my name as if it pains him to say it. His hands gently sliding up my arm until he strokes my jaw. "We can't do this." He takes a deep breath, his eyes imploring me to heed his plea.

"I know." My lids close briefly as he presses his forehead to mine. A single touch that ignites a fire deep in my soul.

"I can't." His voice is barely a whisper.

I swallow back my emotions and separate our bodies.

"It's getting late. I should go." For a moment I think he'll object, tell me to stay, but instead, Preston makes his way to his feet and nods.

"I think that would be smart."

"Goodnight, Dr. Montgomery."

chapter twenty-two

PRESTON

I'M AN ASSHOLE. A COMPETE AND UTTER ASSHOLE. WHEN I held her tonight, everything felt so right. *Nothing* has felt this right in years, not since Sloane. I didn't want to let her go and I didn't want to pull away. But I had to. I can't be close to her. I shouldn't feel the way I do. I'm her therapist and I'm not worthy of her time, her friendship, and I'm certainly not worthy of my title. Doctor of Fucking Psychology, my ass. I should be sanctioned. I should lose my license for the shit I just pulled.

But there is something about this girl. The moment she's around I lose all reason. I can't see anything but her. I feel like I'm going mad. Trying not to watch her, trying not to kiss her. The only thing I can do is keep my guard up, but I swear trying to do that is driving me . . . *mad.*

I won't be able to help her if I continue to blur the lines, and I *need* to help her. I couldn't help Sloane and I won't make that mistake again, no matter how hard it is.

chapter twenty-three

EVE

M Y EYES HURT. THEY BURN. JUMPING UP, I HEAD TO THE bathroom and peer into the mirror. *They're swollen.*

I'll never be prepared for my meeting today.

My pulse races. Adrenaline courses through my body.

I'm going to be sick.

I need a moment to collect myself. *Great.* Just when I think I'm getting back into the swing of things, everything goes to shit again. I thought I was done losing it in the office, but here I am, pacing the bathroom and I'm a fucking mess.

There's no way I can do this. I can't possibly pitch this company. Every part of my body is screaming to push the door open and sprint down the hallway until I reach the exit. *No.* I have to do this.

With a large audible sigh, I head back into the office and look over my notes on my computer. Then I grab my presentation papers. They feel heavy in my hands.

I cannot do this. Not without Richard. I can't even remember my proposal. All the words I've practiced and recited these last few months are gone. It's as though my mind is completely blank. With each step I take, my heart rate accelerates.

Think.

Think.

Think.

I pull out my phone and look for the email Dr. Montgomery sent me a few weeks ago.

Visualization techniques.

Visualize.

Breathe.

Breathe. One. Two. Three.

Visualize a better time, when you knew what you were supposed to do. Breathe—one, two, three . . .

"Okay, from the top. Try to pitch me again." Richard's words ring through my ears. The distant memory breaks apart any of the strength I was able to maintain. Tears well in my eyes. I'm lost. So fucking lost without him. I knew the path. It was clear. Now there's nothing. Visualize!

Richard is standing across from me. He holds the folder with my notes. "Start from the beginning. Clear and precise. Believe in yourself. If you do, no one will doubt you."

My pulse starts to regulate. With an inhale, I re-adjust my skirt, fix my top, and then make my way out the door.

It's two hours later and I nailed it. Not only did I land the client, but I'm already back at my desk starting research on the next project. As I browse the Internet for fresh ideas, I feel a presence hovering behind me. Peering over my shoulder, I see Barry standing over me. My initial instinct is to recoil. Scared of confrontation. But I'm not scared. Not anymore.

I won't allow myself to let the fear win. I know exactly why he's standing beside me and I know exactly what he's going to ask me, so why not answer? Why not end this annoyance now? I have been avoiding his question for weeks but I do know who the new owner is and I know he has nothing to fear for his job, so why am I hiding? I'm not. And I won't.

"Barry, the answer to the question I'm sure you're about to ask me is my mom. My mom is the owner of this company. Your job is not at stake. You will not be fired." *There I said it.* Now he can stop bothering me. Now he can go back to being the office creep, who ignores me. "I have work to do. So now, if you can please stop badgering me for answers, I'd appreciate it. Nothing bad will happen."

I turn my attention back to my computer and continue to type. But he's still there hovering. My back gets stiff.

"Yes?" I say turning back to him. His mouth hangs open. His eyes really stare at me, *maybe for the first time ever.* This is a different side of Barry and I don't know what he wants. I lift my hands off the keyboard and pivot my whole body to face him. "Is there something else?"

"I was—" He nibbles a little more on his lip. "I was wondering if you would have time to go over some of my ideas I have for the Femmes Fetale campaign. I pitched them and landed them . . . but I think I'm a bit out of my element."

My mouth drops. I'm completely taken aback.

"What?"

"Brainstorm," he clarifies, still uneasy and biting his lip. "Can you help me?"

"I don't understand. I thought you hated me. You're always so rude. Why would you want my help?" I feel as if I'm living in a parallel universe and I just can't understand what's happening. This man doesn't speak to anyone. He's like a one-man island.

"I don't hate you."

"But you've been harassing me for weeks."

"I'm sorry."

"You're sorry." I pull at my hair. "I'm really confused right now."

"I guess I was just nervous and didn't know how to approach you. I don't really get along with people. They don't understand me, so I tend to just work alone."

My eyebrow lifts. Is that it? Was I reading him wrong this whole time?

I have a moment of clarity and then I get it. Barry wasn't creepy. He was only like me. Unsure of himself. Scared. Yes, that was it, and I get it. I understand how hard it is to believe in yourself. To not feel comfortable in your own skin, and how that fear can manifest into something you have no control over. For me it's panic. For him it's social awkwardness. Either way it's the same. It's still two sides of the same coin.

I smile up at him. To let him know I understand that putting himself out there must have been hard.

"Okay. I'd love to help."

"Thank you." He pauses. "We can meet during lunch one day," he stutters out and with that, I let my smile turn up even more.

"I'd like that. I'd like that a lot."

———————●———————

With a little less than five minutes to spare, I make it to Preston's high-rise office building. By the time the elevator reaches his floor, my whole body is trembling uncontrollably from the nerves of having to see him after the clusterfuck at his house.

Just thinking of Preston and our nearing session has me in knots. I'm so confused by his behavior, but I need to continue seeing him because I'm still not able to sleep. Last night was horrible, and even the cocktail I had before bed didn't do the trick. I finally did fall asleep, but it was a rough night. When I woke, my heart was thundering, a scream was tearing through my throat, and my hair was soaked from the night terror. I need to talk to Dr. Montgomery about the nightmares.

The fear from last night still consumes and claws at me.

I feel lost and emotionally drained.

In a complete daze, I find myself sitting in the waiting room. It's as if my feet carried me here, but my mind resides elsewhere.

My gaze sweeps across the vacant room. I like the quiet. It allows me peace for a minute, and helps to shut off the distractions from everyday life.

I let out a yawn. *God, today was a long day.*

"Hi. Need some coffee?" I look up to find Preston looking down at me. I'm not sure how I missed him entering the room.

"God, yes," I press out. Every word feels pained today.

"Well, then, let me get you a cup." He gives me a small smile and it feels slightly awkward. As though he doesn't know how to act with me anymore. That makes two of us, because I'm so uncomfortable right now. I feel as if I might pass out from nerves. Being at his apartment made me feel close to him, but now it's weird being here. "I just made a pot. Go have a seat in my office and I'll bring some right away."

I walk into his office and take a seat in the center of the couch. A few minutes later, Preston sits across from me, placing two steaming hot mugs on the coffee table that separates us. He sits back and pulls out my file that's on the table beside him.

He scans the file before he returns it and takes a sip of his coffee. His Adam's apple bobs as he swallows.

"You seem off today." Preston asks.

"I am."

"Is it work?"

"No, I'm just . . . I don't know . . . " I can't speak.

"Is this about what happened the other night?"

"Yes."

He lifts his gaze to the ceiling and blows out his cheeks. The muscles in my stomach tighten into knots. I feel ill. When he finally meets my eyes, I notice a line has appeared between his brows.

"I know we talked briefly on the phone about this, but when you came over we never touched upon it again. I do think we should talk about what happened in more detail."

"Can't we just pretend it didn't happen?" I groan and he shakes his head. "I didn't mean to—"

"It's not just that. The lines have been blurred for a long time. I shouldn't have invited you to my apartment."

"I was upset. You were doing your job." I turn my head away from him and fidget with the material of the couch pillow.

"Eve . . ." I don't turn back. Just continue to tap at the pillow. "I wasn't doing my job when I invited you over. I wasn't treating you like a patient, and you weren't treating me like your psychologist. It's my fault these lines are blurred, but it's not your fault. It's called transference. Or in this case, because of the sexual nature of your feelings toward me, erotic transference. It's very common for a patient to develop feelings for their therapist."

With that, I snap my head back to him and shake my head. "I . . . what?"

"In psychotherapy, it's classified as the unconscious redirection of feelings you associate for one person such as a parent to another, such as me, your therapist." My mouth drops open as I pull in ragged breaths. "Basically, you're replacing the emptiness in your life with me. I'm a figure you look up to. You're replacing the void of losing the caring father, the person you gathered comfort from, with me. These feelings you have are normal, but I think we should talk about why you feel this way."

"Who are you, Freud?"

"It was actually Freud who came up with the theory."

"Of course it was," I deadpan. "Listen, I was drunk. Then I was sad. It won't happen again."

He rakes his fingers through his hair and then nods. Neither of us speaks, and my stomach drops with each passing minute that we sit silent. I rub at my eyes as I stifle a yawn.

His eyes shoot up. "Tired? Didn't sleep well again?" I shrug and he sighs. "What's going on? Please. Talk to me."

"I'm still having nightmares," I blurt out before I can second guess telling him.

"Why didn't you mention it earlier? Did something new happen that I should know about?"

I take a deep breath, and then exhale it slowly. "No, just the same exact nightmare as the night I spoke to you."

"How long have these nightmares been occurring?"

"Since Richard died."

His eyes widen at my admission. The look in them makes me sad. It's as if he's hurt by my not telling him. As though I betrayed him. And seeing it rips a hole in my chest. For some reason, I want to tell him everything now.

He casts his eyes downward and breathes in slowly, "Can you tell me about these dreams?"

"I have them all the time now. It's as if the world is closing in. Sound fades, my vision becomes spotty, and I feel as though

I'm hyperventilating. It's like a nightmare where you're running in the woods and you're not sure who's chasing you."

"What do you remember about them?"

"Not much. They're like a mirage. I can feel them. I can smell them. But just when I think I can touch them, they fade away into the haze of my mind."

"And what is it you feel?"

"Scared. An unimaginable fear."

"And smell?"

"Copper. Almost like blood."

"And you've never had these dreams before?"

"Not that I remember."

He places his mug down and reaches for his note pad, quickly jotting down his thoughts. When he looks up, there is a new clarity in his eyes. "Sometimes these nightmares are actually repressed memories, fighting to find their way out. In a case such as that, I typically would suggest a referral to my colleague who uses hypnosis techniques to retrieve the repressed memories. Is that something you would be interested in discussing?"

"No." My answer comes out harsher than I intended, but he shakes his head with understanding.

"Okay, I understand. But if you change your mind, please let me know."

I stand and stroll to the window, peering out to the city below. A stream of sunlight peeks through the shades, blinding me. I squint and lift my hands to cover my eyes. A cloud must pass because the room that was only seconds ago bathed in white light is dark again and I no longer need to squint.

When I turn back around, I notice Preston is watching me. He's tense, his back upright, and a small line pinches between his brows. I have a desire to keep looking at him, to lose myself in the depths of his blues. He stands and makes his way over to where I am. He's so close to me. His cologne infiltrates my senses—fresh and spicy, and an overwhelming need to bury my head in the crook of his neck and get lost in the smell weaves its way through me. It begs me to touch him, to feel his rough skin against my fingers. It's overwhelming.

Blinding.

I can't think.

My hand reaches out of its own accord across the space that separates us. His eyes flutter shut, and I swear the air around us changes. The tips of my fingers hover above the scruff on his jaw—

Boom!

The sound of a car backfiring or a gunshot rings outs in the distance and I'm suddenly frozen in place. My vision starts to flash, a black haze takes over, and then an image appears behind my closed lids.

An image of flesh.

Of crimson streams.

And brutal cries so sad they break my heart.

My chest pounds erratically. The hum surrounds me. Engulfs me. Suffocates me.

Two arms wrap around me.

Pull me close.

Whispers.

Light flutters across my hair.

"I've got you. I'm here. Breathe. Remember what I taught you. Inhale. Now count, one, two three, four, five, six, seven. Exhale."

The air in my lungs leaves in sudden gasps.

"Slower. Slow. Inhale."

Part of me calms. The flutter in my chest weakens as I continue to follow Preston's directions. As I regulate my breathing, I realize that I'm calm now, Preston calmed it all. He made everything better.

"You're doing great."

His hands rub circles up my back as he lulls me into a peaceful state. Our breathing comes in tandem. Our bodies press close together. Goosebumps spread across my limbs and I lift my head to meet his gaze. His pupils are dilated, the blue almost completely gone. His breath tickles my lips.

"I have you."

I lean closer, allowing the air he expels to fan my lips. *Kiss me. Please, God, let him kiss me.* I'm so close I can almost taste him. His eyes sweep over me. His nostrils flare and his eyes dilate as he assesses me. I can see he wants me.

Right now, in this room, he's not looking at me as a doctor. He's not looking at me as a patient. No. Right now, he's looking at me like a man in lust.

My eyes flutter shut and I close the distance. As my lips find his, my body moves backward. He breaks our connection.

Pushes me away.

I meet his gaze. His is now void. Closed off. The warmth is gone. The compassion no longer exists in his stare.

He walks away and ushers me back to the couch. By the time we make it, my panic has lessened, but now I'm cold from the distance in his eyes.

"Take a seat. I'll get you something to drink. Do you want a cold compress?" he asks and I nod. My strength isn't great enough to find words.

When he returns, his detachment has grown. He won't even make eye contact as he regains his seat across from me.

It feels as if I'm being broken apart but I don't speak, afraid of the outcome.

"I am so sorry about what happened before. It is completely my fault that a line has been crossed."

"Nothing happened. It's okay," I stammer out.

"It's not okay. I crossed a line when I comforted you, and I think it would be best for your healing if I refer you to a colleague."

"No, you can't do that," I beg.

"I can't be your doctor anymore." He won't meet my eyes and it rips me to shreds.

"But why?" Confusion and then anger coil in my stomach as he continues to hide.

"Well, I . . ."

"I understand," I mutter and then his eyes finally meet mine. They look sad and drained.

"No, you don't, but please trust me. I think it will be for the best."

I need to leave. I need to go before the anxiety takes over. If I leave now, nothing has happened.

"It's my fault. I don't need another doctor. I–I'll put distance. It's fine." I stand and walk toward the door. If I leave now, he can't end things. He can't abandon me.

"Eve—"

"I'll see you later, Doc." I shut the door behind me and dash down the hall. If I don't hear him say it, it's not real.

Inhale . . .

One, Two, Three.

It's not real.

chapter twenty-four

EVE

LYING ON THE COUCH A FEW DAYS LATER, I HEAR THE SOUND of the front door opening. Then I hear the click of Sydney's heels as she walks into the living room. Placing my magazine down, I stare up at her.

"Hi," I mutter out beneath my breath as I sit down in the chair. I know I shouldn't be mad at her. I know I need to get over it.

"How was your afternoon?" she asks, gnawing on her lower lip. She's nervous, unsure of how to act toward me. I need to forgive her. I need to tell her it's all right. Preston is right. This is more than Sydney having sex with Richard. *So much more.* This is about him—Richard. I held him to unrealistic standards. In my mind he could do no wrong, and the realization that he was only a man, a human being who made mistakes is liberating. I need to forgive her, because this had nothing to do with her and everything to do with me. My lips turn up. It's a tight smile, but it's all I have to offer right now.

She knows we'll be okay. I know we will, too.

It will just take time.

"You left work early. Is everything okay?" Her lips purse

and she narrows her eyes in my direction.

"Only a few minutes early. I figured I would grab my dry cleaning," she says and I notice she's carrying a stack of mail.

"Anything important?"

"Just the usual bills. Oh, here's one addressed to you." She leans over and hands me a large, rectangular business envelope. It's non-descript and lightweight. I flip it around and check out the return address. Lord knows we get enough crap mail; no reason to open it if it's not important.

Bold lettering jumps off the back of the envelope.

From the Office of Dr. Preston Montgomery.

Shit. I tear at the seal until a folded paper sits heavily in my hands. The weight of it, though less than an ounce, feels heavy . . . ominous. I open it with shaky hands. My eyes burn and my heart thumps rapidly in my chest. What is this? *What the fuck is this?*

> *Dear Eve Hamilton,*
>
> *As you know, a good relationship between a psychologist and his or her patient is essential for quality medical care. Times arise when this relationship is no longer effective and the psychologist finds it necessary to request the patient select an alternative psychologist.*
>
> *This letter is to inform you that I am no longer willing to be your psychologist. My office will continue to direct your care for any emergencies that arise over the next thirty days. It is imperative that you select another psychologist and arrange with our office for your records to be transferred to their office. If you need a referral, it would be my pleasure to assist you.*
>
> *Sincerely,*

Dr. Preston Montgomery

My emotions are like a storm. They batter me. Engulf me. They rip me apart. Anger coils in my blood. The destruction from his words is immeasurable. I knew this was coming, yet I made myself believe I could will it away. *Apparently not.*

I need to see him. I need to talk to him. I need to understand. *Now.*

I make my way to his office in a state of haze and fog. Nothing registers other than the pounding of my heart. Streets, avenues . . . it makes no difference. Muscle memory leads me there.

The building looks ominous. Towering taller than the neighboring buildings, the floor to ceiling windows reflect the gleam trickling out from the cloudy skies. Once through the revolving door, I make my way to the security desk and flash my ID. With a brief nod, I'm allowed up. Step after step, my destination grows closer. A strange feeling weaves its way through me. What will I say to him? What will he say in return?

Trepidation.

Maybe confronting him is a bad idea?

No. It must be done, and nothing but divine intervention will halt me now. I've made up my mind.

Entering the office, I head straight for his door.

"Ms. Hamilton," the receptionist calls out but it's too late, I'm already halfway down the hall. With a heavy push, the door opens, and then slams against the frame. The sound ricochets, slicing through the silence as I step, no *barrel* into the room. Once all the way inside, I close us in together. There he is.

Mesmerizing me with his eyes.

Captivating me with his stare.

A man so imposing I no longer can remember why I'm here.

He arises from his desk. His eyes are wide as he steps toward me. He's noticeably tense. His back is upright and a small line pinches between his brows. When he's only inches away, I raise my trembling hand.

It feels so heavy.

The letter.

"What is this?" I fling the paper in his face. "What. Is. This?" My words come out staccato as I repeat to wrap my brain around what's happening.

"It's a formal letter terminating our professional relationship," he replies. The words are spoken so matter of factly and they slice at me, causing a laceration to form inside my gut.

"You can't."

"I did." His gaze is vacant and I take a step closer to study him, to understand why this is happening.

"How can you do this to me? A letter. You sent a letter. What type of bastard are you? "

"It had to be done." I move past him, walking to the far wall and bracing my arms on it. Tears pool in my eyes. He can't leave me.

He can't abandon me.

"You're discarding me?"

"I'm not discarding you. I just don't think I'm the right doctor for you."

"H-How could you?" I stutter, the anger once harboring in my body recedes into panic. He steps forward and I step back.

"Look at me," he demands and I turn to face him. The expression reflected back at me makes my legs instinctively take a step back. "I think it's for the best."

"Give me a reason. W-why are you leaving me?" More tears well and threaten to fall. "Is it because of what happened? I-I-told you I was sorry. Do you hate me? Is this why you're throwing me out? Is this why you're leaving me, too?" My dad, my mom, Richard . . . I can't stand to lose him as well.

"This has nothing to do with you, or your self-worth. This is completely my fault. It's because of me, not you."

It feels as though every last breath has been extracted from my lungs.

"No, it's because we kissed. It's because we spent time together outside of the office. I know you said it was wrong, but I like spending time with you. You make me feel as if everything will be okay." His jaw clenches at my words. As if they pain him.

"This is my fault. I ruin everything. I promise I'll do better. I promise," I plead as moisture slides down my cheeks. My pulse accelerates at the thought of not having him in my life. Of not talking to him. Of not seeing him.

"No," he affirms. "This isn't your fault. I should have known better."

"Known better than what?"

"This. This is all wrong. I can't talk to you about this. This dependence on me. It's not appropriate. This is—"

"No. Preston, don't you dare say it! Don't you dare say it's transference. It's not that. My feelings for you . . . I am not projecting my issues of abandonment from my childhood and my need for reassurance from an older figure. Damn it, you don't know how I feel. You don't know how long I've wanted you."

His breath is ragged as he rakes his fingers through his hair. He opens then shuts his mouth, pulling at his roots until he finds his words. Swiping away an escaped tear, I stare at him. *If this is transference, I don't care.*

"I could—"

"Enough." My movements halt at the desperation in his voice. "What do you want me to say? You want me to say that every time you walk into my office, my world stops? That when you're here, rather than helping you, I imagine what you would feel like beneath me? Do you want me to admit that all I see is you, and when I close my eyes you're still there? That you've embedded yourself so far in my psyche that I'm the one who needs help, not you? Is that what you want to hear?

"You want to hear that I think the universe is playing a sick joke on me? Yeah, that's what you want to hear. That I have never felt this way before, and of course it's my patient who makes me feel this. My fucking *patient*. The greatest temptation ever laid before me." His voice bleeds with emotion.

"Of all the fucking people . . . Eve." He snatches the letter from my head, my heart racing. "This is self-preservation." It drops to the floor. He inhales deeply, his hand shoving his hair back from his face.

I don't know what to do anymore. I don't know how to feel. All I can do is turn my back on him to gain some distance. My emotions teeter on the brink of eruption and I can't let him see me crack.

"I—" I can't bear the torment in his eyes, and turn toward the wall.

"God, all I want . . ." He steps up behind me, his lips tingling the sensitive skin where my neck meets my shoulder. "All I want is to taste you, savor you, but I can't." Feathery breaths send chills up my spine.

"I was warned in graduate school this could happen. That one day a patient could walk in and knock me on my ass. Make me rethink everything I believed about myself. But what I feel surpasses all that. What I feel threatens everything I know, because this isn't some hunger I need to quench. You've embedded yourself in my soul. And without you I would cease to be."

His lips hover against my skin.

Taunting me.

Tempting me.

Teasing me.

Each pull of oxygen through my lungs releases in ragged bursts. I need him. I need him so much I can barely breathe.

I want to reach for him . . . but I can't.

I want to touch him . . . but I don't.

He needs to be the one.

"Touch me, Preston," I groan. "Stop fighting it."

He reaches out. His fingers fan my rib cage as he pulls me into him and proceeds to spin me around. Our chests brush with each heave of our breaths.

"What are you doing to me?" he mumbles as his heart hammers a familiar beat against mine. It screams of need and want. Of desperation and fear.

"I don't know." And I don't. I have no clue what I'm doing. I'm blind to everything but this man.

"Tell me to stop." His voice is husky.

"Touch me."

"You don't know what you're asking."

"But I do." Hunger courses through me. A new resolve. I have no care for consequences. All I'm concerned about is what I want, and what I want is for him to touch me. For him to kiss me. For him to want me.

He stares at me with an expression that makes my whole body tremble. His emotions mirror my own.

It's unequivocal.

It's absolute.

This man wants to consume me and I yearn to let him.

"God damn it. I'm not supposed to feel this way." The lights from the city trickle in through the window, illuminating his crystal blue eyes that are darkened with lust.

"Feel what way?" I breathe, my chest heaving.

"That I want you. That I need to touch you."

I step toward his voice.

"So, touch me."

"I can't." His eyes dilate. A look passes through them that has my knees going weak. The hot intensity of his stare sets off an inferno inside me.

"I'm not your patient anymore."

And those words break the dam. He crosses the invisible line that separates our bodies. He reaches out and makes feather-like contact with the skin of my jaw. I become lost in a heady trance.

There's a fervor growing inside me.

It's intoxicating.

His hand travels the distance to the hollow of my neck. One touch and it's over for me. Electricity quivers off the pads of his fingers as they trail down to the swell of my breast, peeking out from my blouse. The only thing that matters is his touch. He leans in closer, inhaling me. I feel his breath against me, tickling my skin.

"Eve." It's a warning.

Tilting my head upward, our gazes lock as he traces the lace of my exposed bra. The look in his eyes penetrates me to the core. It has everything inside me halting.

I need there to be no distance between us.

This feeling is all consuming.

I push to my tiptoes and our lips meet.

It's soft.

A gentle touch.

The warmth of his mouth is intoxicating as the kisses grow harder, more passionate. He nips, he sucks, it seems as if he's pulling me in ten different directions.

His movements are full of purpose, full of need.

His hands grip my hips as he presses his body into mine.

Snaking my arms around his neck, I deepen the kiss. The stroke of his tongue is fierce and possessive. Every cell in my body comes alive with this kiss.

I'm lost in the kiss.

I'm found in this kiss.

He pushes me back into the wall and I let out a broken sigh as I collide with the surface. His arms tighten around my waist, pressing us so close together there's no separation between us. Lifting up, I rub my core against him. The hard ridge of his length presses against me. My body shudders at the contact. The feel of him against me makes me forget anything and everything other than my hunger for him.

Sensing my desire, Preston reaches around and lifts my legs to his hips. The movement pulls me in closer, making the friction more intense. He grinds into me. His arms that are still bracketed around me pull away as he separates my legs further. The hand on the small of my back holds me steady.

He drags his mouth from my lips and trails his lips down my throat. A moan escapes and I can't suppress the shivers from the feel of his tongue sliding against my skin. Warm hands lift the hem of my shirt. Fingers stroke my spine, and then graze across the swell of my hip.

My back arches.

His tongue glides across the skin above my breast, and frantic hands pull away at my blouse. Opening, exposing me to him. As the air hits my nipples, they pebble and peak. Continuing his exploration, Preston trails circles across my nipple. His teeth graze the sensitive flesh.

Pulling lightly. Nipping.

His hand slides down my body to the waistband of my pants. He pauses.

The pressure of his hand is a reminder of what I want. Of what I desire. Pushing my body firmly into his, I let him know what I need.

I need his hands on me. His fingers in me.

He finds the button and undoes it. Wedges his hand between the thin material and my skin.

The pads of his fingertips slowly work themselves further downward. Each inch they travel sends a wave of chills to flow through my body; each nerve ending is pricked alive.

He pushes his hand lower and lower until I feel him trace the lace covering my most intimate spot. A whisper against my sensitive flesh.

"Please," I moan, rotating my hips to help alleviate the hunger growing inside me. The flimsy material that covers me moves aside and his fingers trace down the seam of my skin. The movements are so slow, every part of my body quivers with anticipation.

"Dr. Montgomery, your next patient is here." The receptionist's voice slams through our lust filled haze.

Preston's head rears back at the same time he jerks back his hand. I lift my eyes to meet his stare. Regret. That's what I see staring back at me, and it rips me to shreds.

I'm pinned by his eyes. I know I won't like what's coming,

but I can't make myself pull away. He doesn't answer her, but puts distance between us. Our breathing is shallow.

Shock.

I see it in his eyes for what he just did.

They're haunted and hollow. We both inhale and exhale. What the fuck am I still doing here? It feels as if my heart may break free from my chest, it's beating so hard. Pulling away, I fix my skirt.

"You have lipstick . . . " He reaches out, and then catches himself. Our eyes lock in a moment that feels as if it will last a lifetime. There is so much remorse in his crystal blue eyes.

It breaks me apart. Severs me.

"I have to leave." My voice is rough. My stomach crashes, and what's left of my heart rips in two. Grabbing my coat from the back of the chair, I turn my back and head for the door.

"Eve." I look over my shoulder and meet his gaze. With all my strength, I hold back the tears threatening to expel. One lone drop escapes and trails down my cheek. "I'll write you a referral." His mask is back on.

I don't stop. I don't say good-bye. I leave.

chapter twenty-five

EVE

SIT AT MY DESK, SLOWLY NURSING THE ONCE HOT COFFEE IN front of me. The heat has fizzled away as I stare lifelessly out the office window. Grey skies pour ice-cold rain. It bears down, hitting the pavement below mercilessly. *I wonder if you can hear the sound of the tiny droplets when they crash against the concrete?*

As if it matters what it sounds like.

As if anything so mundane matters right now.

I can't concentrate on anything. Not when I'm lost in my own head. All I have done this morning is replay my moments with Preston.

Over and over again. How can something that feels so right be so wrong?

"Earth to Eve."

I lift my head and am met with Sydney's large brown eyes.

"Hey."

"Hey, are you okay?"

"Yeah, I'm fine." I say. It comes out dry and monotone. She grimaces at the tone. Things are still tense. Even though I'm not mad anymore and I'm working past it, it's still a bit odd between us.

"Listen, I know you're still mad at me, but no matter what you think, I'm your best friend, and as your best friend you need to realize I wasn't born yesterday. You got a letter, hauled ass out of the apartment and didn't return for hours. Then you came home, slammed the door and blasted music. I woke up and you were already gone. Seems to me something happened and you don't want to tell me. I understand I broke the trust. But I promise you, with everything I have, I won't squander your trust again. Please let me in."

I let out a huff I didn't realize I was holding. It's time I let it go. I need to stop punishing her for a mistake she made long before she met me. It's not fair to her that I've let it go this long.

"Fine. You're right and I'm sorry. I shouldn't have gotten mad, and I do want to talk to you about what happened, but not here." Standing, I grab her arm and usher us down the hall. We take a step into a more secluded alcove by the bathroom.

"So, what's going on?" she asks, her eyes huge.

"I got a letter from Preston."

"Preston?" She raises her eyebrow.

"Dr. Montgomery." I let out an audible sigh. "I had a mini breakdown after the *drunk* incident, and while he was comforting me, I might have tried to kiss him." I scrunch my nose, waiting for her to erupt.

"You tried to kiss him?" Her voice raises an octave.

"*Shh.*" My eyes jet around the space. "Yes. I tried to kiss him, and, well, he told me I needed to find another doctor. I didn't listen. I apologized and said I would see him the next week. Then I walked out."

"Why did you do that?"

"I guess I figured if I avoided it and ignored it, he would

change his mind."

"And did he?"

"Um, no." I look down at the marble floor. The idea of meeting her eyes right now is too much.

"What aren't you telling me?" With an exhale, I lift my eyes and meet her stare. Her eyes are narrowed and she has a small line forming between her brows.

"He sent the letter," I squeak out on a whisper.

"What! What did it say?" she loud whispers.

"God, Sydney. Can you keep it down?"

"No one can hear shit. Keep going," she says as she rolls her hands to gesture me to tell my story.

"He sent me a formal letter of termination of our doctor/ patient relationship." With that announcement, she covers her mouth with her hand in shock. "He basically fired me as his patient."

"Wow."

Silence descends. An awkward one, where she keeps opening and shutting her mouth in rapid succession. "So, that's why you ran out last night?" I nod yes. "Then what happened?"

"Basically, I barreled into his office, slamming doors and shit. Then I bawled him out."

"Oh, my God! You didn't," she dramatically shouts.

"Sydney, can you *pleeeese* keep it down?"

"Oh, sorry. What did he say then? Not to downplay this, but I think I need popcorn to listen to this story."

I slap my hand against my forehead. As much as I want to yell at her to stop joking, I smile. Because for the first time in a while I feel we're back to us again. It feels good.

"Okay, where was I? Oh, yes, I got heated. Then he got heated, and then . . . " I stop. How can I say this out loud?

"I'm not getting any younger here," she says in a snarky voice and I know she's happy, as well. "Just tell me what happened. It can't be that bad."

I raise a challenging eyebrow and then let it all out with a smug look on my face.

"He pushed me against the wall and started making out with me." *Bam!* Let the explosions begin. She leans against the wall without a word. Just leans there. If not for the tiny heave of her chest, I'd think she's comatose. I'm a bit taken aback and shocked by her lack of reaction, but I know eventually she will gather her words and composure. I tap my left foot on the floor and wait.

"He what!"

I smack her arm playfully and shoot her a look that says "Shut the fuck up."

"Yes."

"He kissed you?"

"Dry humped me against the wall would be more accurate, but yes . . ." My lips turn up in a smile.

"Wow."

"Yep."

"So, how was it?" She smirks.

"Amazing."

"That's all I get?"

"That's all you get," I deadpan. I couldn't tell her this was the kiss to end all kisses. That his kiss ruined me for all other men. That his kiss left me breathless and desperate and begging for more.

"What will you do now?"

"What can I do? He doesn't want to see me."

"Wait! What? What do you mean? And what about therapy?

The nightmares. The panic attacks. You can't stop seeing him."

"He freaked out and told me I had to go. He offered me a list of referrals."

"Okay, good," she says and I pinch the bridge of my nose. "What?" Her eyebrow lifts.

"I kind of forgot it at his office."

"What do you plan to do about that? Because if your answer is nothing, I'll smack you upside the head."

"What do you expect me to do about it?"

"I expect you to man up, head to his office and get it back." I look down to the floor, playing with the hem of my skirt. Sydney takes a step closer to me. "It will be okay. You just need the referral list. In and out." My eyes must bug out of my head at her choice of verbiage, because she busts out laughing.

"Grow up." I roll my eyes and step away.

"That's it? No more gossip?"

"I would have thought that was juicy enough for a lifetime."

" I don't know about a lifetime. I'd say a week, maybe two." She shrugs and I shake my head. I'm a few steps from the office door when I realize she's no longer next to me. Turning back to where I was, I see she's still standing there.

"Come on, Sydney. Before you catch flies in that mouth."

She lets out a laugh and then rights herself. *It's good to have us back.*

"If you don't hurry, we'll be late to the meeting," I say to her as I stand waiting for her to catch up. She doesn't say anything but I know the previous conversation is far from over.

Everyone on our team is already in the conference room when we make it back into the office. Grabbing my notepad from my desk, we jet inside and all eyes turn to us. I sit down and stare up at Michael, who is already going over the budgets and objectives for the rest of the week. We're working on a campaign for a new fashion publication that's set to launch in six months. Around the room everyone throws out random hashtags and concepts for an Instagram program we will kick off the beginning of the next week.

It seems the office has returned to normal. The excited energy is back from before Richard's death. This should make me happy. I know Richard would be pleased. Instead, it tightens my chest. Rubbing at the muscles there, I concentrate on what is being said. Breathing in and following Preston's techniques helps keep the panic at bay. Every day that passes, the anxiety lessens when I'm in the office. I only wish the nightmares would stop, too. They're so strange. They make absolutely no sense. I have never seen blood like I have in my nightmares. I have never felt fear like I do in my night terrors. As I rub the fatigue out of my eyes from another restless night, I know I need to follow Sydney's advice and get the referral list from Preston.

When I get back to my desk, I grab my cell phone and dial the number for his office. On the third ring the phone is answered.

"Park Psychology. How may I help you?" A high-pitched voice answers. I know instantly I have never met this receptionist. Her breath comes through the phone in a ragged burst and sounds as though she's just run a marathon.

"May I please speak to Dr. Montgomery? This is Eve Hamilton calling. I wanted to get a referral from him."

"Ca-Can you hold on a minute? Let me see if he's with a patient." The phone drops and echoes on the desk. Then I hear the sound of her heels on the wood floors. A little laugh escapes me as I realize she forgot to put me on hold. *I wonder if she's new?* A few seconds later, she returns out of breath again. "I'm sorry, Ms. Hamilton. He's on a call, and will be on and off calls for the rest of the day. He said he will send a courier to you with the chart and referral list." Courier? *Wow.*

"No, that's okay. If he can just leave the file with you, I have a lunch meeting in the area so I can stop by afterward. Say two p.m.?"

"Um, okay. I guess that's okay. He has a patient then. I'll just grab it from him before he goes in."

"Thank you." Hanging up, I pinch the bridge of my nose. *He won't even speak to me.* I shudder at the thought, then let out a deep sigh.

It will be fine. Everything is fine.

Don't get upset.

In. Out.

In. Out.

I turn back to my computer and start my search for stock images for the new Instagram campaign.

chapter twenty-six

EVE

PEOPLE SCURRY PAST ME AS I MAKE MY WAY UPTOWN TO MY meeting. The sky is its usual shade of New York City grey. It's dark and dingy and utterly ominous. I pull my coat tighter around my body. A skirt is not appropriate for this weather. Neither are the Louboutins I'm wearing as I walk the ten blocks to StreetSide Grill where I'm meeting Nicolette from Posh Life. We are meeting to go over and finalize the details for the #PerfectlyPoshLife campaign. When I enter the restaurant, my heart picks up until it's pounding rhythmically in my chest. *"Believe in yourself. If you do, no one will doubt you."* I straighten my posture and walk toward the hostess.

"I'm meeting—" I start to say but I stop speaking as I notice a tall, lithe brunette waving at me. "I see her." I smile and make my way to Nicolette.

For the next forty-five minutes, I run over the ideas we pulled together to build hype for the launch. I gathered a group of the top trendsetters in the fashion industry to launch the hashtag as well as a living storyboard of what it means to live the #PerfectlyPoshLife. I knocked it out of the park. She loved the idea. What an amazing feeling to believe in myself and succeed because of it. Sure, I second guessed myself—but then I did it. I used Preston's technique of remembering Richard, but now I see that I can do it and I didn't need anyone's help. I succeeded on my own merits. Preston would be proud—

Preston.

Looking down, I glance at my watch. 2:45. Lunch ran a little later than I anticipated, but once we started to talk, we couldn't stop. The ideas just kept flowing. I debate whether to call before heading to his office. I said two o'clock, but I'm sure the forty-five minutes I'm late won't be a big deal.

I smile to myself and turn in the direction I need to go. When I see Preston's large, ominous building spanning in front of me, my grin drops off my face. *You can do this. As much as you want him to be your doctor, maybe he's right. Maybe you need space from him.*

Stepping inside, I present my ID and head for the elevators. You would think after coming here for months, maybe just maybe they would let me pass, but alas, I need to present my ID every time.

Once I make it to his floor, I'm met by an empty reception desk. I push open the door and look down the hall. I wonder if she's in the bathroom? Maybe she left my file on her desk. I scan the neatly organized surface but don't see anything. Not wanting to rummage, I walk down the narrow hall to investigate whether someone who works here knows where she put it. As I pass Preston's door, I expect to see it closed. Instead, I'm met with cerulean blue eyes staring up at me.

"What are you doing here?" he says from his desk and I take a step into the room.

"I needed to get my file. She told me to come."

"Who told you?"

"Your receptionist." He shakes his head and groans to himself, "Of course she did." Then he pulls himself from his chair and stands, "I told her I would send a courier," he mutters more to himself than to me.

"I know, but I was in the area. I said I would pick it up."

"Did you do this to see me?"

"No." His eyes widen and I swallow. "Maybe."

"You can't be here." The muscles tightening in my neck tense as he watches me. His unwavering gaze has me on edge.

"I needed—"

"What did you need?" No more lies, or false truths. As easy as it was to have the files sent over, I chose to come here, and it's time I lay my cards on the table and be honest.

"To see you," I admit on a sigh.

"Why?" The mesmerizing blue of Preston's eyes swallows me whole. They unnerve me as I step closer. A small frown line develops between his brows.

"Because I can't stand the idea that I never will again." His gaze softens at my words. He takes a step toward me and I move further into the room.

"I know this is wrong," Preston says as he takes another step. "I know we have to stop." *Step.* "But this feeling weaves through me every time I see you. It takes control of me. It's like I can't . . . I can't stop myself." *Step.*

"I'm not your patient anymore." I breathe out. One more step will place him directly in front of me. My chest heaves as I wait.

"Semantics." *Step.* His voice drips with heat. It sends shivers down my spine as he reaches out and pulls me toward him. "God dammit, I fucking want you but I can't be with you. This shit is fucked up. I'm fucked up. You are . . . *were* my patient.

There is a statute of limitations. Two years. There's a reason they say a minimum of two years after terminating the doctor/patient relationship, and even then . . . Even then it's frowned upon. This thing between us could do irrevocable damage to you. Statistics have shown—"

I lift my hand, place my finger on the soft skin of his lips, and silence him as I shorten the length between us.

"I don't give a fuck about statistics. Don't fucking care about any of it." Lifting onto my tiptoes, I place my lips almost to his. Our mouths barely touch, but as the seconds pass between us all I feel is the soft caress of his breath fanning over my lips.

I could breathe him in.

Inhale him.

Consume him.

Ours breaths mingle in a slow beat. One so hypnotic, I have been placed under his spell.

Finally, he closes the remaining distance that separates us. He reaches for me, pulling me into his arms. Soft fingers turn my chin up. I soften my body into his as he hovers . . . almost touching

His exhales caress my lips.

"What do you want? What are you doing to me?" he mutters more to himself than to me. But I answer him breathlessly nonetheless.

"I don't know, I don't know." The real words I want to say won't come out, so instead I answer the question with the only answer I have . . .

I press my mouth to his.

He responds eagerly, his lips spreading against mine, his tongue seeking entry until he's kissing me with abandon. His hands cup my cheeks and our movements slow until we are left panting.

"That kiss, did it feel fake? Did that feel like transference?" He doesn't speak as I wind my hands up to wrap around his neck. "Does this?" I pull my body closer and grind up against him. "Does this feel like transference?"

Our mouths crash together again. If it is at all possible, it's even more frantic than before. This kiss is a fire. One that is sure to burn us, but neither of us cares. We can't get enough.

On a gasp, I realize I'm being lifted off the floor, carried a short distance, and then lowered onto the smooth top of his desk. My skirt lifts and I feel the cool surface against my exposed skin. I shudder and Preston pulls away and surveys me. A primal groan escapes his mouth as he takes in my now exposed garter. His normally blue eyes have grown dark and needy, almost black with heat.

He reaches out and traces my swollen lips then passes a hand down my neck to the hollow of my chest. He continues a trail until he unbuttons each button on my blouse. Slowly.

One.

Two.

Three.

I shiver as he passes lightly over each breast, his fingertips stroking each pert nipple. He touches me, but it's not enough. I need him inside me. Wrapping my legs around his waist, I pull his body in toward me. His rock hard length presses against my core. He looks at me through hooded eyes as he pulls his hand away from my chest and tips me backward so my back hits the broad surface. Leaning down, he removes my legs from around his waist and traces up the exposed skin of my thigh. When he reaches my thong, he runs circles over the sensitive flesh hidden beneath. Teasing me. Torturing me.

"Please," I moan.

"What do you need?" He rubs a little harder. "Do you need me to touch you? Taste you? Or do you want me inside you?" A ragged moan leaves my mouth as I push up to apply more pressure. He nods in understanding, then drops down.

Soft fingers pull at my thong.

Remove it.

Leave me bare.

Soft lips touch my skin. Traveling at a punishingly slow pace, sure to drive me mad with need.

Preston's mouth kisses up higher. Inch by inch.

Sucking.

Nipping.

Drawing it out, making me pant.

When I think I can't take much more, his hands cup me from beneath, lifting my pelvis to meet his mouth. Warm currents electrify my body. His arms are braced around my hips and pull me closer. His warm breath hits me where I need him most.

Desperate.

I'm desperate for him to touch me there. To feel his tongue lap at my sensitive skin.

His fingers part me. One slips inside as his tongue swipes at my buddle of nerves.

I lift my hips and he buries his face deeper into me.

He licks with a ferocity I have never felt before. His fingers keep up the pace, matching the swipe of his tongue.

A demanding rhythm.

His assault drives me higher and higher.

Faster and Faster.

Until the ripple of sensations flood my senses.

When I come down from my high, I find him staring down at me with hooded eyes.

"God, you're beautiful when you come undone." Lifting to a seated position, I reach for his belt buckle.

"What are you doing?" he says as I start to unzip his pants.

"I want to taste you now."

"Jesus, we can't do this here! We're lucky Maggie hasn't returned from lunch yet." He looks toward the half open door to his office and then back to me. "Fuck it," he groans out as he frees himself from the confines of his pants. "If I'm on borrowed time, I want to be inside you."

Gripping his shaft, I guide him to where I need him.

"I got you," he whispers in my ear, sending a shiver to spread down my body.

He settles between my hips. My heat pulsates around him as he dips just a bit inside.

Teasing.

A whimper escapes as he pushes deeper within, then withdraws.

Then with one powerful thrust, he's fully seated in me, stretching me open as my body tightly fits around him. This feels too good. As though our bodies are meant to be joined together.

I wrap my arms around his shoulders. My nails grip at his skin.

His movements increase. His body slams into me at a punishing pace. Like a man exorcising his lust for something he cannot have. Again, an all-encompassing bliss spreads through me. My whole body tenses with the need to release. With a final slam of Preston's hips, I fall into a heavenly bliss. With one last shudder, he falls, too.

As our breathing regulates, he lays panting on my chest. When we finally calm our breaths, he separates our bodies and stands. The haze of desire has left his eyes and something else is there that I can't pinpoint. I straighten my own body and lift up to sit on the edge of the desk.

Preston runs his hands through his hair. "Shit. We didn't use a—"

"I'm healthy and on the pill."

"Me too, but still. *Shit.* I can't think when you're around." His brows knit together as he studies me. "You're a dangerous temptation. You're an addiction. One I fear I'll never kick now that I've tasted you. Now that I've felt you." His words are barely audible.

"So don't."

"We can't be together. We shouldn't. If this came out, I would be ruined. All my work at the hospital—" His blue eyes morph into swollen red-rimmed slits as he rubs them furiously. "But I'm not willing to stop."

chapter twenty-seven

PRESTON

WHAT THE FUCK HAVE I DONE?

This girl renders me fucking blind. Hell, when she's around I don't know up from down. She clouds my judgment. But I've never had a choice. Not with her. There is *no* choice when Eve's involved.

Even now I can't get her out of my mind. She just walked out the door and already I'm itching to call her back.

I'm not done. Not nearly done.

Sitting back in my chair, my eyes roam over my desk. *The kiss...my mouth touching hers...*

One kiss, I'd told myself. What a lie that was. I knew the moment I kissed her that everything inside me would implode.

But I kissed her anyway.

And it wasn't enough, it wasn't nearly enough.

I'll never forget how my tongue felt against her skin. How it felt as I licked the soft hollow of her neck. I can still taste her. I can still smell her. She lingers in my office like a sin.

She's my sin.

Not my salvation.

And I don't give a damn.

chapter twenty-eight

EVE

GLANCING DOWN AT MY WATCH, I SEE IT'S AFTER FIVE P.M. *Where did the afternoon go?* Heat spreads across my face. I know exactly where it went. *Preston.*

When I walk into my apartment, I hear water running in the kitchen. I hang my coat in the closet, then make my way inside and find Sydney filling a pot with water.

"I'm making pasta. Want some wine?"

"Sure. What's the occasion?"

"Well, for one, I hear you landed the Posh Life deal."

"And two?"

"Well, it's obvious you didn't come back to work for a reason, and from the look of your clothes . . ." She looks me up and down and I notice that in my haste to get dressed, I forgot to button two of the buttons on my blouse. "I'm thinking you have some explaining to do." I swallow and open the fridge to grab a bottle.

"But first a glass of wine," I say and she lifts her eyebrow.

"Wow, that bad? Or by the looks of things that good?"

"The best, but yeah. I'm royally fucked. Figuratively and literally." I pop open the bottle, grab two glasses, and pour. I drink my glass so fast I barely taste it.

"Wait, what?" Sydney places her hands on her hips as she taps her foot. When I don't answer right away and then pour myself another glass, she gestures with her hands for me to hurry it along and talk. I can't meet her eyes and confess what I'm about to, so instead I look down and pick a piece of lint from my skirt.

"I slept with Preston," I admit on a sigh and she slaps a hand over her mouth. "I would say I didn't mean for it to happen, but that would be a lie."

"What happened?" I purse my lips at her and raise an eyebrow. "You know what I mean. How did it . . . Oh, just tell me everything." Reaching over, I hand her a filled glass and take a seat at the island in the small kitchen.

"So, right after the meeting, I went over there to get my referral list and file from the receptionist. Well, my meeting ran long and by the time I got there, the girl I was supposed to meet went for a late lunch. I went looking for someone to help me, and, well, I bumped into Preston. One thing lend to another . . . "

"And you fell on his penis. Got It." Sarcasm drips off her words.

"Sydney! God. Really?"

"What? You know that's how you made it sound."

"Fine. It was a little bit more elaborate than that. The moral of the story, we had sex . . . on his desk." And with that she jumps up and down, sauce from the spoon she's holding spraying across the room. "Shit," she says, eyes wide at the mess.

"Don't worry about it. You cook, I'll clean. It's my fault, anyway." Standing, I set my wine down, grab a rag from the counter, and get rid of the sauce splattered on the cabinets.

When I'm done, I turn to find Sydney staring at me.

"What?" I ask and she frowns.

"Now what? He's your doctor. It's not like you can date him."

"Was my doctor," I clarify, and then let out a deep breath. "But yeah, you're right. We can't be together."

———•———

When my phone pings a few days later, I almost fall off my chair. Preston? I didn't expect to hear from him so soon, or ever again. What does he want? Does he miss me?

Preston: You left your referral list

I shatter at his words, or lack thereof. I want him to miss me. I want him to beg to want to see me. For him to feel what I feel, but instead, it's as though my soul is broken into thousands of glass shards, so small you can never piece them back together. My shoulders tip forward and I continue to walk. Normally this walk is too far for me to trek in this weather, but after Preston's text I need the air. I need to be able to breathe. The air tastes bitter on my lips, or maybe that's just my pain manifesting in all aspects of me.

In. Out.

In. Out.

My gait is unusually short today. Each step a feat. But no matter how hard I try to abandon my funk, to look up at the world around me, to take in the beauty of the day, it doesn't matter as my body continues to trudge along the pavement until I reach my mom's apartment.

"Mom, are you up?" She doesn't answer as per usual, but I find her soon enough. The last rays of sunlight stream through the window illuminating her. She looks like an angel. Beautiful and fair, sitting up in her bed. There is a glow about her and for the first time in forever she seems lucid. Together.

"Hi." I step closer, assessing her before I get too excited that I finally have the chance to talk to her about some things. "You look good. How are you feeling?"

"I have a headache." She shifts in her bed, slouching her back. It's as if a light switch was flipped. She's a different person now. Is she always so lucid when I'm not around? Does she only do this to get my attention? Ignoring her comment, I take a seat alongside the bed and glance at her. What is it about my presence that makes her act this way?

"Mom, a few weeks ago I asked you about Richard's company. Why did you invest your money in The Stone Agency?"

"Do we have to do this now?"

"I'd like to. I just don't understand anything. You never talk about Dad. You won't tell me about his accident. You don't tell me why you invested. You're my mom and I know nothing about you at all."

"It's the past. Can't you leave it in the past?" She closes her eyes and leans back onto the pillow behind her, essentially shutting me out again.

"It's not my past, Mom."

She opens her eyes. They're no wider than a squint.

"After your father passed, I wasn't well enough to work. Richard gave me the opportunity to invest some of the insurance money in his startup company. It was a gamble but it paid off in the end."

"Why did you risk it?"

"I owe everything to Richard. Everything. If it weren't for him, I don't know where we'd be." She reclines again and I know she's done with me.

But at least I have one more piece of the puzzle, whatever

the puzzle might be. Richard saved us. How I'm not sure, but I need to find out. Next time she seems better I'll find out more.

Once my mom's breathing becomes shallow with sleep, I head back toward my apartment. When I'm only a block away, my phone rings.

"Hey." Preston's voice is low and raspy. Just hearing it makes me forget all the sadness I felt on the walk to my mom's. Instead, it makes my whole body warm.

"Hi," I breathe.

"You left the referral list again."

"I know."

"Why didn't you respond?"

"There was nothing to say." Neither of us speaks for a few minutes until I hear him swallow.

"I can swing by tomorrow," I say. He's quiet for a second before responding.

"That might not be the best idea after what happened last time." I let out a chuckle and he follows suit.

"Yeah, you might be right. Maybe we should meet somewhere else. Somewhere a bit more public?" I close my eyes and take a breath, then silently pray he doesn't offer the courier service again. I want to see him. If only for a moment.

"I have a patient tomorrow night. But I can stop by your building and leave it with the doorman."

"Call me when you get there and I'll grab it." There's a pause on the other end of the line and I wonder if the call disconnected. "I want to briefly go over the list with you."

"Yes, that makes sense. Okay, my next patient is here. I'll see you tomorrow."

Hanging up the phone, I swear I feel every muscle in my body loosen and then tighten again. I'm not ready to let him go. I'm not ready to move on.

———— ———•———— ———

ONE DAY LATER . . .

I should still be at work. I should be finishing up the last of the details for the Posh Life launch. I definitely shouldn't be home pacing my apartment. But here I am, in front of the mirror, reapplying my lip-gloss for the umpteenth time. Truth is, it's already five p.m., but with the new project, this will be my first chance to prove myself as more than Richard's family. Landing the project isn't enough. Nailing the pitch isn't enough. I need to knock it out of the park, but instead, my head is too distracted with what I'll wear to see Preston. Black skirt and a silk blouse, black pumps. That way it appears as if I'm coming home from work.

Finally, after what seems like forever, my phone pings with a new text.

Preston: Downstairs in lobby.

Me: Come up.

I type before I can second-guess myself. I wonder what he will say. My heart leaps in my chest as I wait.

In. Out.

In. Out.

The intercom buzzes.

"Hello?"

"Hello, Miss. Hamilton. I have a Preston Montgomery here to see you."

"Send him up."

When I swing the door open, my chest tightens. It's only been a few days since his lips touched mine, but I'm hungry for him all over again. As my gaze reaches his, I know I'm not the only one affected by this pull. He still feels it. His breathing is shallow as he surveys me. It makes my pulse race. With one step, we are practically touching. So close that if I reach out, my hand would be on his. Desire pools in my belly. Lifting my hand, my fingertips connect with his jaw. A sharp inhale of breath echoes through the room.

"No matter what's wrong or right, or even if I can lose my license, I don't fucking care." He pulls his lower lip between his teeth and I'm afraid he might draw blood. Finally letting go, he speaks. "Go away with me." There is finality in his voice. As though this is my one chance to be with him.

"What?"

"I need time with you. I need to see you again before I let you go. I'm not ready for this to end." I can hear him take a deep breath and in my head I hear the word he didn't say . . . *yet.* "I know my job is on the line but maybe we can figure out a way to make it work." I wonder if he hears his own lie or if he, like me, so desperately wants to believe that he's still clinging to the hope of a chance.

"But how? What if someone sees us?"

"We'll go somewhere. Just you and me." He motions his hand between us. "I know it's so wrong for me to ask but I'm aski—"

"Yes."

"Yes?" His face contorts. Awe, fear, and then resignation cross over his face. This might be our only shot to be together again.

"Yeah, one trip. One perfect trip and then . . ." I take a breath but don't have the strength to say the rest of words I know will one day break my heart. *"And then I'll let you go."*

chapter twenty-nine

PRESTON

THIS ISN'T A GOOD IDEA. WE SHOULDN'T BE GOING AWAY. IF the APA finds out, I can lose my license. Do I trust her enough to know she won't tell?

We're asking for trouble. Or at least, I am. But like an addict, I need my next hit. What the hell am I doing? What the hell are we doing?

Maybe it can work out . . . *who am I kidding?*

Shit. I need to think straight but around her I can't.

She's beautiful. Gorgeous. She's everything I want and don't deserve. I'm being selfish but I don't care. I need to have her, even if only for a brief moment. I know the ramifications of my actions. But fuck. How can I not have her?

Just once.

Maybe twice.

One taste.

God, it's wrong. I guess I'm a bigger asshole than I thought, but she's pure temptation.

Consequences be damned.

chapter thirty

EVE

I HURRY BACK TO MY APARTMENT. I HAVE TO PACK. TOMORROW we will be going somewhere after work. I'm not sure where, as Preston finalized the details.

I don't think one weekend will be enough, though I lied and agreed to it because the thought of not having this time with him makes me sick. The thought of not feeling his hands again is too much to bear. So I agreed and made a promise I know I can't keep.

"So, what are you going to do?" Sydney's asks after I tell her Preston invited me away for the weekend.

"Fuck him out of my system." I laugh and she giggles, too. She thinks I'm joking. When I stop laughing and give her a serious look, she stops as well.

"What do you mean?"

"Since we can't be together here, we're going away. We're going to get each other out of our systems." She crosses her hands in front of her chest.

"You think that's a good idea?"

"Nope."

"So why are you doing it?"

"Because I can't not." She nods in understanding.

"When do you leave?" I take a gulp of my wine before answering her question.

"After work tomorrow."

"Where you going?"

"No clue."

"I hope you know what you're doing." *Me, too.*

———————•———————

I'm a basket of pent up energy at work. Not only did I not sleep well, but I'm also super nervous about leaving with Preston today. Luckily for me, at least my anxiety at work is almost under control. I have become well versed in self-soothing techniques. That, and I'm popping homeopathic remedies like they're candy. If only they made a drop for calming my subconscious mind when asleep.

To make matters worse, the lawyers are here again. Who knew settling someone's affairs would take so long? That Richard left his shares of the company to my mother leads me to believe maybe he needed psychiatric help as well. I'll never understand why he did it or why my mom had anything to do with anything, but as long as Michael has control of the show, I feel secure we'll all continue to have jobs.

After answering emails and basically fidgeting at my desk, I see Michael step out into the hallway and wave me into the conference room. With long strides, I make my way in and take a seat.

"Thanks for joining us. I'll be stepping out shortly, but I wanted to ask if your mom was okay?" His comment makes me narrow my eyes.

"Yeah, sure. I mean, no different than always. Why do you

ask?"

"Well, Mr. Swartz has been trying to contact her to sign some papers in regard to the will and she hasn't responded to his request. We wanted to make sure she was okay."

"From what she's said on the phone and when I've seen her, yeah, but I can follow up with her next week if you want?" Normally I would go straight to my mom with this news and make sure she's okay, but I'm tired of not living my own life and I need to stop enabling her. She needs to learn to be more self-sufficient. Finding out why she hasn't answered the lawyers will have to wait.

"That would be great. Thank you so much." He stands and straightens his suit jacket. "I'll leave you two." I smile up at him, then turn my attention to the attorney.

"Thank you, Ms. Hamilton, for taking your time to meet with me again. I wanted to discuss how you would like to proceed with the apartment. At the last meeting you said you didn't wish to keep the property. I wanted to see if you had changed your mind, and if not, whether you'd like help selling it?"

"I have thought about it and yes, I have no wish to keep it. As much as I love it, it's too close to my mother." I try to laugh. The idea of living so close to her again makes my whole body crawl. I love my mom, but she sucks the life out of me.

"Okay, I can help you find a listing agent, and when the time comes, I can handle the closing with you."

"Thank you so much, Mr. Schwartz. If that was it, I do have to get back to work."

"Oh, yes, of course. I only have a few more papers to go over and then I'll see myself out." He's already looking down and scribbling in his notepad.

Once back at my desk, I type Manhattan realtors into my

computer search engine. I've been putting this off for too long. It's time to settle it.

———— ————•———— ——

It's official. By the time my desk clock says five, I'm bouncing off the walls. Sydney and I bolt out the door and head home. He should be there soon. My stomach is a ball of knots, as are my shoulders and the muscles in my back. Just as Sydney opens the door, my phone vibrates in my pocket and I jump to retrieve it. Sydney pads down the hallway and I head to my room and check my message.

Preston: I'm outside your building in the illegally parked Range Rover.

Me: There in one minute.

I grab the tiny carry-on bag I packed last night and make my way to leave. When I start walking to the door, I hear Sydney call my name.

"Escaping without saying good-bye?"

"He's downstairs." She nods.

"Be safe, okay? And if you need me, no matter when, call."

"Okay."

She pulls me into a hug and then lets me go. I turn my back and head for the door. Biting my lip, I enter the elevator, and swallow hard as I make my descent.

My heart rams in my chest with each step that brings me closer to the outside world, and by the time I see his parked car, I fear it might explode. *Am I making the wrong decision?*

But then my world stops and my question is answered. *No. I'm not.*

The late afternoon sun reflects in his eyes, twinkling crystals and sapphire specks dance across the distance. *God, those eyes.* He pulls me toward him. His mouth brushes over mine and my lips part on a gasp. Taking advantage of the opportunity, he deepens the kiss. His tongue fights mine in a frenzy of passion and desperation. Of hunger and need. As our mouths collide, it's as if he's fighting for ownership of me. To possess me.

But what he doesn't know is there's no need. The moment I saw him, I was his.

"I shouldn't have done that in public, but when I look at you I lose all reason," he mutters as he pulls away from me. "Here, get in the car before someone sees us." He opens the door for me before slipping around to the driver side and getting in.

"So, where to?" I ask as I fasten my seatbelt and he pulls away from the curb.

"Ever been to Rhode Island?" A grin tugs at his lips.

"Can't say that I have."

"Good." He smirks.

"That's it. That's all you're telling me?"

"Yeah, it's more fun this way." I playfully swat at his arm and he gently encases my hand in his, then places our entwined hands on his lap. It's an intimate gesture that makes me fall a bit more than I want.

As we drive out of the city, my shoulders uncoil. The idea of spending a few days with Preston is exhilarating. Soft music plays throughout the interior of the car and I get lost in the skyline vanishing into the horizon the further we get. We sit in comfortable silence. Preston's fingers trace circles on my own as we continue to our destination.

"How was work today?" He finally breaks the silence and I turn to him and smile. He looks away from the road for a brief second, his eyes soft.

"It was okay."

"Just okay?"

"Well, I was a bit anxious to get away, so the day dragged. Then Richard's attorney came to speak to me about the apartment."

"Have you decided what you want to do with it?"

"I'm going to sell it." His hand squeezes mine. "Other than that, the day was good. Just working on a new campaign I landed."

"That's amazing."

"Thanks." My lips split into a smile. It was pretty amazing. "What about you?" Although his face is forward and turned toward the road, I see his lips pucker. "You don't have to tell me about your day if that makes you uncomfortable." He nods and I can see him let out a big exhale. "How about you tell me something about your family."

"I can do that." His lips tip up in a smirk. "What do you want to know?"

"How about everything," I blurt out, eliciting a hearty laugh from him.

"Okay, everything. Hmm. Well, for starters, I'm one of three. I have an older brother named Jace, you already met his twins. Jace works at my father's hedge fund, and then there is Madeline, my younger sister. She actually works in fashion. You would love her," he says before he catches the implication and frowns. Getting to know her isn't in the cards for us right now. He knows it and I know it. There's too much for him to lose. After a brief silence, he shakes his head and appears to right his thoughts.

"Where does she work?"

"She's the merchandising director for She." I recognize the

name instantly—She is a cutting edge fashion line that's carried at all the high-end department stores and upscale boutiques in the city.

"Are you close with your siblings?"

"Yes, very. We speak on the phone almost daily and we try get together every week for dinner. Well, not this week. But typically."

"That's so nice." My voice betrays my emotions. I might see my mom every week, but we would never have what he has with his family. It just isn't possible to get that from her. Needing to let my mind drift from my own dysfunctional family, I continue to drill him about his own.

For the rest of the drive, we talk of everything and nothing. Mundane details that for most would seem unimportant, but for me, getting these tiny glimpses of the man who makes up Dr. Preston Montgomery is everything. I love hearing him talk about his parents. Married for thirty-seven years, they are still madly in love. And when he speaks of his siblings, it makes me smile from ear to ear.

As we pull off the highway, I'm giddy with excitement. Two days alone with this man . . . I can't wait.

chapter thirty-one

EVE

WE PULL DOWN THE LONG PENINSULA IN NEWPORT, Rhode Island. With a sharp inhale of breath, my mouth hangs open. *Castle Hill Inn.* It's everything I've ever imagined perfection would be and more.

Perched high up on the hill is a beautiful white-shingled mansion that overlooks the ocean. It's one of the most magnificent homes I have ever seen. Preston pulls the car into the circular drive and we depart with the little luggage we have. The air is crisp, as most of the bitter winter has passed, making its way into spring.

After checking in, we proceed to the quaint cottage set on the beach. Preston has secured a private residence for our weekend on the property.

Before the door fully closes, he's on me. Lifting me into his arms and sweeping me over to the giant canopy bed set in the center of the bedroom. Once I'm lying there, he lowers himself over me. I feel the pressure of his lips as my eyes shut with a moan. His mouth probes my own. His tongue tastes my tongue. In a haze, I feel his hands lifting at my blouse. He pulls away and I open my lids. He lifts my shirt above my head, then with slow, precise steps removes all my clothes. Lying on the bed naked, a shudder runs through my body as he undresses as well. His tall frame is long and lean. Each muscle well defined. This is the first time I'm seeing him naked.

He's perfect.

Mesmerizing.

He looks wild with lust and it lights me on fire. I want him to touch me, but he just stares down at me. Like a predator stalking his prey until he finally pounces.

I position my legs further apart to allow him to cradle between them. When he aligns himself with my core, I lift my pelvis. Every part of my body quivers with anticipation. *With need.* My skin is a live wire. Ready to be set ablaze. He brushes against my entrance and a moan escapes me. He continues to tease me, running his length back and forth against my heat.

Sweet torture.

"Preston," I cry out in a desperate plea. Our eyes lock. The blue of his irises is completely gone behind the black of his dilated pupils. He looks at me is as if he wants to devour every single inch of my body. Slowly, he pushes inside me. He cups my face and peers into my eyes as he enters me inch by inch. The movement of his body stills, and with one swift lift of my hips, I close the space separating us until he is fully seated. Preston holds his body still until my muscles stretch to accommodate him, molding completely around him.

"Please," I moan, pleading with him to move. He silences my cries by covering my mouth with his and rotating his hips in a painfully slow circle. When I think I can take no more of his sweet torture, he retracts his body from mine and hovers again on the brink of entry. Then slams back in.

Over and over again.

Each time driving harder and harder.

Deeper and deeper.

He thrusts in slow strokes, in long ones.

I welcome each pull and drag of his body.

I cling to him, bracing my hands against his shoulders, my nails gripping and scratching across his sleek skin. He keeps me on the edge of my climax.

Torturing me.

With each move he makes, I hang on the precipice of bliss.

Until I finally fall over the edge. Just as I return from my haze, I hear a fierce growl escape his mouth as he claims his own release.

We lay panting, each of us needing to catch our breaths. Preston's body is heavy on mine. His heart beats erratically against my own. They beat in tandem. As if we are one, and at the moment we still are. After a minute, he lifts up and places a soft kiss on my swollen lips.

"That was amazing." He kisses me again and I smile against his lips. He runs his tongue along the seam of my lips, and then pulls away.

"Perfect," I mutter. He removes his body from mine and rises from the bed. He crosses the room, and I feel as if I'm living in a wonderful dream—one I hope I never wake from.

He returns wearing a robe, and in his hand is one for me. My lips spread at the gesture.

"Thank you." I stand from the bed, the sheet dropping away from my body. He sweeps his gaze across my naked form and I can see the desire in his eyes.

"How is it possible I just had you and I already want more?" his voice is low and smooth, and makes my body shiver with desire.

"I'm not sure, but if it makes you feel better, I feel the same way."

He gives me a lopsided smile and shakes his head.

"Nope . . . Doesn't help."

I walk to where he stands and wrap the robe around my body. "So, what do you want to do tonight? Do you want to go into town and grab dinner?"

"Truth?"

"Always."

"I want to stay here with you . . . naked."

"Oh, thank God." He laughs at my words and pulls me toward him. Sweeping me into his arms, he plants a soft kiss on my lips. "Want to order in room service?" he mumbles against my mouth."

"Mmm hmm." My arms attempt to wrap around his neck but he pulls away before I can and I groan out in protest.

"After dinner." He walks over to the coffee table and grabs the room service menu. "Here, let's take a look and I'll call it up."

"Fine." I pout, grabbing the menu and turning the page. "I'll have the club sandwich."

"A girl after my own heart." He smirks as he picks up the phone and dials. "Hi, yes. I would like to place an order for room service. Two club sandwiches, side of fries. Yes, that would be perfect. And a bottle of . . ." He stops talking and mouths to me, "Wine?" I nod. "Yes, and what bottle of Sauvignon Blanc do you recommend? Okay, yes. That would be perfect. Thank you." He places the phone back down and turns to me. "We have thirty minutes to kill. How should we spend them?" His lips turn into the most wicked smile I have ever seen, and I swear I melt into a puddle in the middle of our cottage.

"Shower." I raise my brow suggestively.

"I like the way you think."

Together we walk into the bathroom and into the shower. The hot water relaxes every part of my body as Preston lathers and soaps my body. Each pass of his hand causes my body to shiver, even under the heat. When he drops to his knees in front of me, I'm sure my own legs will give out. *But they don't.* Well, at least not until his lips find me and he spreads me open and devours me.

Under the water, he makes me quiver and quake once again.

An hour later, and with our stomachs full, we find ourselves sitting in front of a roaring fire drinking wine. Night has fallen and the fire crackles in the dark room, casting a shadow over Preston's face.

Hooking my feet around the chair legs, I lean back and take of sip from my glass. Preston stares at me from across the coffee table.

"It dawned on me that for as much time as we've spent together, I barely know anything about you," I say as I lift the glass again to my mouth.

"That's not true. I told you about my family." I let out a laugh at his statement.

"Preston, that was today. You just told me that."

"Well, I couldn't really tell you anything before . . . with me being your . . ." His forehead creases.

"I have an idea. How about for the rest of the weekend that subject is banned." He opens his mouth to speak, but I hold up my hand. "No, really, Preston. I don't want to waste my time with you arguing why we shouldn't do this. We both know the ramifications of us being together, of us getting caught. There's no need to discuss it further."

"Fair enough. What do you want to know?"

"I have no clue. You can't put a girl on the spot like that. What the heck am I supposed to ask, some dumb question like if you were stranded on a dessert island, what would you take?"

"I'd take my iPad. That way I have books, music and I can Skype." His eyes glint with humor and I roll mine in return.

"That's cheating. And p.s., you wouldn't have Wi-Fi on this island."

"You need to specify that kind of information before you ask the question," he teases and I laugh.

"I didn't even ask the question."

"Touché. What about you? Barring no Wi-Fi in this version, what would you take?"

"My collection of Jane Austen books."

"What? Not a vampire book, or one with a rich CEO?" He opens his eyes wide in a mockingly shocked expression.

"Har har har. No, smart-ass, and it's witch books I'm into. But if I was stranded on an island I wouldn't bring them." My laughter dies and I narrow an eye at him. This is my chance to discover everything I ever wanted to know about him. I can't possibly waste it on stupid trivia type questions. But at the same time, if he's opening up I don't want to scare him off. *Keep it simple, don't get too deep.* I grow silent for a minute as I try to think of something . . . anything. "Did you grow up in the city?" I finally ask. He lifts his head so our eyes lock.

"I did. Born and raised."

"Where in the city?"

"Upper east. I moved downtown for college, and then when I was in school getting my doctorate, I purchased my brownstone in Murray Hill."

"How do you like living there?"

"It's a bit young for my taste," he says before he realizes. "I mean—"

"It's fine. I have to agree. I can't imagine a . . . Wait. How old are you, anyway? Is it weird I don't know this about you?" My hearts races as I realize just how much I don't know and how much I'm dying to find out.

"I'm thirty-four." *Ten years older than me. How am I just finding this out?* But I guess in the grand scheme of things his age is the least of our problems.

"A bit old to be going to the bars every night."

"Way too old to be doing that." He chuckles.

"Did you ever? Like in college, were you a big partier?"

"I was."

"What made you stop?"

"When Sloane died, I stopped." He leaves it at that, and I swallow at the revelation. I want to ask more, but I don't dare. If he wanted to divulge, he would, and I know better than most never to push someone who's not ready to open up. We watch the fire, neither of us speaking. Just enjoying the silence—a comfortable silence as if we've known each other our whole lives. The seconds pass, become minutes, and soon our glasses are empty. The wood has sizzled to small crackling embers.

"I'm not a big drinker," I say finally. His gaze sweeps over me and it's as if he's looking at me for the first time.

"You could have fooled me," he says as he raises an eyebrow in challenge. A genuine smile lines his face and he lets out a sigh and relaxes into the couch.

"Believe it or not, I'm really not. With the way my mom is, I never know when I need to be on call. So typically, I stay sober. Since Richard's death, I've been indulging far more than normal."

"That's common. Everyone grieves in their own way." I pucker my lips at him and then smirk.

"Are you doctoring me right now?" His eyes widen and then he lets out a laugh.

"Oops. Sometimes I just can't turn it off."

"It's okay. It's one of the things I like about you."

"And what are the other things?"

Preston sets his glass down and stands. He stalks over to me and sweeps my body into his arms, burying his lips in my neck and tickling the sensitive skin with his jaw.

"Again?" I giggle as he places me on the bed and starts to pull my robe off.

"If this is all I have, I plan to savior every second. I don't want to waste a minute of our time together. I don't want to waste a second. "

And for the third time since we've been alone together at Castle Hill, he ravishes me fully and completely.

chapter thirty-two

EVE

THE SMELL WAS EVERYWHERE. I COULDN'T ESCAPE IT. I looked down to see my hands were shaking so badly as the thick crimson flowed through my small fingers. It clung and coated the surface. A high-pitched scream echoed through the room. I looked for the sound but then realized it came from me.

Jolting forward, I clasp at my chest. My eyes won't adjust to the darkness and I'm frantic to see. A wrecked sob tears through as I search for where I am. Tears pour from my eyes and through the dark haze of the night, light flitters in.

"*Shh.*" Searching hands find me. They pull me forward and into his warm body. "I've got you. You're okay."

"I'm not. I'm not okay," I cry out, pulling my hands from his and touching all over my body, trying to find the origin of the blood.

"What are you looking for?" Ragged breaths leave my lungs. Preston holds me and rocks me in his arms. As much as I try to pull away, he holds me tighter. "There's nothing on you."

"I need to wipe it off," I whisper in defeat.

"There's nothing there." He lifts me his lap, and I curl into him. My whole body goes limp. I allow him to soothe me.

Slowly, my pulse regulates and I take smaller pulls of oxygen. When I'm finally breathing normally, he lifts my jaw to look at him. His brows are knitted, and he looks sad as one finger reaches out and swipes at a tear that runs down my cheeks.

"What can I do?" he implores.

"Just hold me."

"I can do that." And he does. He holds me. He holds me until all the tears drain from my eyes. Until every last bit of panic has passed. His heart beats against my back and eventually it slows to a soft lull. Looking up, I see he's fallen asleep with me in his arms. My heart is full. He takes care of me. Never have I felt so safe. Cared for. In his embrace the world stills, and it's just him and me and nothing else matters.

When I'm sure he's fully asleep, I creep out of bed, moving quietly to not wake him. I grab my purse and pull out my notebook. Perching at the end of the bed, I sit and stare. Every move, every breath I take note of—recording them in my heart and memory to always cherish. The feeling pulsing through me right now for this man is so concrete and absolute. I'm falling for him, and every moment I spend with him, my emotions become more complicated. Because this isn't just sex. This isn't something I can get out of my system.

There is no removing Preston Montgomery from my system. He's embedded so deeply inside me I fear I have no hope but to one day fall in love with this man.

———•———

Last night I sat and watched Preston sleep, and somewhere between the inhale and exhale of his breath he pulled me against him and I drifted off to sleep. As my eyes flutter open, he looks across the bed at me. He's studying me.

"What?"

"I'm watching you."

"Creepy much," I groan, but in my head I'm laughing. *Pot, meet kettle.* "Stop looking at me. I probably look like a mess."

"You know what makes you so beautiful? That you don't know how beautiful you are."

"I do not look beautiful right now."

"Baby, no matter what you do, you could never not be beautiful."

My eyes widen, first at his statement, then at the moniker. Both make me melt in equal measure. Warmth spreads across my cheeks.

"Thanks."

"Come here." His voice is husky. It makes me want to run to him, but first I have to brush my teeth. No matter how much I want him right now, making myself presentable is my number one priority. I move to leave the bed and two firm arms bracket themselves around my waist.

"Hey."

"Where do you think you're going?" Preston's arms trail up from behind as his face buries in my neck. His breath fans my skin, and the feeling is incredible. It causes goose bumps to prickle my skin.

Soft kisses first, and then his tongue licks with abandon.

When he circles the back of my neck, my whole body shivers. As much as I need to get up from the bed, this man renders me completely useless as he drops kisses down the length of my spine.

Before I know what's happening, I'm flipped over to my back and Preston is hovering over me. He leans down and plants a series of kisses over my abdomen. His tongue traces a path down to my belly button, then to my pelvis . . . and across my hipbone.

Small kisses.

Soft nips.

"What is it about your skin?" he mutters into my body.

All of a sudden, Preston lifts my legs to rest over his shoulders. He opens my body to him. His fingers press deep inside me in tempo with his masterful tongue. My breathing becomes erratic.

I feel myself come apart as he feasts upon me.

"That's it, baby," he mumbles against my body as I become lost in my pleasure and explode.

When I come down from my high, he's just staring at me.

"What about you?" My lip lifts into a small smile.

"That was for me." A deliciously sexy smirk spreads against his face. Who is this man? He's so different from the Preston I was falling for before. Lord, am I in trouble. *Screwed, really*. Because heaven knows I was not prepared to guard my heart against this Preston. This Preston owns me already and it's only been one day.

Together we shower. This time we're in and out. No distractions. Preston was determined to not let me have my way with him, claiming I needed breakfast.

After breakfast of our favorite—waffles—we find ourselves sitting in Adirondack chairs on the large sprawling lawn that appears to cascade down into the sea. The view is awe-inspiring, as we have a panoramic view of the ocean below crashing upon the beach.

"Are you cold?" Preston inquiries from beside me. My arms are pulled tightly around me, but inside my coat I'm not cold.

Just comfortable. It's been so long since I felt this peaceful that even if it were the dead of winter, I wouldn't move.

"I'm perfect." He leans across the space separating our chairs and captures my lips. His are soft as they gently nudge my lips to part. I tremble in his mouth. It might only be one kiss, but I am lost, and if this is what lost feels like, I never want to be found.

Our faces pull apart and our eyes lock.

In his gaze I see the possibility of *more*, and the thought scares me. How am I supposed to let him go? How can I let someone go who makes me feel so much?

He makes me feel beautiful. He makes me feel special. He makes me feel free.

"You happy?" he asks.

"Beyond." I smile back.

"Good, because this is only the beginning. I have a whole day planned for us." He jumps up and reaches his hands out toward me. As I stretch mine out to him, a part of me wants to pull back. Freeze time. Once I get up, the end has started. Like tiny sand grains slowly spilling. The end is near.

I decide that I won't dwell on what the future brings. Instead, I plaster on the biggest smile in the world and vow that Preston will never see my inner thoughts. We walk in the direction of the main building, but instead of going inside, he asks for the keys to his car. Once inside, he grabs my hand in his and squeezes lightly.

"Since we never left the cottage last night, I thought it would be nice to see Newport."

"I would have been fine staying inside." I bat my eyelids and he laughs.

"I'm sure you would have."

"So, what's there to do in Newport?"

"Well, typically it's more of a beach town, but I figured we would do a bit of sightseeing. Then we can grab lunch."

"Sounds like a great plan."

A few minutes later we pull into the quaint seaside town. Historic buildings line the streets and I can see how lovely it would be in the summer. Although the weather is losing much of its chill, it will still be months before Newport is in its full glory. Preston pulls the car into a parking spot, and then like a perfect gentleman, comes around to my side to help me out. My hair whips against my face as the ocean breeze picks up.

I pull my light coat tighter around me as he rests an arm over my shoulder, bundling me to him. His heat radiates through the material, warming me instantly.

With each store we pass, we peek inside, looking over the cute accessories and knick-knacks Newport has to offer.

Removing Preston's arm from around me, I make my way to the opposite wall of a shop we're investigating. My fingertips trail over glass apothecary jars on the shelf. I pick one up and study the image. When my eyes roam the room, I see Preston walk toward the register. He has something in his hand but I can't see what it is. The sales woman is quick to wrap it, and charges his card by the time I make it over to him. When he turns around, the beginning of a smile tips the corner of his mouth when he sees me. Exiting the store, Preston grabs my hand and I turn towards him.

"There's a great little lunch restaurant down the block. Are you hungry yet?" he asks.

"I can always eat."

Along the way we pop into a few more stores to shop, and all the while Preston continues to hold my hand—as if we're couple on a romantic trip, and not a doctor and his patient stealing a moment in time. The caress of his soft fingers makes me want to believe the lie.

Once we cross the street, I spot the restaurant, but before we step in I notice that right next door is a quaint little bookstore. *It's perfect.* The outside of the building has a whimsical look to it. Painted mushrooms decorate the plate glass windows and giant flowers accent the front façade.

"I need to go in there. There's a book I'm dying to get." I announce and together we walk into Book Time. Stepping inside, I'm transported into a faraway world. It's a darling little store with Alice in Wonderland themed décor. It even has little tables for tea service. Pulling my hand from Preston's, I head straight to the section that houses the Young Adult new releases. He follows a step behind. As I step forward to grab the book I came to purchase, so does Preston. My hand brushes against his, sending an electric shock through my body.

His touch is intoxicating, enticing . . . primal.

His dazzling blue eyes meet mine, showing me he's feeling the same connection and thinking the same thoughts as me. That I want to put my hand back on his. Touch him again. Relive that feeling when our hands and body connected. But we're in a bookstore, so I calm my growing hunger by looking at the stack of books in front of us.

"I didn't know you read YA."

"YA?"

"Young Adult. Obviously. I didn't know you read young adult books."

He laughs at my silly comment. "I don't, I just wanted to see the cover, I didn't know you read YA?" He winks.

"They're the best!" I exclaim and a smile lines his face from my excitement. Butterflies fly in my stomach at the sight. That spark when our hands touched has rendered me useless—and apparently melted all the strength I have to keep my distance.

He laughs again. This time it's a boisterous laugh and it warms my heart. "Little old for flying witches, aren't you?"

"Um, no."

"Well, then, I guess we're lucky they still have two copies, or I'd have to fight you for that one." My eyes must bug out, because his face lights up with a huge grin. "Relax, I'm kidding, but if you say they're the best, I'm going to buy one for my sister. She loved the vampire one." His crystal blue eyes shimmer at me as he talks of his sister. He pulls the second copy from the shelf and takes mine from my hand. "Come on."

We head to the front counter and he hands the saleswoman our books. She smiles at us.

"Will that be all, sir?" she asks as she scans the two copies.

"Yes."

"That will be twenty ninety-nine."

I reach for my purse.

"Nope. My treat."

My whole body turns to him, my eyes wide. "You can't buy me a book."

"Sure I can."

"But—"

He looks so serious—insistent. So I agree.

"Okay." I nod.

He pays and we walk to the exit door.

We arrive at the restaurant sometime later. It's a darling little bistro, with only a few tables inside. Most are outside overlooking the boats in the marina. After the hostess hand us our menus, I lean over and smile at him.

"So, what do you want?" I ask and a grin curls up the side of his face at my comment. "For lunch, Preston." He winks this time and I just sigh. "Can't take you anywhere, can I?"

"Fine, fine. I'll have the tuna. What about you?"

"Caesar salad."

"Well, that's an interesting choice," he says and I tip my eyebrow at him.

"Meaning . . ."

"Well, every time we eat, you manage to order the item with the most sugar or calories on the menu. I assumed you would get something a bit crazier than a salad."

"Hey. I eat stuff other than junk," I whine and his smile broadens. "I do." He lets out a laugh and I pin him with my eyes "I do."

"Okay, then. What's your favorite food?" I fold my arms across my chest and let out a dramatic huff.

"Fine, you're right." His lips part into a big grin at my response.

"Not everything you like is junk. You do like me." He smirks and I shake my head, but I can't hide the giant grin lining my face. This Preston is playful, and a part of me wishes we could live in this fake world forever. Unfortunately, I know we're on borrowed time.

"I do like you." I nod in agreement.

"I like you too, probably more than I should. But when I'm with you, everything fits together. Everything makes sense." We both grow quiet.

"So, you obviously have been to Newport before. Do you come here a lot?" I say, essentially changing the subject.

"Not anymore. Growing up in the city, my family had a house in the Hamptons where we spent our summers, but when I was older, my friends and I from high school spent a week in the summer here."

"So, you travel a lot?"

"Honestly, not so much. Between my volunteer hours at the hospital and the private practice—"

"Wait, you volunteer there?"

"Oh, yeah. I though you knew that. I do a few hours a week volunteering with patients." I sense there is more to the story than he is letting on but I don't pry. "What about you? Did you travel?"

"No, never."

"Because of your mom?"

"Yeah." He nods and it's comforting to realize this man knows me and understands. "I always wanted to travel, but Mom always came down with something right before we were scheduled to go. As amazing as Richard was, his company was just taking off, so I never traveled. By the time I got to college, I concentrated on studying and graduating. So really, the only place I have ever been is nowhere."

"Well, now you've been to Newport, Rhode Island."

"And it's my favorite." I don't say that any place with Preston would be my favorite, but from the way his trained eyes assess me, I think he knows.

"Where would you like to go? If you could go anywhere in the world, where would it be?" *With you? Anywhere.*

"I love history and architecture, so I'd have to say anywhere in Europe. Being a huge Jane Austin fan, I would love to go to England."

"You would love it."

"You've been?"

"When I was in college I was a theater major. So me and

. . ." He pauses and swallows. "Sloane and I went to see the Globe Theater."

"Wow. That must have been amazing."

"It really was." He looks as if he's lost in a dream or a memory. With a shake of his head, he rights himself at the very same moment the waitress appears and takes our order.

A little less than thirty minutes later, my plate is empty. After Preston pays the bill, he cocks his head to the right.

"Now, what do you want to do?"

"Go back to the hotel?"

"Do you want to see the beach?"

"No."

"The lighthouse?"

"No."

"What do you want, Eve?" I tremble at the way he says my name.

"You. Only you." He looks down, his chest rising and falling with his rapid intake of breaths.

"You have me," he whispers so low I can barely hear him. *For now.*

———·———•———·———

When I look at him, I lose all reason.

I want him to devour me.

Body, mind, and soul.

And that's exactly what he does the moment we enter our cottage.

My body quivers as I wait. The anticipation of his touch is almost too much for me to bear.

I'm intoxicated with desire. I rip off my clothes and stand naked before Preston. Taking slow steps, I make my way to him and run my hands down the soft T-shirt covering his chest. When I make it to the hem, I lift it to expose his torso, and then pull at his belt, I work to free him, but he stops my hand.

"Patience."

"I can't. I need you," I beg, but he shakes his head at me.

"I want to take it slow. I want to savor every touch, every taste, every feel." My brain wants to scream *No, don't savor it*, because I know what that would mean, but I don't say anything. My eyes will betray me. So I stand and stare and watch as Preston's eyes sweep the length of me.

His lips trail down my torso. When he reaches my breast, he captures my erect nipple into his mouth and nips and tugs at the peak with desire. Pulling away, he moves further down my body as my hands pull at his unruly hair.

I need his lips. I need his mouth on mine.

Sensing my urgency, he moves back up my body and kisses me. As our tongues tease one another, his hands continue to explore, parting my swollen flesh and sliding inside. I gasp at the sensation, panting heavily as his fingers pump in and out of me. When he pushes his digits up, my inner walls clench around him. My head thrashes back and forth as I reach my climax. Preston continues his ministrations until my orgasm crests and peaks, and then he removes his fingers and pushes me down onto the bed. I watch through hooded eyes as he undresses then crawls up my body and starts to tease my entrance with his hard length.

"God," he groans out as he inches himself in. "I want to burrow myself inside you. I want to be so deep, I don't know where you end and I begin." His movements are excruciatingly slow. My own body is so desperate for more that I push my center up to fully impale him inside my still quivering body.

Wanting more.

Needing more.

"Fuck." He pulls out. "So fucking good." He slams back in.

He keeps up the pace until once again we are both chasing the high. With a final thrust of his hips he plunges inside me and I welcome the bliss, falling over into an endless abyss of pleasure. Every muscle clenches around him until his body has no choice but to follow me.

Together, we lay panting on the bed. My blonde hair fans over his chest as our breathing regulates.

The light seeps in through the windows, reminding me that it's still daytime and we will be returning to reality tomorrow.

"Anything else planned for the day? Or can I keep taking advantage of you?" I say into his chest as I alternate between speaking and kissing him.

"As much as I would love to do this all day, I do want to take you to the lighthouse. Then we can have dinner."

"Fine." I groan, kissing further down his torso. Just as I begin to run my tongue down the carved V of his pelvis, he pulls me up. Bracketing his arms around me, he moves his mouth to mine.

"Later. Come on, let's get dressed," he says and I give him a playful smirk. "Nope, none of that. You're showering alone or we'll never leave. Actually, forget the shower. I like the idea of you . . . dirty." He grins.

Burnt orange streaks the sky as the sun starts to set for the day. It casts a soft shimmer across the translucent blue of the water. With each pass of the wind, hints of pink burst through the clouds. It's one of the most beautiful sights I have ever seen, and witnessing it with Preston makes it even more meaningful.

Preston's gaze drifts to the horizon and his hand lightly

squeezes mine. I wonder if he feels what I'm feeling. The wind teases my hair, making it flutter across my face as we climb closer to the lighthouse.

Preston ventures closer and closer, the path giving way to nature. When my foot slips, he turns around and reaches for my hand to help me. As our hands meet he smiles down at me. It's earth-shattering.

God, he's beautiful. *But I can't think these thoughts.*

If only we were two different people. If only this was allowed. Instead, it will fade into a memory of a once perfect time. It will become a chapter in a closed book.

"You coming?" He laughs and I realize I was caught gawking at him.

"Um, yeah. Can we go inside?"

"No, unfortunately it's not open to the public."

I feel as if I'm living in a fairy tale as we take a seat at a small picnic table and watch the last bits of sunlight dance against the sky. A shiver runs down my body as the wind picks up. Preston pulls me into him, and runs his hands up and down my back to warm me.

We don't speak for the remainder of the time we sit there. I know I can't voice any words to reflect the emotions choking me. As beautiful as this moment is, as perfect as our time together has been, it's bittersweet.

When we arrive back at the cottage, I see that Preston has had a candlelight dinner prepared. Tiny teas lights flicker against the walls, and a bottle of champagne is waiting. Letting go of my hand, he walks over and pops open the bottle, then pours it into two waiting flutes. He employs careful precision to not spill, then hands me a glass.

"To the most perfect weekend in my life," he says and tears

pool in my eyes. "Don't cry." My chin trembles and I force my lips to part in a smile.

"I'm not." He brushes his finger across my cheek and wipes away the moisture.

"Would it be better for us to talk about it?" His eyes narrow with concern and I shake my head adamantly.

"No." I tilt my head into his hand and stare up into his cerulean eyes. The ones that have hypnotized me in the past, and I open my heart and allow them to put me under their trance once again. In that moment, I let myself fade into the fairy tale story you read with a happily ever after.

I wasn't the patient and he wasn't the doctor. We were merely two people falling in love.

"Please, let's just enjoy this time together." He sets his glass on the table and lifts mine from my hands. He wraps his arms around me. I inhale his scent, and immerse myself in the comfort he brings me. With one whisper of a single kiss against my forehead, he pulls back and leads me to the table, and although I want to cry, I vow to enjoy every moment of this last night together.

After dinner, he draws me toward him. Our mouths collide. We tell each other everything we can share with each sweep of our tongue.

This kiss makes me believe my lie. His lips tell a tale of their own, and as our bodies join, I let myself go. I let myself become immersed in the imaginary pages of what we could have been.

chapter thirty-three

EVE

Bittersweet. That's what this is. As we both pack our belongings, sadness hovers in the air. It lingers and bathes us. It's all-encompassing and tangible. Choking us as the seconds pass.

My own heart breaks a million times before we even leave the room. As I step outside, I turn back one final time to memorize each second we spent here together.

If I could push reset, I would, but I can't. So I hold my head high and walk with Preston to our car.

The drive is silent. Neither of us dare speak. I watch out the window as the city comes into view. I want to ask if there's a chance for us. Not now, but maybe in the future. He cares for me. I know it. It's in every gesture. Every look. Every touch. But love me, or even care about me enough to risk his future? Well, that's a question I don't know the answer to. A question I'm not willing to risk. *No, I won't ask.* I'll bite my lip and not beg him to give me a chance.

"Eve," he says, his head turning slightly to see my eyes. "I bought you something." He reaches for the bag on the back seat and hands it to me.

"Should I open it now?"

"No," he says, but nothing more. He doesn't need to. The implication is there, laced behind the pain etched in his voice. It's a parting gift. There is no future here. These will be the last minutes spent in the bubble we created.

I will leave it as it was meant to be.

A stolen moment.

One chapter of a book.

My whole body hurts from the weight of emotion hanging above us. The tension is so high I might suffocate.

Through the windshield, I see my apartment building. It looms in the distance, but as the seconds pass, the space separating the car from my home disintegrates until we are back where we started two days ago, his Range Rover parked in front of my building.

Two days.

A lifetime.

Everything between us has changed, yet it all stays the same.

This is it. This is the end. I want to beg and plead. Tell him to never leave me. Tell him to risk it all for me.

Tell him I'm falling in love with him. That he is everything I've ever hoped and dreamed about. Instead, as a lone tear drips down my face . . .

I say good-bye. I want to crumble to my feet, but instead, I square my shoulders and hold my head high. Plenty of time later to fall apart. I will not let him see how badly I hurt. I know he's hurting, too, but unfortunately, the timing isn't right for us.

———————•———————

Later that night, I lie in bed with his box in my hand. I need to open it, but do I dare? Once I do, it's official. Mustering all the strength left in my body, I tear away at the paper. There is a note inside the box.

> *Eve, I want you to have this. It will catch your nightmares and help you to the other side.*
> *Preston*

It's a tiny gold dream catcher necklace, and with all that I have left, I fall to pieces on my bed. Sometime later, I hear a knock on my door, but I don't answer.

"Eve?" *Silence.* "Sweetie?" Sydney pops her head in through the crack of the door. I don't bother to answer or even move from where I'm submerged under the heavy blanket. "Are you okay?" When I still don't answer, the door creaks and her feet pad against the floor. The bed dips as she sits at the foot. "You're worrying me. You've been in here since you came back from your trip. Do you want to talk about it?"

I lift the blanket and look into her deep brown eyes. "Not much to tell," I say under my breath and I hope she takes the hint . . . I don't want to tell.

Sometimes the most amazing moments are the ones we can't talk about.

That's how it felt every time Preston was near.

His proximity alone lit me on fire, and I won't tell her that. I want to keep the memory to myself. I don't want to share it with anyone.

"I can't help you if I don't know what happened."

"Nothing happened, Syd. It was amazing. It was perfect. It was the best two days of my life. But that's all it was. That's all it will ever be—two days. Two fucking days is all I get." Anger and sadness bleed from my words. "Want to know how I am?

I'm a mess."

"You're not a mess."

"I promise you, I am." Her eyes meet mine and the air is tense. I plaster on a fake smile and gleam up at her.

"This isn't like you. Sure, you've had a tough go the last couple of months, but normally you're the strongest person I know. Even after Richard, you managed to land one of the largest accounts the firm has ever seen. That's not a small feat. If you can do that, you can get through a little breakup."

"It's not even a breakup." I pout.

"It is."

"How can we call it a breakup when he was never mine to break up from?"

"A break then. After the shit you've been through, you'll get through this break.

"I know you're right. I just wonder how much a person can take. Like my mom. What was the final straw for her?"

"Have you ever thought to ask her?" I narrow my eyes at Sydney.

"Every day. Every time I'm there I try to ask her questions but she's too sick to answer anything. To be honest, I don't even think she realizes her behavior isn't normal."

"Maybe she needs a therapist. Know anyone?" she jokes and I shoot her the look of death. "Too soon?"

I grimace at her. "Yeah. I think so." She gives me big puppy dog eyes and I can't help but laugh. "Okay, I'm going to hop in the shower. Do you want to go out for dinner or order in?"

"I say we get Chinese and get drunk off food. A little MSG will make you feel better."

"Syd, I'm pretty sure that statement is actually reversed. I think they have banned MSG for being really bad for you."

"Tomato, tomaaatoe." I snort at that and she giggles.

Once dressed after my shower, I follow the smell of Chinese permeating the air. It leads me to the living room, where little white cartons are sitting on the coffee table.

"Wine?," Sydney screams through the walls of the kitchen.

"Sure." A few minutes later she comes out with two glasses filled to the rim with Pinot Grigio. I hope and pray this night with her with help drown my misery. Somehow I doubt anything will, but I smile anyway and try to forget.

chapter thirty-four

EVE

WEEKS PASS SLOWLY WHEN YOU'RE SAD. THEY DON'T EBB and flow like a passing tide. Rather, they are like quicksand, and the harder you attempt to pull away, the more stuck you become.

It's been one month since my trip with Preston and I've sworn to Sydney I'll get out of my funk, but really I'm learning to fake it better. By Friday after work I can no longer pretend to smile. I have nothing left in me.

I throw myself into work and organizing Richard's estate. Today I've decide to take up the task of cleaning out his closet.

Walking into Richard's apartment wakes up all sorts of feelings. Sadness is laced with smiles. There were some great times here. There were also some not so great times, but the good outweigh the bad. I'm overcome with emotion. I blink away moisture, and the room comes into focus. It's just like the last time. Except it's different now . . . empty. A picture on the console table pops out at me. It's the same picture I have in my apartment, the one from my graduation. Instantly a smile forms.

Right after Richard died, I had the apartment professionally cleaned. Since the windows haven't been opened in weeks the air is stale; bleach still wafts through the air.

All the furniture has been sold through an estate sale, and all that remains to be done is to go through Richard's personal belongings. With a deep inhale I set off for the master bedroom. Suits still hang in the closet. Shoes are still displayed along the wall. *Goodwill.* Or maybe a charity that helps men get back on their feet. I've heard of a few that train and dress the unemployed for interviews. Richard would like that. Yeah, that's what I'll do. Grabbing my phone, I make a note to look into companies that provide that service, then I set off to do my task.

There's a step stool in the back of the walk-in closet that Richard obviously used to store boxes on the top shelf. For twenty minutes, I rummage. There are bills and receipts in one box. The next box has old pictures. They make me smile as I take a few out and remember the better times. Every muscle starts to ache after two hours of sorting, and by the time I'm ready to give up for the day, I see one more box in the back corner. In order to grab it I have to climb to the highest step of the ladder and lean my whole body up and onto the shelf. My fingers are barely able to reach it, but as I stretch one more inch, I secure it in my hand.

It's marked "Miscellaneous." As I pull the box down and almost have it safely on the floor, it slips and it crashes, turning over on its side.

Papers spread against the hardwood floors.

Just my luck, now I have to go through everything. I hop down to clean up the floor. The first thing that becomes apparent is that some of these papers are actual legal documents. Some are contracts. There's an operator's agreement between my mom and Richard. LLC paperwork. Banking information. With a huff I pull the lid fully off and decide to see what else he has in here. There's a picture of Richard and myself. A few small envelopes, nothing that seems too important. A book. I pick up the book and notice it's a Jane Austen. It looks to match my mom's old collection—the ones that sat in our library growing up. When I lift it to get a better look, a piece of paper falls out. I reach out and turn it over.

My heart stops.

An arctic chill runs up my spine.

Every last bit of oxygen leaves my body.

I'm stuck. My feet heavy like cement.

What the hell is this?

I see crimson.

I crumble to the ground.

I'm desperately gasping for air.

I can't breathe.

I can't stop the memories that flow into my brain.

All at once consuming me with pain.

There was blood on my hands.

Get it off! Get it off!

A rush of broken visions flashes in my mind. Take shape and tell me a story.

My heart races in my ears and I can no longer hear anything.

The vision of me is so clear, and I bite back a sob.

I was small.

So small.

An innocent child.

I sat on the floor, my doll in hand and I gently brushed her hair. In the distance I heard a sound. I wasn't sure what it was, but it was loud, like the fireworks we saw on the Fourth of July. It made my ears hurt and the walls shake. I hugged my doll to me tightly. Where was Mommy? Maybe she knew where the loud bang came from. The sound was scary.

"Mommy?" She didn't answer. My feet pressed against the cold wood floor as I peered out of the playroom. "Mommy?" Where did she go?

Maybe Daddy knew. A smile grew on my face and the fear I felt left my body. He always knew everything. Mommy always said he'd protect us from harm. The house was silent as I padded down the hallway toward the library. He often sat in there for hours.

"Daddy?" My little hands pounded on the door, but he wouldn't answer.

Turning the knob, I peeked my head inside. "Daddy, are you in there? I can't find Mommy," I said as I flung the door open. "Daddy." I couldn't see him. Where was he? The room smelled funny, like he had blown out a candle. What was that smell? I walked in further and from where I stood I could finally see him.

"What are you doing there?" I walked to where I saw my dad.

"What are you looking for on the floor? Did you drop something?"

He was turned to face under the desk. "Daddy?"

My foot slipped out from under me and I fell and hit the floor. My hands hit the wood first, then my stomach.

"Ouch!" I yelped as I brought my hand forward to lift myself back off the floor.

I slipped on something warm.

It was thick against my fingers.

It was all over my dress.

My hands were red.

Why were my hands red?

Everything was red.

Looking around me, I noticed I was sitting in a pool of red liquid. Red spread over the surface of my skin. Was this blood?

Why was I bleeding? I shook my head. My heart rate sped up.

I wasn't bleeding.

It wasn't blood.

It was . . .

"Daddy!" I could barely call out to him.

The blood was flowing from the back of his head.

I tapped at his shoulder and fear spread throughout my body when he didn't answer. "Why aren't you answering me, Daddy. Daddy!" I shook him with all my might, and his head flopped forward. His open eyes stared at me. But he still didn't answer. "Please, Daddy. Answer me."

Why wouldn't he answer?

"No!" I manage to scream. I press my palms against my eyes to force the memory out of my mind. "No. No. No. No." I rock in place.

A knot is lodged in my throat but I can't swallow. I can't breathe. I can't move.

My father.

Dead.

I found him.

It was a suicide.

The blood.

I run my hands down my shirt as I wipe away the memory, but there's no point.

The visions tear at my soul. I'm holding my father's note. His last words. It grows heavy in my hand.

The note that brings it all back. That makes me remember.

A suicide note.

With a shaky hand, I force myself to read his last words.

I'm so sorry, Laura. My intentions were never to harm you. I don't want to bring you pain. I don't want you to be ashamed of what I've done. Sometimes I think this will pass. That I will get through this, and you'll look at me like the husband you were once proud of. But now I know I have failed you too many times. I have failed our family. This is the only way out, the only way I can stop the pain I'm causing you. You were right. Everything you said was right. I failed you. I failed Eve. For that I'm truly and forever sorry. I hope you find the happiness you seek. This is the only way. I can't stand the disappointment I see in your eyes.

Please don't be sad, for I'm not worthy of your tears.

Please forgive me, and what I've done to us.

This is the only way. I know how to make it all better now.

Tell Eve that Daddy will always protect her. Tell her I love her.

My hand shakes. A sob breaks lose. Everything trembles. My body collapses forward. Every tiny shred of remaining strength breaks. What is this? What the hell is this? I have no idea what's going on. No clue, but I can't move. I can't think. The world is shutting down. The walls are closing in. It feels as if I'm drowning. Ice-cold liquid fills my veins as I realize my entire life is a lie. Everything I know is wrong. Nothing makes sense.

Time stops. Everything ceases to be. Lying on the floor, I think of nothing but the betrayal. As the seconds turn to minutes and then hours, I realize I haven't moved from my spot on the floor.

Nothing will ever make sense again, but in truth, it all makes sense. Every vague answer. Every sidestep. All to avoid this. But she won't avoid it any longer. I need to know everything and she will tell me. I have that right. I deserve to know.

My anger fuels my body. I make my way out of Richard's apartment and storm into hers. The hallway is quiet. No doubt she is curled up in her bed, hiding from the world. How nice it must be to hide from everything in your life.

"Mom?" She doesn't answer, and I step further into the room. "Mom. I'm talking to you."

"I'm not well. Can we speak after my nap?"

"No. You will speak to me now!" With that her head rises from her pillow.

"What is this about?" She seems more alert than normal, but when I lift the paper into her line of vision she flinches, and the look in her eye fades as she shrinks back into herself.

"I'm dizzy. Can we talk about this later?"

"No, Mom. I deserve answers. How could you not tell me? How could you keep this from me? How could Richard?"

"I had to. We had to." Her voice is so sad. She's broken.

"I–I don't understand."

"I don't even know where to start. I'm not sure I have the energy to tell it."

"Please, Mom," I plead and she finally relents.

"You were so young. We lived a good life. Your-your father was a good man. It was my fault. Everything is my fault." She starts to sob uncontrollably. I don't know how to help her. Her tears break out like a river. Never stopping. Always flowing.

"I don't understand."

"I said things. Bad things," she whispers.

"Mom, please. I think you owe it to me to tell me the full

story. What happened? And no more saying you're sick. No more hiding. No more lying."

"I told him he was a loser. That he wasn't good enough for us. That if he couldn't . . . he couldn't provide for us we were better off without him."

"But how is that your fault?" She looks down.

"What else did you say, Mom?"

"I-I . . . Don't make me say it."

"Please."

"I told him we'd be better off if he was dead. I didn't mean it. Oh, God. Oh, God. It's entirely my fault. Everything is my fault." I crawl into bed with her. Hold her in my arms. Tears seep through my blouse. They're coming from my own eyes. I cry and I cry until I have no tears left to shed. When they finally dry, I turn to her.

"But why? Why did you lie to me?"

"I can't."

"You have to, Mom. For the first time since Dad died, put me first. I need to know everything. Tell me everything."

I wait for her to wipe her own tears and then she looks at me. There is so much sadness. So much remorse. "When we found you—"

"We?"

"Yes, Richard came over to discuss finances with your father. You see, we were bankrupt. Your father was always a dreamer. One scheme after the other, each one riskier than the last. The bigger the risk—"

"The bigger the reward." I nod.

"I had no idea we were financially destroyed until I overheard him begging Richard to come over and help him. I stormed into the room after he hung up the phone and he came clean. We had lost everything. When I found out, I flew off the handle, screaming and yelling at him.

The last investment was a property in South America. The developer was supposed to build a hotel. He was assured it was a sure thing. When he first told me about his new project, I begged him not to do it, but the return on the investment was supposed to be incredible. He couldn't say no.

I'm so ashamed of myself. It's my fault he did it. I didn't hear the gunshot. I left you in the house with him. I needed air. I threatened to leave him, to take you. I-I . . ." She starts to tremble. "I didn't . . ."

"Please, Mom," I plead to hear the rest. To know about those fateful minutes before my dad took his own life.

"When I pulled into the driveway, Richard was outside knocking. No one was home, he said. But I knew that wasn't true. I left you with your dad. He was out of his mind when I left but I didn't think. I didn't. You were in your room watching a TV show, playing with a doll. I thought you'd be okay. I thought he would be okay. Oh, God . . . He could have hurt you. What kind of a mother leaves her child?" She swipes at her tears again.

"When Richard said that, I knew something was wrong. The TV was still playing when we walked through the house, but you weren't there. We found you, and you were covered in blood, lying on him. I don't know how long you were like that. B-but you wouldn't speak. You wouldn't cry. You were catatonic."

"But why, if I found him, why did you tell me it was an accident? What are you leaving out? What are you not telling me?"

"When we found you that way, we weren't thinking straight, or at least I wasn't. Richard brought us to my room. He took care of us. Th-then he called the cops. He didn't tell me he took the note until much later. He knew we were in financial ruin, and with your father's life insurance policy—although there was a stipulation allowing payout—he didn't want to risk it. So, he took the note, and he said it was an accident. When you finally came out of your trance and started to speak again, it was as if you forgot. So we never told you."

"But there was no accident."

"No."

"And Dad killed himself."

"Because of me," she says through sobs. I'm numb. I stand and walk toward the door. "You're leaving me?"

The walls are closing in. I have to leave. I can't stay here. I need to get out. Get far from this hell I've been thrust in. I know I will break, but not in front of her.

"But I need you—" she cries out. I'm already out the door.

It's too much.

My heart crashes in my chest.

Too much information.

It as if like my heart has been ripped out.

Too many lies.

I'm not okay.

My shoulders constrict. All my muscles have become corded. I place my hand on my shoulder blades and massage.

Needles tingle down my arm.

I move about uncomfortably.

The panic is starting. Spreading through my veins like a poisonous venom suffocating me.

It's all in your head.

It's all in your head.

You can control your own fear.

Own it.

Inhale.

Exhale.

In. Out.

In. Out.

My chest is still pounding.

The truth has broken me.

I don't know how long I've been walking or how far my feet have carried me. I fall to the ground. The tears come heavier now. My broken soul bleeds out all over the streets of New York. I sob for everything I thought I knew. I sob for my dad, who felt so desperate that he had no other choice. I sob for the pain and guilt my mother carried inside her, and I cry for a decision Richard shouldn't have had to make.

From a haze, I lift my phone and reach out for help. For someone to help me. My fingers do the dialing. It rings and rings, but no one answers, and all I can do is sob harder. But then I hear a voice coming through the earpiece.

"Eve?"

But the sobs don't stop. They only increase in tempo at the sound of the voice on the other side of the phone. "Shh. Please don't cry. Are you hurt?" Still no words come out, only endless whimpers. "Please." He pauses a beat. His breathing pulls me out of my haze. "Where are you?"

"I don't know where I am," I finally say. My voice is raspy from the strain.

"Are you home?"

"No."

"Are you out?"

"Street."

"Okay, you're doing really well. Tell me the street. What

street are you on?"

"I don't know."

"Can you look up? Can you see anything?"

"Thirty Seventh."

"Okay, do you know the avenue?"

"Lexington. I have to go."

"Please, stay on the—" Without another word, I drop the call. I break. I fear I will pass out from the racing of my heart. Slumping down on the stoop of the apartment building, I let it all out.

It hammers to the point of pain as my small hand touches the ice-cold pavement.

A light sheen of sweat collects down my back. In the distance, through my fog, I hear my name.

There he is. His gaze sears mine.

"What are you doing here?" I mutter out, drained and hollow.

"I needed to make sure you're okay."

"So you found me?"

"Of course, I found you."

"Are you here as my doctor or as my friend?"

"What do you need me to be?"

"Everything. I need you to be everything."

"Then that's what I'll be." My shoulders shake on a sob. "I'll be anything you need."

"Please hold me," I plead. He nods and sits down on the stoop beside me. "Don't let me go."

"Never." He pulls me closer into his embrace. Cradles me. My body wracks with another waves of sobs. They won't stop. They just keep coming.

"What happened? What's going on?"

"I-I can't. It's too much." He tilts my chin up, locking our eyes together.

"Please."

"It wasn't an accident."

"What wasn't an accident? I don't understand."

"My dad . . . Not an accident." With that, I slump forward, laying my head against his legs. He traces soft circles on my back. They comfort. They soothe.

"Breathe. Inhale. One, two, three. Exhale. One, two three." The air once restricted, flows back. He must feel it as he waits, trailing circles until I calm. "What do you mean it wasn't an accident?"

"I-I found a letter. He did it."

"Did what? What did he do?"

"He took his own life," I say. "He lost everything and took his own life. He left us on purpose. He left me on purpose," I cry. "Why am I never enough?"

Preston holds me. He holds my trembling body against his until I can't cry anymore. Until no sobs leave my body. Until I'm numb.

"Please don't abandon me," I whisper.

"Shh. Shh. I have you."

"Please don't leave me," I cry out again. This time I raise my head to meet his stare. I have said so much more than words can say, but he understands every word.

"Never." He stands and lifts me to my feet, taking on my weight.

"Where are we going?"

"I'm taking you home." With slow, steady steps, Preston guides me down Lexington until we get to Thirty-Fifth. I expect him to keep going, but instead he turns down the block and up to his brownstone where he fishes for his keys.

"I thought . . ."

"I didn't want to leave you. I needed to make sure you were okay. So I brought you to my place."

"Thank you, Preston."

Together we walk into his apartment. He takes my coat and hangs it by the front door, then leads me to the living room.

"Tell me what happened?"

"It's so hard to say. To understand." He nods and takes my hand in his, squeezing with reassurance.

"I was at Richard's apartment, cleaning out his closet and I found a box. Inside were all types of personal belongings. The papers from my mother's investment, the deed to the apartment that the company bought for us in the building. Then there was a book. A Jane Austen book. When I grabbed it, a letter fell out." All the words dry up. They feel like chalk.

In, out. In, out.

"I got you."

"He said he was sorry. He said my mom was right about him." I take gulps of air. "Mom t-told him we were better off without him. He had lost everything, and she told him that." He nods in understanding. "How could she say that? How could she tell him we were better off with him dead? It's her fault."

"I know you're angry right now. And it's understandable for you to blame your mother. But your father was obviously going through something very emotional and not thinking rationally. He felt he had no other way out besides taking his own life. As much as you want to blame your mother, you can't. From what you've told me about her, it's obvious she blames herself enough. You need to forgive her."

"And him? How do I forgive him? How do I forgive the fact

he didn't love me enough to stay?"

"You have to know it in your heart, that he truly felt he had no other option. He was in pain. Forgive him and love him despite his actions."

"I don't know if I can."

"You can. And you will. You're an amazing person, and if anyone can forgive, it's you."

"How do you know that?"

"Because I believe in you."

And again he says the words. The words I'm so desperate to hear. The words that I need to hear.

"It will be the salve for your heartbreak. Forgive her. Forgive him."

"You speak as if you know."

"I do." I quirk my eyebrow up at him.

"No, this is about your loss. I don't want to make it about mine."

"Or you just don't trust me with that part of yourself."

"I do." He lets out an exhale. "I told you when I was in college I had a girlfriend. We'd dated since high school. She was amazing, but there was another side to her, as well. I know she suffered from bipolar disorder now, but at the time, well, obviously I didn't know. She was reckless and fun, but when she was off, it was bad . . ." His voice trails off. "She committed suicide our sophomore year."

"I'm so sorry. Is that why?"

"Is that why I became a psychologist? Yes. I never saw the signs. If I only knew, I could have helped her get through her nightmares." My eyes grow wide at his choice of words. My heart beats frantically in my chest.

"Nightmares?" I whisper to myself, looking up at him,

letting the piece of the puzzle fit together.

"Oh, my God. All this time you've been so scared that what I had was transference, were you with me because . . . Am I a replacement? Am I some way for you to right your wrongs?"

Preston's self-restraint snaps. He leans forward and cups my face, and before I know what's happening, I find myself kissed with abandon.

When we pull apart, his ragged breath tickles my lips.

"How can you doubt me? How can you imagine this is anything other than what it is?"

"And what is it? What is it you feel for me?"

"Everything. I feel everything for you. You're all I think about. You're all I dream of. Every second I'm not with you is a second too long. Don't you think this is killing me? Don't you think I'm hurting, too?" And with that, our mouths collide and my lips part again.

Tasting each other's mouths, savoring each swipe of the tongue.

The feel of his thumb running alone the curve of my jaw makes me open fully to him.

He takes me in an all-consuming kiss.

Strong arms pull me closer. They surround me, engulf me. They pin me to him.

His touch is electrifying.

Every inch of my skin burns to feel more. To experience more of this heady sensation.

Preston eases back until our eyes lock.

The feel of his breath tickles my lips.

Our breathing mingles.

Our mouths barely touch as we inhale each other.

Steam puffs between us.

I curl my arms around his neck as he lifts me into his arms and pads his way to the bedroom.

Once in the room, he eases me onto the bed and lays another deep kiss before lifting off me. His icy blue eyes study me.

He's silent as he removes his clothes . . . and then removes mine.

My body shakes and trembles from the emotion swirling around us.

This is more than sex.

This is more than comfort.

He might not say it, but I see it in his eyes. This is two people falling in love.

When he gets back on top of me, he presses tiny kisses to my neck, trailing them down to the hollow of my chest. His warm hands feel me.

My body arches into his touch. To the feel of his fingers caressing each nipple. To the feel of him stroking them into hard peaks. The tip of his tongue circles them. One, then the other. He licks with careful precision until I'm writhing with pleasure.

I need more. So much more.

"Please," I beg and he answers my pleas by crawling up my body.

A ragged gasp echoes through the room. His fingers are the catalyst for my frantic desire. His hand slips between us, aligning himself with my core.

Urgency fills my blood. The need to feel him inside me is all I can think of.

Greedily, I grab at his hard length, teasing my sensitive skin.

He pushes forward, and when he enters me, he takes my breath away.

My head falls back on the pillow, and my lids flutter shut as he takes me over and over again.

With each push and pull, I lose myself more to the feeling.

"Open your eyes. I want to see you. I want to see all of you."

As they flutter open again, I get lost in a sea of blue. The entire world drifts away.

Through gasps and shudders, the connection is broken. Through trembles and sobs we hold each other. My body clamps around him.

His hands dig deeper into my flesh as his whole body jerks inside me.

Preston leans in and kisses the soft hollow of my neck, soft lips, tantalizing tongue.

"I keep doing this, and I feel like I'm taking advantage of you. I want you, I want you more than you will ever know, but this was supposed to be about more than my pleasure. This was supposed to be about me helping you."

"You did. By being here. By opening up. By telling me your story. Every part of you that you gave me, helped me." He looks away from me. "What is it, Preston?" He won't look at me. "Just tell me."

"Eve."

"No, you don't get to *Eve* me. Not after that. You know it meant something. You know it meant more. Can you see that?"

"We still can't be together. I'm your doctor."

"You're not my doctor anymore."

"Semantics."

"How can you say that after everything? What we have, it means more than that. How can you push me away now? Are you scared? Is that it? Scared of what I could become? That I could be like her? Because of my father."

"I am scared. But not of that. I'm scared of everything else, all that we have done, and everything you've learned, it would be all for nothing if I do this. If we continue down this path. Even though you're no longer my patient, that doesn't mean I won't get in trouble if we're found out. I could still lose my license to practice. I wouldn't be able to volunteer at the hospital anymore. I wouldn't be able to help people. And to be honest after, what we just found out about your father, this is even a stronger case for transference. Between losing Richard and now the repressed memory surfacing of your father, you could be unknowingly projecting your feelings of abandonment to me. You could be looking for an older figure to protect you and until you, know you're not, that it's not transference you're feeling, we can't."

"Please don't let me go. You're all I have."

"But that's the problem. I can't be your crutch. You need to learn to hold yourself up." His words hang in the air. They steal the oxygen like a poisonous gas, slowly killing pieces of me.

"So, now what?" I say, still lying in his arms. Our hearts still beat in tandem.

"We go back to the way it was before."

"And how was that?

"Me wishing every day that I could rewrite history, and that I never walked into the hospital for work that day."

I have wishes too, but mine I won't speak . . . *Say I'm enough. Sacrifice for me. Fight for me. Wait for me.*

chapter thirty-five

PRESTON

HAVEN'T SEEN EVE FOR THREE WEEKS AND I'M MISERABLE. SO fucking miserable that basically all I've done since I told her we couldn't be together is work and be completely anti-social.

I finally successfully pushed her away and severed our professional and personal relationship, and I should feel relief for it, but I don't. Instead, she's all I think about, day and night. I feel all the things I thought I would never feel again. All the things I tried to shut out all these years after I lost Sloane. But this is different. It's so much worse, because the way I feel for her is so much more.

With my glass of scotch in my hand, I flop my body on the couch. Just as I start to relax, my phone vibrates across the coffee table. I know who it will be. *It's going to be Jace.* I peer down and low and behold, I'm right. It's him. Since I haven't been to the last three Sunday night dinners it's no wonder he's calling. Avoiding my family like the plague has obviously not gone unnoticed.

"What," I answer, not even pretending to hide my attitude. I'm not in the mood for a lecture about how Mom wants to see me again. That was last week's call. *I know already.*

"What the hell is up your ass?" *Everything.*

"Nothing."

"Is this about that girl?"

"She's not "that" girl. She's not some girl," I blurt out before I realize what I'm saying. *Shit.* Now he's going to ask questions.

"Okay, spill. It's time to tell me what the hell is going on with you?"

"I met a girl." I let out a deep ragged breath. "It's more than that, though."

"I'm listening,"

"She was my patient." There I said it, the truth is finally out there. No more avoiding the truth. Now all I can do is brace for his response, for his judgment.

"Fuck."

"Yep."

"So now what are you going to do?" There's nothing in his voice but concern, and it make my shoulders drop in relief. It's bad enough losing Eve, but having Jace disapprove would have sucked right now.

"I had to let her go."

"So what's the problem?"

"I want more," I admit on a sigh.

"Yeah, I can see how that could be a problem. I understand, but don't you think some things are worth risking everything for? I don't know who this girl is but if she's the one Logan won't stop talking about, I would say she's worth it." *She is.*

"It's not that easy."

"Why the hell not?"

"Well other then the obvious, her being a former patient and all, there's also the small problem of Sloane."

"What about her?"

"Well maybe I'm suffering from counter-transference?" I whisper. I can still hear Eve's words replaying in my head. Was this because of Sloane? *Was* Eve some sick sort of replacement?

"I think it's time you go back and start speaking to someone again. The fact that you're even considering that, means you aren't over what happened. I think this girl is special. I think that she might be worth risking it for, but you'll never know until you face your issues about Sloane."

He's right. I have to. When Sloan died, it left a stain on my soul, one that years later has still not left me. Sloane called the day she overdosed. I was mad at her, so I sent her to voicemail. She needed me and I didn't answer. I should have seen the signs. I should have answered the phone. That decision still haunts me every day. And although I don't believe my feelings for Eve are misguided, I still need to find out. I need to know, not just for me but for Eve as well.

———————•———————

Therapists really do make the worst patients. Sitting here waiting for Dr. Audrey Kenner to speak is agonizing. I'm ready to bolt out the door, when I finally see her pull out her notebook and turn to me.

"Why are you here? You haven't seen me in quite some time. Did something happen?"

I consider what to say. I can't tell her about Eve. Or at least I can't divulge that she was a patient, so I come as close to the truth as I can without stepping over the edge.

"I met a girl." My teeth gnaw at my lip as I determine how to proceed. "She looks like Sloane and she's been through a lot. She's . . .troubled. I'm afraid my feelings might be misplaced."

"Do you think you are falling for her in an attempt to heal

her, to fix her the way you weren't able to fix Sloane?"

"I'm not sure."

"When did you start having these feelings for her?"

"I always thought she was beautiful, but when I saw her, the *real* her, I knew she was more than a pretty face."

"And when was that?"

"When she made my nephew smile."

"I think you just answered your own question, Preston." I quirk my brow at her and wait for her to continue. "You didn't fall for her because she was weak, you fell for her compassion, her strength, her resilience. When she was able to put her own sadness aside and put your nephew first."

She was right. Everything she said was right. This was more than Sloane. I fell for her . . . *I'm in love with her.*

"I have to go." I need to tell her.

"Preston. I'd like to talk to you a little about Sloane now, actually. If you can give me a few more minutes, I'm a little concerned about this. It's been years since you came to me and spoke about this. You became a therapist because of her, but at what point is it enough? At what point do you forgive yourself and stop punishing yourself for not seeing the signs? You were a kid. You were still in school. You weren't a psychologist then, so how could you have known? How could you have saved her? It's been years. You really have to stop punishing yourself and live your life. Be happy. She would have wanted that for you."

She's right. I do. I know exactly how to do that. I need to allow myself to be happy.

chapter thirty-six

EVE

Journal entry

Was he right? Am I projecting my feelings, my abandonment issues, my need for comfort with him. No, I don't believe that. I won't believe that. It might have started that way, but that doesn't mean that's what it is. It doesn't matter where you start, it's where you end up. Maybe the initial attraction started in the wrong place, but when your heart grows to love someone it doesn't make it any less real. Right?

This has been all I've been thinking about for the last three weeks. Even as time passes, I can't stop wondering if he's right. That this is how it started. I'm lying in bed when my phone rings. It's late on a Friday night, Sydney is out, and I'm sulking in my room. Picking it up, I check the caller ID.

Holy shit, it's Preston.

"Hello?"

"Where are you? I need to speak to you." My stomach bottoms out. Why is he so desperate to see me, to speak to me? Did something happen?

"I'm home. Are you okay?"

"I need to see you."

"Can you tell me what's going on? You're scaring me."

"I'm coming over. I'll see you—"

"No." I cut him off. I hop out of bed and head out of the room. "I'll come to you." I hang up.

When I knock on the door, he flings it open.

"What's going on? Why were you so desperate—" He pulls me toward him and seizes my mouth with his. I push at his chest to separate us.

"Stop it. What are you doing?" I pant, trying to catch my breath.

"Did I lose you, Eve?"

"What are you talking about? Why am I here? What did you need to say that was so important?"

"I needed to tell you I love you, that I don't want to lose you. That I'll give up everything to be with you. I lost you before. I'm not willing to lose you again."

"No, Preston." I step to turn away.

"Where are you going?" he asks as he pulls me closer.

"I'm doing the right thing, I'm saving you from yourself right now."

"Fuck the right thing."

"But you said before you would be ruined."

"I know what I said, and I don't give a shit. I need you. I need to touch you. I need to taste you. I need to feel the heaven I know your body encompasses. And most of all, I need to love you. There are not enough words to tell you how wrong I was. You're not some girl. You're not just a forbidden desire. Don't you see what you are?"

"No."

"God. You're everything. We're everything . . . Together. When I'm with you, everything is possible. I never thought I would meet somebody who would make me feel this way. After Sloane, relationships were not an option, but with you it's so much more. With you, the possibilities are limitless. Love, breathe, smile, laugh . . . I can't do these things without you, and I would never want to."

I want to cry, but mostly I want to forgive him and jump into his arm and never let him go.

"Everything I said was wrong. Everything but I love you. Because no matter where we are or what we become, that love will always be right," Preston declares.

"But what about—"

"I don't give a damn about any of it. I'd walk out this door right now hand in hand with you it meant you would be mine, that we'd be together."

"What about your career? What about your patients?"

"You are my only concern. I don't give a fuck if I lose my job, my practice. I don't give a shit if I lose everything, as long as I don't lose you. I have spent the last few months torturing myself to fight this feeling, and then I had you. If I thought it was bad before, now that I know what you're like, I can't give you up. I would rather give up my work. I would rather find something else to do. I could work for my—"

"No. I can't let you do that." I cut him off. "You love helping people. It's what gives you joy. I would never take that away from you. I won't let you do that."

"Try to stop me. I love you, only you, forever you . . ." Preston's lips find mine, his soft tongue delving inside my mouth. At first it's soft, loving. But as the seconds pass, our mouths collide in a frenzy.

Desperate.

Passionate.

My arms wrap around his neck of their own accord. A primal and desperate need to intensify the kiss.

I know it's wrong. I know I need to leave but I allow myself to be swept away. I let myself believe one more time that this is just a dream and we can be happy together.

He grins and pulls me closer. "I love you." A fingertip traces across my jaw. I wrap my hands in his disheveled hair.

Kissing.

We move together as if we are one being.

I let go of any resistance or argument still seeking refuge in my body. Instead, I cling to him. He reaches for me, pulling me into his arms. Soft fingers turn my chin up. I soften my body into his as he hovers close, our lips almost touching.

His breath caresses my lips.

"Do you love me?" he asks through heavy pants.

"Yes. I'm in love with you. It's you . . . It's always been you." He is everything. My air, my soul.

Taking a step back, my fingers trail along his shirt. One by one I unfasten each small button. Then I slide my hand down to the belt of his pants. The material hits the floor. The sound echoes as I wait for him to undress me.

His hands find the hem of my dress and lift it up, and when he reaches my panties, he pulls it aside and swipes his finger against my core.

Teasing.

But his fingers don't continue the ministrations. Instead, he lifts the material over my head, exposing my almost naked body to him.

Blue eyes sweep across me. They dilate and flash with

hunger.

He groans as he pulls me closer. We are so close that I feel his heartbeat against my chest.

"I need you." Rough hands. Fingers unsnap my bra. "It's been an eternity since I felt you against me, since I've been buried inside you." My panties are next, leaving me completely bare to him. With a force I didn't expect, he mutters out one more word and then his mouth descends. Claiming me. Owning me. I answer him with my own desperation, frenzied and hot.

Desperate and needy for more. With one last sweep of the tongue our bodies separate on pants and gasps.

Light as a feather, Preston lifts me up, cradling me until we reach his room.

He covers his body with mine, letting me lead. Allowing me the control. My tongue jets out and licks at the seam of his lips. Then I pull back, nipping as I go. A moan of protest escapes him, but I just give him a coy smile as I press kisses down his neck and over his torso to the V of his abdomen. With each inch I travel, Preston's breath becomes more ragged. Each pull of oxygen becomes harder to take in. When I reach my desired destination, I find him hard and ready. My tongue sweeps against him, eliciting a string of curses and groans.

"Fuck." He pulls back, and I look at him through hooded eyes. "I need to be inside you." Crawling back up his body, I align him with my core and then slowly sink down. A feeling of power weaves through me as I take him fully. Once he's all the way seated, my hips begin to circle, and then I rock up and down.

Nothing has ever felt this good.

Flipping me onto my back, he thrusts in and out of my body. My nails scratch at his shoulders as I brace for each push and pull of his body. He slams in over and over again, moving his hips at a faster clip. Strong hands catch my chin.

"Look at me." We both climb toward release together. I'm breathless.

Ragged bursts escape. Our movements become frantic. Grabbing. Thrusting. Panting.

Gasps.

He makes love to me like a desperate man. Like a starved man. Like a man trying to take possession of me. Like a man trying to own me. My body shivers and quakes as he pulls out and then enters me again. "I," *slam* "Fucking love you." *slam* "You're mine." He thrusts in deeper. "Do you understand? I don't care how, but you're mine."

At this moment, in this bed, I give myself to him fully. My body contracts and pulses around him, just as his whole body jerks with his own climax.

"God," he shouts out his release. "You belong to me. This connection will never break. You will always be mine."

Sometimes, even though it will hurt beyond measure, you have to do the right thing. As I look at him from across the bed, I realize that's what I need to do. As much as I see the future, as much as I can see myself in an all-consuming love with him; as much as I envision that together with him my panic attacks will fade and my nightmares will turn to dreams, I can't do it.

I can't be with him. It wouldn't be fair. I'm not the woman I should be yet, and he deserves that woman. I deserve to be that woman as well. I need to come to him complete, not broken parts of myself.

I need to be strong. I need to prove to him that I can stand on my own two feet. That this isn't transference. That I'm not in love with him because of some void I'm filling.

Although my heart hurts to walk away, I know I have to. Not only for my growth, but also for his.

He might not think he has counter transference, but a small part of him still thinks he does.

We both need to find ourselves.

When the time comes after I have grown, and if the feelings are still there, we can see what happens, but right now my priority is me, and he needs to make peace with his own tragedy.

With a trembling hand, I start to write. And when I'm done, my shaking fingers take the letter and tuck it into my journal. I wonder if this is where our story ends. Will this be my only gift to him?

My journal.

All of what's in my heart.

Turning around, I walk away. I can't look back. I know if I do, I'll never go.

chapter thirty-seven

PRESTON

ROLLING ACROSS THE BED, I REACH OUT FOR EVE. TO HOLD her body tight to me, to feel her warm body beneath me. As my hand searches her out, I come up with nothing and the spot is cold. My eyes fly open but I'm met with emptiness.

Where is she? I start to get up from the bed to find her when everything inside me stills. There, siting next to my side of the bed is a journal. But it's not my journal. It doesn't belong to me. It belongs to *her*. I move swiftly to grab it. To understand why she left it here. And as I open it a piece of paper falls to the bed.

Dear Preston,

I have written and rewritten this letter, and the truth is I will never truly be able to tell you how hard it is for me to write it.

In the last few months you have helped me learn so much about myself and have inspired me to find my happiness. You are my happiness, but to have you right now would be selfish and unfair to you. I love you. But what I have learned is that sometimes love isn't enough. Sometimes it's not nearly enough.

    Thank you for believing in me before I knew how to believe in myself.

    Please don't forget me. One day I hope to be in your arms again, a healed woman. A complete woman. I won't forget you, either. For as long as I live, I will love you.

But now, I'm setting you free.

Eve

She left me. She fucking left me. My heart pounds in my chest from the emotions raging inside me. Set me free? I'm not free. I'll never be free, not when she owns my heart. Not when these words she's written have ripped me into a million pieces. It feels as if there's a wind whipping through my heart, pulling it apart and shredding it to pieces. The feelings drag me under until I fear I might never survive this storm.

I lie back in my bed. Hours must pass as I let it all sink in. As I realize it wasn't enough. I might have tried to give it all up for her, but it wasn't enough. I was too late. I'm not able to comprehend what to do now. How do I move on from this? How do I let her go? Do I fight for her? Despite what she says, should I fight? But then my rational side kicks in. *She's right.* I know she's right. I have to let her leave. She needs space to figure out who she is and to believe in herself. She needs to focus on rebuilding her relationship with her mom and forgiving her dad. Doesn't mean it won't break me apart every day for the time that separates us. I know it will. But I'm willing to risk it, because there is no question that I love her. *Why do we fall in love with people we can't have?* Maybe I can't have her today, but I have to have faith that maybe one day we'll have a future. We are two pieces of a puzzle and eventually we will be put back together.

chapter thirty-eight

EVE

I would be lying if I didn't admit to myself why I was walking past Thirty-Fifth Street. Sometimes I find myself walking past his street when I want to feel close to him, when I want to remember the lessons I learned when seeing him. Today, I need his strength. Today marks three months since I've seen him and I need to find the strength to get out of my funk and make a change. Every day since I got the referrals from Preston, I have stared at the names, but I haven't found the strength to call them. I know I have to, but I put it off. Sydney thinks I'm holding off for some crazy notion that Preston will charge in and demand I change my mind. I know he won't. He can't. Deep down, he knows this is right.

Today I walk down Park, and as usual I peer down the street. That's when I see him. He's across the street. *Preston*. The man I can't get out of my head, and worse, the one I can't get out of my heart. I squint my eyes to get a better look. He's perched on the stoop. His head is bowed and fine lines paint his forehead.

When he finally lifts his head, the look in his eyes haunts me. They speak of a deep-rooted pain that I could never imagine. I put that pain there, and I would do anything in my power to take it away, but it wouldn't be fair to go to him now. Not when I'm still so screwed up and when we still can't be together. No. Today isn't the right time. But hopefully it soon will be, and I know what I have to do.

Lifting my hand, my fingers find the necklace he gave me and I stroke it gently. It's time I stop hiding. It's time I face my nightmares and learn to forgive. Today is the day I make the change.

I turn on my heel before he catches me looking and walk in the other direction, leaving a part of me on that corner with him, but vowing to find all the other pieces and put myself back together.

I scan the intersection from right to left. There are a few choices I can make. Home to pretend my life isn't happening and continue to hide in my bed, or send Sydney a text and finally start living again. Seeing Preston makes my heart hurt, but I also know he wouldn't want me to be sad. So I pick up my phone and send a message to Sydney.

Me: Bar?

Sydney: Hell yes.

Me: Ten minutes?

Sydney: DONE!

The Corner Bar is packed as usual. From across the room, I see Sydney waving at me. My mouth spreads into a large smile. For the first time in a long time, I feel as if I might be okay.

"What up, chica!" Sydney throws her arms around my neck and starts bouncing up and down "I've missed you."

"Syd, you do know we live together right? You see me every day. How can you miss me?"

"Eve." Her eyes narrow. "You have been in a funk for weeks. I wouldn't call that living anywhere."

"You're right. But I'm back now."

"Well, you know what that means?"

"Tequila shots?" I flash her a megawatt smile and she starts to laugh.

"A girl after my own heart." Sydney turns to Austin. "Two shots of Patron, extra chilled," she exclaims.

He comes back and places the two chilled shots in front of us.

"Celebrating something?" he winks.

"No," I say as Sydney says yes. I turn my attention back and quirk an eyebrow.

"We are?"

"Yep."

"And what, pray tell, are we celebrating?"

"You, of course," she replies.

"I don't understand."

"It's good to have you back." She smiles and I grab the shot and take a swig.

"It's good to be back." I nod. It is. *And tomorrow, first thing, I'll call the names on the list.*

"What are you smiling about?" Sydney asks.

"Nothing. Just happy, I guess." And for the first time in a long time, I do feel happy. I feel hope. Because I know what I need to do and I'm going to do it. I'm going to stop running from my past. I'll confront my fears and figure out me, and that is worth celebrating.

Once again I stand at the precipice of change, but this time instead of walking into Preston's office, I find myself in a small room, waiting to see my new therapist. Her name is Dr.

Beckett, and from the look of things, she will be nothing like Dr. Montgomery. Where he was upscale, this space is homey. Comfy couches line the walls of what seems to be an old parlor of a brownstone in the west village. It's quaint and feels like home.

With everything I've been through, I welcome it. Dr. Beckett wasn't on the list Preston gave me. I needed a clean break. So I asked around the office, only this time I didn't hide that I'm having a hard time coping with Richard's death and some other things in my life. Surprisingly, everyone was supportive. And now that they knew my mom had no interest in taking control, they reach out more and more. It isn't only Sydney and myself for lunch anymore. Now Natalie comes along, and Barry too. After apologizing for harassing me, he really isn't that bad.

Today begins the next step in my journey. I'm not sure how this new story will end, but I hope eventually it leads me back to Preston. All I can do is take a deep breath and vow to conquer my fears and learn to forgive.

The door creaks open and out walks a taller middle-aged woman.

"Hello, Eve. I'm Dr. Beckett."

"Hi," I say as I stand and extend my hand.

"Are you ready?" She smiles and I nod.

I am. I finally am.

⸻ • ⸻

As my sessions with Dr. Beckett come and go, the weather turns from sweltering to brisk days. Orange and red bleed from the leaves and the air is crisp with fall fragrances. The weeks have turned into months. We talk about everything. Well, everything except Preston Montgomery. He's one topic I won't breach. I keep our time together tucked firmly in my own heart and memory.

Right now the focus is on me. I'm working on forgiving Mom and Richard for lying to me. Richard's omission of the truth has been easier for me to move past. He was in an unimaginable situation and made the only choice he though he could. It's taken me a long time to forgive Mom, and an even longer time to forgive my dad.

Day by day and week by week, I get closer to forgiveness. Like Preston said, I'd never understand the pressure he was under. But little by little I move past the anger and open my heart to love.

Today is a day to move forward.

"Mom, are you decent? Are you dressed?" I say as I knock on the door.

"Yes."

"I have someone here to talk to us. Can we come in?"

"Um," she mumbles through the door. I crack it open a little. "I'm a little dizzy."

"I know, Mom, but it will be fast. She just wants to talk to you. We want to talk to you together. Dr. Beckett thinks it will be good for us. I think so too. We can no longer let our future be dictated by our fear of the past. We need to move forward."

"Okay," she croaks out.

Dr. Beckett and I walk through the door and into the room. Mom is sitting on the bed. I had called previously and warned her that she should be dressed today. I'm happy to see she is in lounge pants and T-shirt. She's even wearing a light dusting of makeup. She's trying, and that thought makes tears fill my eyes.

We sit in the chairs situated along the window inside her room. She stays where she is. Dr. Beckett begins, and then we let my mom talk. For the first time in as long as I can remember, she tells me what it was like to be married to Dad. I sit with welled eyes as she relates stories she never shared before. Tears pour down my face at the idea that they were once in love. That my mom was once more then she is. It's almost too much to take in, but as I do, something strange happens. I find myself laughing, smiling and forgiving.

When Dr. Becket asks me if I have anything to say, I do.

"Mom, it's time you forgive yourself. It wasn't your fault. Every year that passes, a bigger part of you dies. Your guilt has eaten away at you. It has to stop. Every day that we have is a gift. You need to keep living for Dad. You need to live for yourself. And for me. I need you to be my mother. I need to know you're there." She nods and we sit in silence. Eventually, I take her hand in mine and ask her softly if she can tell me how she met my father and she does.

The stories encompass topics of all types, from hobbies they had to all the places they travelled. After the moisture on my face evaporates, it makes me happy to think of a better time. Hearing her stories reminds me a little of Preston. He's the reason this is happening right now. He was the catalyst for me doing this. In order to go to him in the future, I need to heal my past. This is the first step—my mom and I forgiving ourselves. This won't be an overnight success. It'll take time before she can talk again about what happened that night. But I'm willing to try. I'm willing to wait.

chapter thirty-nine

EVE

TEN MONTHS LATER...

STEPPING INSIDE PARADISE DINER, I PREPARE FOR THE impending assault of memories. They wash over me like a tidal wave but I embrace them. Losing Richard. Meeting Preston . . . walking away, and then gaining my strength, it all lead me here to this moment. Having spent the past ten months focusing on myself, I'm finally ready to face my fears...to face *him*. Every week that I've seen Dr. Beckett, I've grown stronger, and today I'm ready to confront the man I had to walk away from. I've come here with a purpose. It's not by accident I'm here at the very place I know he frequents. We have unfinished business that I intend to resolve. Perhaps it isn't fair that I'm ambushing him, but I need him to look at me and see that I'm better.

As I wait, I peer toward the window and watch as people pass by. A young couple walks hand in hand, and my heart swells at the sight. Months ago seeing this might have hurt me, but not now. I'm ready for what they have.

To live. To breath. To love.

My lips part into a smile as I watch them fade into the horizon, a sigh escaping my mouth. The chime above the door rings and pulls me out of my thoughts. I don't have to look to know who's walked in. The air has shifted around me.

I've imagined this moment so many times. Replayed how I would respond to seeing him again, but as often as I fantasized about this moment, I'm finding myself ill prepared for the emotions coursing through me.

My eyes find him. God, he looks gorgeous. As if no time has passed. His shoulders are pulled back and he's wearing a blue hoodie and jeans. I love him like this. I'm reminded of our trip together. The weekend I began to fall in love with him. A stolen moment where we were able to live in our bubble and just enjoy each other with no consequences.

I want to run to him.

I want to jump into his arms.

Kiss him madly.

Never let him go.

I hold back the tears of joy that threaten to fall from my eyes.

He walks towards me, but hasn't yet seen me. The closer he gets, the more I have to secure myself to the seat as to not make a fool of myself.

Patience. You've waited this long.

He twists his body speaking to someone behind him. As he turns back around, I get a peek at who he's talking to and my heart stops. All of the oxygen leaves my body and an all-encompassing sadness slithers its way inside me.

He's not alone.

She's tall and lithe. Long brown hair cascades down her back in waves.

She's beautiful.

The woman says something which causes Preston to throw his head back and laugh in joyous abandon.

He's happy.

Familiar ghosts are gnawing at me, the panic that wants to overtake my body consuming. It claws at me. Wanting desperately to take over and pull me into it's wicked trance. I almost fall prey, but I've come too far.

Instead I straighten my back and stand taller.

You're strong. You're brave. You're better.

She mouths something to him then places her hand lovingly on his forearm, leaning up on tiptoes to place a tender kiss on his cheek…every last piece of me dies.

I'm too late. He's moved on.

Everything in me says get the hell out of here, but I'm too late. Before I can make my escape, our gaze locks. Preston's dark eyes go wide, his pupils taking up the entire circumference. Every muscle in his body seems to tense.

Inhale. One. Two. Three.

Exhale. One. Two. Three.

Through my breathing, memories of everything I've learned since I met Preston flood my mind. My journey to forgiveness, overcoming my fears about life and myself. I will not falter. I will square my shoulders and hold my head high. I will remember to be strong, and not to let the sadness take over.

At least not here…not where he can see me fall.

He steps toward me.

"Eve?" he says confused. Like he's trying to gauge whether it's really me he's seeing. I close the distance between us, standing in front of them, my teeth gnawing viciously at inside of my cheek.

"Hello, Preston." I turn my head toward the brunette, smiling wide despite the very real need to cry.

"Oh. Um, this is Heather. Heather this is Eve Hamilton," he stutters. The awkwardness of the situation only grows worse with his obvious discomfort. I extend my hand, hoping to alleviate the tension.

"Nice to meet you, Heather."

"Nice to meet you too, Eve." She smiles warmly at me.

She's sweet.

"We were just grabbing breakfast," he offers lamely. Heather moves closer to him. The way she's staring at him makes every muscle in my body feel as if it's being pulled tight.

She's in love with him.

"Are you coming or going?" Preston asks, pulling me out of my haze.

"Going." I step aside. "I'm going." He nods and opens his mouth to speak but stops himself.

"Ready to sit, Preston?" Her hand rubs up his arm. She's touching him, her hands are on him—I am barely masking the pain this is causing. Desperate to leave, I nod and begin to slowly retreat.

I have to go.

As strong as I am now, this is too much. Seeing him here. Seeing her with him is too much. I need to be alone. I need to feel this pain.

"It was good seeing you, Eve." I don't miss the way his voice cracks when he says my name.

I smile. It's weak and fake, but it's the only thing I can do to not fall apart right there in the middle of the restaurant.

My eyes meet his one final time as a single tear I can no longer hold falls.

THREE DAYS LATER...

"I saw Preston the other day, " I say to Dr. Beckett as I lean forward hugging my knees to my chest. "He was with another woman." She pauses what she's writing, and looks up at me. The lines etched on her weathered face becoming more pronounced.

"And how did that make you feel?"

"It tore me in two. That day I arrived feeling on top of the world and ready to move forward. The ambush backfired in the cruelest of ways. It hurts to know that I lost him, but at least he looks happy and that makes me happy. The hardest part is that I have so much I need to say to him, and never had the chance. I couldn't get past the hurt to just say it. The strength to pull him aside to talk was not there."

"I know it must feel hard and I'm sure you're scared of what you will find out, but I do think you need closure. I think your next step is you reaching out to him, thanking him, and then you might be ready to move on."

"Okay." My fragile heart doesn't want to know if he's moved on with Heather. From the looks at the diner, he has. I can't blame him. She was perfect in every way. How could I expect him to wait for me? It was unrealistic for me to think he wouldn't.

So much time has passed, and my feelings have never wavered. Unfortunately, I was too late. Regardless, I do agree I need to thank him for being instrumental to me finally finding peace with my mother and with myself.

Once back at my apartment, my eyes are glued to the blank screen in front of me. I know I have to dial. I need to find the strength, swallow my pride and stuff my emotions as far down as I can. With a shaking hand, I type the one number I've avoided for so long.

"Eve?" It's him. His voice sends my heart soaring despite my every move to suppress it.

"Hi," I squeak. "Listen, I know this is long overdue but I needed to speak with you."

Silence fills the space between. My nerves are getting the better of me, so I rattle on. "I wanted to say thank you." Still he says nothing. At this point I have nothing to lose, so I go on. "Meeting you, loving you…it was my saving grace." I sigh. "No matter what happens, I need you to know." I prepare to hang up as it appears he has nothing to offer, but finally he speaks.

"Meet me. I need to talk to you." My stomach tightens in nerves.

"I don't know if that's smart. I don't want to cause problems between you and Heather," I whisper so that he doesn't hear how my voice cracks.

"Eve, we need to talk about that." My heart hammers in my chest and I nod to myself, not that he can see me. "Is that a yes," he says through the phone.

"Yes." I stutter.

"Have you had dinner?"

"Not yet."

"Okay, Paradise. Eight Thirty?" An hour and half to prepare to see him… Am I ready? Can I do this? Will I have the strength to hear whatever he has to say?

I am.

Good or bad it's time I put this part to rest.

"Okay." The line goes dead.

AVA HARRISON

I'm going to be late. Shit. With fast steps, I move through the crowded streets and to the corner. My skirt flies up as a cab whooshes by.

I wonder what will happen. How everything will go down. As I wait for the light to change and the cars to pass, I look into the passing traffic. It isn't so bad for a Tuesday evening, and walking in the crisp air is invigorating. New York City isn't usually this chilly this time of year, but it seems spring is lingering in the air. This thought reminds me that we are only nine months away from the statue of limitation running out. I shake off the thought. No need to set myself up for more disappointment.

In a rush, I step in the door.

A short line has formed in front of me, but when the crowd parts, I come face to face with all I was hoping for. All I've dreamed about. *Preston.* His lips part into a smile as he sees me.

"Am I too late?" I whisper to myself. There's no way he can hear me but the way his eyes pierce mine, I think . . . no, I believe he can. As I close the distance between us, it's as though there is something tethering me to him, pulling me closer.

"Am I late?" I blurt out, my heart beating erratically.

"Nope, your timing is impeccable." His words swallow me whole. Invade every crevice of my mind that still dares to dream.

"I was scared I was too late." The way he looks at me, I know he understands my meaning.

"It's never too late. It will never be too late."

"But what about—"

"What about nothing. There was never anyone else. There is no one but you. The other day when you saw me with Heather, it meant nothing." He extends a hand to me, his finger sweeping lightly against my jaw. "Jace was sick of me moping around, so he said I needed to date. Get out there again. Heather works in the hospital with me. She's made her interest in me known for a long time, so I asked her out."

"She's in love with you." My head tips down to look at the floor. "I should know," I mutter.

"Yeah," He takes a deep breath and my eyes snap back up. There's so much emotion in his eyes but I can't place it. "He said it would be good for me," he repeats.

"And was it?"

"Yeah." His voice dips low, it sends a wave of chills down my spine as I wait for him to continue. *To seal my fate.* "It was good because it made me realize there's no one else for me but you."

My mouth trembles against his fingertips as all of my pent-up emotions come pouring out in fresh tears. He reaches up and collects the wetness. "I was so scared. I knew what I had to do, and I did it. But then I had to wait for it to be okay for us to be together. It felt so long, this time without you. I was so scared you'd moved on. That you forgot about me," I stammer out.

"How could I ever forget about you? Don't you know by now that I love you?" He pulls me into his arms and buries his head in my neck. "I love you," he whispers into my skin before he moves his head back and his mouth connects with mine, showing me just how much.

"Okay, I get it," I laugh into his lips. He pulls away and gives me a heart-stopping smirk.

"I'm glad you're finally starting to catch on." He says with a wink.

"God, I've missed you. It feels as if I've been everywhere and nowhere. Does that make sense?"

"More than you know. That's how I've felt, too. But there is a light at the end of the tunnel. We only have to wait—"

"I don't want to wait anymore. I don't want to waste another minute not being with you." I say.

"Okay, so we won't wait. We just have to be careful until the time passes, but are you sure you're ready? As much as it would kill me to let you go again, you have to be sure."

"I swear, I've been to hell and back. But when I lost you, I found me. God, I had so much to learn, but knowing there was a chance for us . . . I fought. I hired a new therapist, not one from your list. She's wonderful. She's been working with me to not need approval. She's been helping me to forgive, and she's been working with Mom." His eyes widen at my words.

"Yeah, the three of us have been meeting. Dr. Beckett has been helping her to understand that it's not her fault Dad took his life. She's really come a long way." Tears fill my eyes. "Last week, she came to the office with me. She's leaving her house again. Do you know how amazing this is?"

"I'm so happy for you." He smiles.

"You saved me, Preston."

"No. You saved you. I only gave you some of the tools you needed." His arms wrap around me and he holds me in his arms.

"I used to be scared, but now I'm controlling it. I'm learning new coping mechanisms and I'm building myself up one day at a time. I have more to learn, but I'm working on it. I'm not perfect, and I still have nightmares sometimes, but it's okay, because no one's perfect."

"To me, you're perfect." He runs his hand up my spine. "To me, you're everything. You are beautiful inside and out."

I exhale the last bit of fear that still resided in my body. The fear that I had lost him.

epilogue

EVE

NINE MONTHS LATER . . .

WATCH OUT THE WINDOW AS THE STREET PREVIOUSLY blanketed in white starts to melt away. Spring is coming, breathing warm winds and change. Like a soft lullaby to my ears, each pass of the breeze against the glass pane speaks about the promise of a new beginning. A new beginning for us . . . *finally.*

Warm arms slip around me and I lean back taking his embrace.

"So now that we can finally be together, where do you want to go?"

"It doesn't matter, as long as I'm with you." And that's the truth. The last nine months we have spent every free minute we could together, maybe not in public because we couldn't be seen together. But we learned to make do. We've become quit creative in fun dates to take in Preston's brownstone. We cook. We watch movies. We even have picnics in his living room and make love as often as possible. We have fallen further in love. Into an all-consuming love, the kind of love that stories are made of.

He leans down and places a kiss on my exposed shoulder.

"Now that you're stuck with me, you promise you'll love me in five years?" I ask and he doesn't respond but I feel his mouth hovering over my sensitive skin.

Kiss

"In ten years?"

Kiss

"Fifteen years?"

Kiss

With that he spins me around and places his lips on mine, robbing me of my breath. "I'll love you until forever and a day," he mumbles against my mouth. "Don't you understand by now? I want to kiss you till forever. I want to love you until forever, and when forever ends, I want to start all over again." His voice touches places within me I had almost forgotten were there. It touches the place in my heart where dreams do happen. "Because I will never have my fill of you. Even eternity won't be enough. I want to be the reason you smile today. I want to be the reason you smile every day." He pauses and gently opens up his closed hand revealing a beautiful solitaire diamond.

Crystal blue eyes gaze back at me. They speak to my soul, to every facet that I am. In his eyes, I see a future. I see hope, and I see love. It doesn't matter where we started.

Or how many obstacles we'll have to overcome.

All that matters is where we're going, and that we go there together.

"Will you marry me? Will you give me all of your forevers?"

"Yes," I say through joyful tears that drip down my cheek. His arms encircle me as he sears me with his kiss.

I have learned so much over the last two years. I've learned that I'm more than my past. I'm more than the nightmares that haunted me. I'm able to forgive and move forward and have a second chance.

Life does provide a second chance.

This is ours.

the end

acknowledgments

I want to thank my entire family. I love you all. Thank you to my husband and my kids for always loving me, I love you so much!

Thank you to all the amazing indie companies that helped mold my words.

Champagne Formats
Write Girl Editing Services
Indie After Hours
Hang Le
Virginia Tesi Carey

Thank you to Linda, Kristi and Melissa from Sassy Savvy Fabulous for your help with EVERYTHING!

Thank you to Heather White and Kylie McDermott from Give Me Books.

Thanks to Leonardo Corredor and Rob Rea for the most perfect picture of "Dr. Preston Montgomery"

I want to thank all my friends for putting up with me. I know it's no easy task!

Melissa: You're my Soul Mate and I love you and would be lost with out you.

Livia: You're high maintenance but I love your ass. Thank you for always being there!

Trish: I love you girl, even when you are making me do re-writes, and I'm screaming at you . . . I still love you.

Lisa: There is no one I'd rather drink Champagne and eat

truffle fries with!

Leigh: Thank you for staying on the phone and not hanging up when I get "panicked"

Mia: Love you! Thanks for your help

Vanessa Renee Place: Thank you for your help!

Linda: Thank you for bearing with me through my "theories"

To My "Sisters" Thank you for being there for me. Love you guys!

To all my author friends, thank you for giving me great advice and being my friend!

My Beta's… Leigh, Argie, Liv, Christine, Trish. Thank you for your wonderful and extremely helpful feedback. I appreciate it more than you know! I wouldn't have been able to write this book without you and to Mel, thanks for the final push, lord did I need it. Love you all!

To the ladies in the Perfectly Flawed Support group, I couldn't have done this without your support! Perfectly Flawed Group: http://bit.ly/2e67NYi

Thanks to all the bloggers! Thanks for your excitement and love of books!

Last but certainly not least. . .

Thank you to the readers!

Thank you so much for taking this journey with me.

I hope you will, please consider joining my Perfectly Flawed Support Group on Facebook. The goal of this group and my books is to help women own their imperfections and flaws. This group is to help us remember that every single one of us. . .is perfectly imperfect.

For future release information please sign up here to be alerted: http://bit.ly/2fnQQ1n

by Ava Harrison

Imperfect Truth

Perfect Truth

Through Her Eyes

about the author

Ava Harrison is a New Yorker, born and bred. When she's not journaling her life, you can find her window shopping, cooking dinner for her family, or curled up on her couch reading a book.

Connect with Ava

Newsletter Sign Up: http://bit.ly/2fnQQ1n

Facebook Author Page: http://bit.ly/2eshd1h

Facebook Reader Group: http://bit.ly/2e67NYi

Goodreads Author Page: http://bit.ly/2eNjYwX

Twitter: http://bit.ly/2fnRP1v

Instagram: http://bit.ly/2f5H5RT

Made in the USA
Coppell, TX
28 February 2023

13521922R10173